Praise for Christy Award-winning author

Vanessa Del Fabbro

and her novels

SANDPIPER DRIFT

"The fabulous scenery is vividly described and places
the reader in the story.... Overall, the plot
and characters are enchanting."
—*Romantic Times BOOKreviews*

THE ROAD TO HOME

"Del Fabbro, who was born and raised in South Africa,
offers a fascinating window into the stark beauty and
random violence that characterize the 'Rainbow Nation,'
where racial hatred still threatens the fragile peace that
has been won. Through dynamic characters and an
unflinchingly honest perspective on human weakness,
Del Fabbro concocts a winning story of the triumphant
power of female friendship."
—*Publishers Weekly*

"This touching debut novel is well worth purchasing."
—*Library Journal*

"Intricate, vivid, and lyrical, a story that transposes the
dark era of South African racial struggles with the healing
brilliance of two women who risk everything to reach for
each other, *The Road to Home* is an amazing first novel."
—Deborah Bedford, *USA TODAY* bestselling author

"I was deeply touched by Vanessa Del Fabbro's poignant
account of an unlikely friendship in a brutal land.
With lyrical prose, this gifted author illustrates
Christ's great teachings about the true meaning of love.
The Road to Home is both powerful and heartbreaking."
—Catherine Palmer, Christy Award-winning author of
The Heart's Treasure

"Eloquently penned, this is a poignant story of a
redemptive friendship that triumphs over generations of
prejudice and social injustice. Recommended."
—*CBA Marketplace*

Vanessa Del Fabbro

A Family in Full

Steeple
Hill®

Published by Steeple Hill Books™

STEEPLE HILL BOOKS

Steeple
Hill®

ISBN-13: 978-0-373-78590-2
ISBN-10:   0-373-78590-9

A FAMILY IN FULL

www.SteepleHill.com

Printed in U.S.A.

For my sister and brother, Lesley and Roger, with love

Acknowledgments

I am grateful to my agent, Helen Breitwieser, for her persistent support and charmingly frank counsel, my editor, Joan Marlow Golan; line editor, Lee Quarfoot; and copy editor Sherry Noik-Bent for their wisdom and vision, and Emily Rodmell for all her assistance. I would like to thank Joyce Zulu, in Johannesburg, South Africa, for patiently sharing with me her knowledge of Zulu culture and customs. As always, I am grateful to my wonderful husband and sweet little daughter, for their love and encouragement.

1

«««««««««

"I'VE FOUND THE TREASURE, MONICA," SHOUTED SIPHO.

Monica Brunetti's eleven-year-old adopted son never called her Mom, and she noticed he sometimes wore a wounded expression when his younger brother did. But Mandla had only just turned two when his mother died, and although it might be difficult for Sipho to hear his brother replacing their mother, it was to be expected from a child Mandla's age. If Monica ever admitted to herself that she would like Sipho to call her Mom, it was only fleetingly, and she always felt a twinge of guilt afterward. Ella Nkhoma, the boys' mother, had been a close friend.

"I want to go home," complained Mandla, his breath warm on her neck.

Below they could see Lady Helen, the town that had been home to them for a year. Monica had found the climb up the koppie tiring with four-year-old Mandla on her back, but he had walked for an hour on his own and could go no farther. Sipho had strode ahead, breathing hard, sweating in the midafternoon summer sun, driven by the vision in his head of what he was about to find. Monica was astounded at his stamina; he was small for his age and not athletic. He had his father's slender build. Before his death from AIDS, Themba Nkhoma had been a member of South Africa's new military, a combination of the old South African Defense Force and Umkhonto we Sizwe, the armed wing of the African National Congress, a political party that had been banned for many years. Slim and wiry, Themba had always been clean shaven and neat in his pressed silk shirts and dress pants.

Mandla looked more like his mother. Monica first met Ella in the hospital. Ella was being treated for bronchitis—or that was what she told everyone—while Monica was recovering from a bullet wound after a violent carjacking. Ella was a large, muscular woman, with broad shoulders and a laugh that could be heard four wards away. Only later, after both women had been discharged, did Ella confess to Monica the true reason she was losing weight and felt fatigued. Themba had passed his disease on to her. Two years had gone by since Ella's death, and Mandla had stopped asking about her.

The limp in Monica's right leg, the result of being shot in the carjacking, was more pronounced now from carrying Mandla up the steep koppie. Out of breath, she reached the spot where Sipho was crouched at the entrance to a cave and let Mandla slide to the ground.

"No," moaned the little boy. He was too tired to stand on his own. Then he spied the cave, and Monica had to catch his shirt as he charged past her.

"There could be black mambas in there," said Sipho.

Mandla stopped in his tracks. With a nature expert for a big brother, Mandla knew a drop of poison from one of the world's deadliest snakes could kill a grown man.

Monica squatted next to Sipho to examine his find. Although in shadow, the fine lines of the artist's quill on the rocks were surprisingly clear. The figures held spears, calabashes and the carcasses of dead animals. Steenbok, eland, kudu, giraffe and elephant were easily recognizable in varying shades of red and ochre. This was the first time Monica had seen San paintings in the Western Cape.

"It's as good as Oscar said," said Sipho, his eyes shining. From his backpack, he took out a sketchbook and pencil and began to copy the rock art for his history project.

Oscar, the unofficial curator of all the artifacts from the town's namesake, Lady Helen, was a good new friend to Monica and her family. Oscar had discovered this site on one of his walkabouts to find Lady Helen's burial site. Some believed that she was murdered by her husband, Lord Gray, for freeing fifty slaves and running away with his horses and supply wagons. But Oscar believed that Lady Helen had stayed on in the small town she'd founded, perhaps with the assistance of the nomadic San tribesmen who roamed the area at that time.

"I'm going to make my class promise not to tell anyone about these," said Sipho. "Maybe Oscar can build a fence around this cave."

Fences were Oscar's passion. He had built one around the statue of Lady Helen in the park next to the ocean, and another, an ornate one topped with curlicues and shields, around the cemetery. It was Oscar's ambitious goal to discover the identities of the townsfolk buried in the cemetery so that he could replace the piles of rocks at their grave sites with proper tombstones. This would not be an easy feat since the town had been abandoned and reestablished too many times to allow family lines to be traced.

"I want to go home," moaned Mandla.

If he was not allowed to enter the cave, then this outing was no fun at all. Mandla had gone to bed at seven o'clock the previous evening and had slept for thirteen hours, but he was evidently still in need of one of the daily naps he had stopped taking before Christmas.

"I'm almost finished," said Sipho. "This is going to be my best history project ever."

Last year, Sipho had taken the end-of-term exams for his grade and the next and he had passed both. The principal of his school—which everybody called Green Block School because of its modern architecture—had decided on a fluid approach to Sipho's education. This pleased Monica because Sipho had been bored at his school in Johannesburg. He was studious by nature and enthusiastic about his lessons at the new school. His accelerated pace might slow as he reached higher grades, but if it didn't, he would go to university early and South Africa would have a new young doctor sooner than expected.

There was one weak area in his education, and Monica blamed herself for it. As Themba had lain dying, she had promised him that his sons would continue to speak their native language, Sotho, but it was proving to be difficult. Of all the errors she had made while learning to become a mother to two young boys, this one pained her most, and she had decided that in their second year in Lady Helen she would rectify things by finding friends for Sipho who spoke Sotho and by learning the language herself.

"Okay, I'm finished." Sipho held out his drawing for her to inspect.

"Very good."

She had offered to take a photograph of the paintings, but he had insisted on copying them himself. Like Sipho, some people in Lady Helen often seemed to make choices that were unnecessarily labor-intensive, but the slower pace of life was one of the attractions the town held for Monica.

The discovery of the San paintings would make an interesting story for her newspaper, the *Lady Helen Herald,* but Oscar had told Sipho first, and Monica had decided to allow him to break the news to his classmates before she ran the story. She would never have allowed this delay when she was a reporter in Johannesburg, but life in Lady Helen was different. And so was she. She was a parent now.

"Let's go home," she said.

Mandla reached out his arms and she picked him up. Sipho put his sketchbook in his backpack and took the lead down the koppie.

Monica remembered the first day she had driven down the steep road that was Lady Helen's main entrance from the outside world. She and her cameraman had stopped at the top of the koppie, just a little higher than they were now, and climbed out of the car to look at the view. She had felt as though she were in a glass-bottomed boat looking down at a brightly colored coral reef. Cerise, burnt orange, brilliant pink and sunshine-yellow bougainvillea billowed over walls, scaled fences, crept under the eaves of houses and along the gutters. The sun, reflecting off the green, blue and deep red tin roofs, gave the whole town a bright glow. Monica had been entranced.

As she looked down on the little town now, she was not any less impressed than the first time. The cerise bougainvillea she had planted alongside her carport was too small to add to the spectacle, but it would one day. On the western edge of the town, a pile of rocks separated the land and the cold Atlantic Ocean. Perilously balanced, these were evidence that the ocean was not always this calm. Less than a few hundred yards off the coast lay many wrecks, covered in seaweed. North of the town, a lagoon stretched inland in the shape of a horizontal question mark. The tide was out, and the mudflats surrounding it glistened in the sun.

A small boat bobbed around in the water two hundred yards from shore, and Monica knew that if she looked through binoculars, she would see the red-and-white flag of scuba divers. Lady Helen, the small but respected art town, had become a popular location for divers, especially those who wanted a glimpse of the ocean's fiercest predator—the great white shark. In the distant past, the men of the town had gone out in boats to fish for their living, but now dive boat operators took tourists out to see snoek, tuna and hake from under the water—the great white from the safety of a steel cage.

Monica did not draw attention to the presence of the boat for fear of upsetting Sipho. He said that this new sport, shark diving, made sharks associate people with food.

The sun glinted off two rows of cars parked up and down Main Street. Since it was Saturday, these likely belonged to people who had made the ninety-minute drive from Cape Town to browse the art galleries and enjoy a cup of coffee at Mama Dlamini's Eating Establishment.

Main Street ended in a park that ran along the beachfront for about a quarter of a mile, palm trees forming a natural break between the lawn and the white sand. In the middle was a grass amphitheater with a stage at its lowest level, and behind it a rock garden with flowers indigenous to the region: poker-red aloes, pink pincushion proteas and red African heather. On summer evenings the amphitheater hosted concerts, usually by visiting musicians, and the townsfolk turned out with their picnic blankets, baskets and excited children. This was one of Mandla's favorite activities in the world, but unlike other children who ran among the blankets chasing each other, Mandla got as close as he could to the stage to dance and, if Monica's attention was diverted, join the performers onstage.

From Monica's vantage point on the koppie, it was easy to see what some called a lack of zoning restrictions in the town and what she called perfect planning. Interspersed between the single-family homes were small farms with pastureland and fields stretching out behind them to the foot of the koppies. Mandla loved to watch the milking at Peg's Dairy Farm. Children, who would normally not have known where their food came from, saw it firsthand in Lady Helen.

The hospital and cemetery, too, were surrounded by family homes. The hospital was Sipho's favorite place to visit. When his mother fell ill, he'd decided that he wanted to become a doctor. In his rare spare moments, the hospital's doctor, Zak Niemand, took Sipho on guided tours. The boy was not intimidated by the sight of injuries, burns, illness, needles or blood. Monica, too, was secretly pleased with any excuse that took her to the hospital. Now that Zak's divorce had been finalized, she didn't feel as though she had to keep her distance from him.

They'd met when she reported on the new burn unit at the

hospital for *In-Depth,* a television program for which she had filled in for a staffer on maternity leave. He hadn't been able to give her an interview because he'd been delivering twins, but she had been intrigued to learn that he'd washed and dressed the babies afterward. One day his wife would regret her decision. How could a woman leave a man who did that? A very attractive man... Zak was six foot three with dark hair that looked as though it might curl if he allowed it to grow a little, and he wore small rectangular glasses that made him seem more serious than he really was. Monica wondered if Jacqueline Niemand had left Zak for a wealthy man. Zak was employed by the government. His salary was not near to what it would be if he had his own practice.

Zak had once joked that his last name fit like a glove. Niemand meant *nobody* in the Afrikaans language. But Zak was far from that. Many people in Lady Helen owed their lives to him. Zak would not think of this, though, not even as he drifted off to sleep at night. His dreams, Monica was sure, would not be of patients he had helped but of those he had failed—or of new ways to get around bureaucratic red tape so he could purchase more equipment or supplies.

A breeze had begun to blow in from the ocean, and Monica could feel Mandla perking up on her back. January was supposed to be the hottest month in Lady Helen, but March seemed intent on topping it. Still, they were comfortable with only ceiling fans to cool their bedrooms at night. The climate of Lady Helen was close to perfect, with breezes to cool the hot, dry summer days and a natural drop in temperature at dusk. Unlike the rest of South Africa, where it rained during summer, the Western Cape received its rain in winter. Monica missed the quick afternoon thunderstorms that cooled the hot summer afternoons in Johannesburg and filled the air with the smell of wet soil and crushed flowers. The winters were mild, and if they experienced biting-cold days with driving rain, it was pleasant to sit indoors and watch the wind whipping the waves into a white froth. Best of all was the light, which was bright and clear and always made the landscape look as though it were begging to be painted.

Sipho had slowed down, and Monica knew that she would have to motivate him for the rest of the journey home. Though he was tired, the fresh air and exercise were good for him. The promise of activities such as this was another of the reasons Monica had been lured from Johannesburg.

As they neared their house, Monica saw that the bougainvillea she'd planted had started to climb the trellis she'd erected to give the plant a foothold onto the roof of the carport. With restrictions on new buildings and not many people leaving Lady Helen, they'd had to wait for their house. Like most buildings in Lady Helen, it had a tin roof—this one green—lace filigrees, shutters, wood-frame windows and a wide covered veranda with a polished-concrete floor. The only thing that had set it apart was that it did not have a mature bougainvillea. The newcomer, however, seemed to be thriving.

Oscar had built the carport after converting the garage into a studio flat for Francina Zuma, the Zulu woman who had been a longtime housekeeper, first for Monica's mother and then for Monica and her adopted sons. Francina and her new husband, Hercules Shabalala, might have stayed there after their marriage, but Hercules had invited his mother to live with them and there was not enough room for three. In Italy this past Christmas, Mandla had told Monica's parents that the Old Garage, as he called the flat, was ready and waiting for them. Monica had watched her mother's eyes light up, but her father's face had shown no expression and the subject hadn't come up again. If Monica could have her way, her parents would be here already, but her father was content in the seaside town of his birth after decades of living in South Africa. His widowed brother lived next door, his nephews in the next village with their families. Before she'd left Italy, Monica had extracted a promise from her mother to visit Lady Helen this year. An artist had told her that once you discovered Lady Helen you always returned. It had been true for Monica, and now she was bargaining that her mother, too, would be smitten by Lady Helen's charms.

"There's Dr. Niemand!" Sipho pointed toward the end of their block, where two mismatched figures were walking slowly, as though unsure of their destination.

Monica had never seen Zak on foot near her house, but Sipho was right: that was Zak and his thirteen-year-old daughter, Yolanda.

Sipho ran the rest of the way down the hill, took a shortcut through one of the neighbor's gardens and almost tumbled onto the road in his haste to greet his hero. Monica followed his route as quickly as she could, knowing that the lady who lived in this house didn't mind them using her garden to gain access to the koppie. Before stepping out onto the road, she ducked behind a hedge, took off the ridiculous sun hat she was wearing and redid her ponytail. The hairdresser had recently cut her shoulder-length blond hair, and now too-short strands were falling free around her face. She swiped at them with clammy hands and they stayed back as securely as if she'd used gel. She dabbed at her perspiring face with a tissue. This morning she had been more concerned about lathering sunscreen on her pale complexion than about applying makeup. There was nothing else she could do now to improve her appearance. When she stepped onto the road, Sipho had reached Zak and Yolanda. They turned to watch her approach.

"Hi." There was something in Zak's voice and manner that made Monica instantly hopeful. He was uncomfortable, which might mean he had chosen this route for a stroll because it passed her house.

"Hi," she said, looking first at Zak and then at his daughter. "Hi, Yolanda."

The girl looked down and muttered a greeting. Monica knew from Francina that Yolanda was having a difficult time adapting to her new schedule. She lived with her mother in Cape Town during the week and spent weekends in Lady Helen with her father.

Zak looked at his daughter with an expression bordering on agony. It was not the first time Monica had seen his dark eyes filled with worry but the first time his concern was not for a patient. He put an arm around Yolanda's shoulders, but she shook it off. Monica hoped that Zak's ex-wife was not filling this girl's head with lies about her father.

Monica had never seen Zak in jeans and a T-shirt before. Scrubs were not nearly as revealing. Even though he worked long hours at the hospital, Zak obviously worked out, too. He was muscular without being burly.

"Let's go, Dad," whined Yolanda. "I'm tired. I don't know why you wanted to walk all the way here."

His discomfort became obvious embarrassment.

"Would you like to come in for something cold to drink?" Monica hoped her relaxed attitude would put Zak at ease.

Yolanda shook her head.

"Say, 'No, thank you,'" Zak told his daughter. "Thanks, Monica, but we'd better head home. Anyway, I think you have other guests waiting for you." He tilted his head in the direction of her house.

Monica was not expecting anyone, but that didn't matter in Lady Helen. It had taken time for her to get used to the townfolks' practice of dropping by unannounced. There were obvious advantages. If an elderly person fell in Lady Helen, he or she would not lie for long on the floor before someone breezed in with a smile and a tin of biscuits or butterscotch drops.

"Can you come to the hospital sometime soon?" said Zak. "I have a new project."

She rolled her eyes dramatically. "What piece of equipment are you after this time?" Zak wanted his hospital to be adequately equipped, but government funds were severely stretched. There were many hospitals that did not have basic necessities. Zak saw his fund-raising efforts as obligatory.

"You'll find out." The smile on his face was different now; it made the corners of his eyes crinkle. Monica had been off the dating scene for many years, but she was almost sure that he was flirting with her.

"So it's a mystery project. I'll have to come soon then." She wondered if Sipho noticed that her tone had become playful.

"Good," said Zak firmly.

"Well, enjoy the rest of your walk," said Monica, looking at Yolanda.

The girl's mouth was a thin, pinched line. She watched with detachment as her father shook Sipho's and Mandla's hands. When they left, Zak reached for Yolanda's hand, and this time she did not reject him, but took his hand firmly, possessively even, thought Monica, as though she were trying to convey that he belonged to her.

"She's mean," said Sipho once Zak and Yolanda were out of earshot.

"Be kind," said Monica. "She's having a rough time."

"She was mean before she left Green Block School to go and live in Cape Town," Sipho persisted.

"She may have been aware that things were not right between her parents," explained Monica. "We should always put ourselves in the other person's shoes."

This was one of the lessons Ella had taught her when they first met.

"Won't Yolanda be angry if you take her shoes?" asked Mandla.

"It's just an expression, sweetie. It means try and understand why others feel the way they do."

"Okay," he declared as though this were easy. "Can we go home now? I feel hungry."

"Do you think Dr. Niemand was hoping to see us on his walk?" asked Sipho as they approached the garden gate.

"I do."

He smiled and Monica found herself smiling, too.

The visitors had let themselves into the back garden and were sitting in the skinny afternoon shadow of the syringa tree. They stood up when Monica came through the gate with the boys. Monica had seen the four ladies around town. She had even stopped once to admire the baby boy who was with them now, sleeping, wrapped in a light shawl. During the busy time of the annual art festival, the young mother worked at Mama Dlamini's Eating Establishment.

"Good afternoon," said the largest woman of the group. She wore a bright yellow head scarf tied at her neck. "We read in the newspaper that you saved Sandpiper Drift. We've come because we also need your help."

The story the lady was referring to was one Monica had written about the opening of a new golf course fifteen miles up the coast. The owner, Mr. Yang, had initially wanted the land on which the small neighborhood of Sandpiper Drift was built. Monica hadn't intended to be part of the story, but an editing oversight on her part meant the facts were there for all to see. She had played a role in helping to save Sandpiper Drift. A big-city newspaper had no qualms about publicly taking credit for saving a neighborhood, but Monica was mortified when she saw the printed issue. She preferred to think of herself as someone who did not bring about change but enabled it. She prodded people's consciences while there was still time for them to reverse their actions, and when other people took the lead—as the women of Sandpiper Drift had done when they'd climbed onto their roofs to stop the bulldozers from demolishing their houses— she supported them in any way possible. The thorn in everyone's side, she often called herself. She wasn't an activist, but the article had painted her as one.

"Someone is taking our *perlemoen*," blurted the young mother with the baby.

"From your nets?"

The women looked at each other with exasperated expressions.

"Come on, let's go home," said the oldest of the group, who had remained silent until now.

The young mother, who introduced herself as Anna, explained that *perlemoen*—the local name for abalone—was a delicacy in restaurants and that these sea snails were not snared in nets but with a sharp scraping tool. Every day at low tide the women waded into the ocean to search under the rocks, and the money paid to them for the abalone by the chef at the golf resort was enough to feed their families for the day. But lately someone had been beating them to it and taking all the abalone in the shallow water.

"There's plenty in the deeper water—" Anna threw her hands up in dismay, startling her young baby "—but I can't swim, never mind dive under the kelp."

The ladies nodded in agreement. It was dangerous work. Anna put the shawl over her shoulder and, still standing, began to nurse her crying baby.

Monica hoped her question would not offend them. "Sometimes overfishing—"

"No." Anna's voice was adamant. "We've been doing this for years. Someone is stealing our *perlemoen*." There were murmurs of assent from her friends. "Everyone knows you're good at solving problems."

"I'll see what I can do," said Monica.

Anna wrote her telephone number on a tissue and handed it to Monica.

"Would you like some tea?"

The surprise on the ladies' faces indicated that tea was the last thing on their minds.

"No, thank you. We all have to get back to our families," said Anna.

Monica accompanied them to the gate and held it open.

"Thank you." Anna looked intently into Monica's eyes.

Monica closed the gate. Why did she feel such trepidation about looking into this mystery? It was a routine task for any day in the life of a journalist.

Monica's neighbor, S.W. Greeff, the man who had rediscovered Lady Helen and turned it into an art center, waved from across the fence. He was filling his birdbath. Monica hadn't seen him lately since he was preparing for a large exhibition in Johannesburg. His latest project was rumored to be in a new style, but Monica could not confirm this; he never invited anyone into his studio. The only piece he'd wanted her to see was the tombstone he'd designed for himself. After looking at it for only a couple of minutes, she'd rushed out of his studio because his efficiency both depressed and shamed her. She couldn't even seem to find the time to put all her photographs of the boys in albums.

Mandla was itching to try out S.W.'s watering can.

"Never mind about the birds' bath, you need one," she told him, wiping dust from his nose.

The boys were so different. Sipho despised getting dirty, but Mandla would find the only patch of dirt for miles and manage to spread it all over himself.

"After your bath we can play Chutes and Ladders."

Sipho groaned. His brother liked to win at all costs, and Sipho had to check the moves he made or Mandla would skip over chutes he was supposed to slide down and climb ladders he was not.

Satisfied with the deal, Mandla followed Monica inside without protest.

After his bath, Monica started her special Saturday-night dinner. Francina was not required to prepare dinner when she looked after the boys every afternoon, but after years of doing it for Monica's mother it had become a habit. On Saturdays it was Monica's turn, and she made the most of it, cooking homemade soup and preparing pastas with inventive sauces. Sipho's favorite was olives, anchovies and capers, but Mandla, a less adventurous eater, preferred plain marinara. The boys laid the table in the dining room and, just before she served the dinner, Monica lit candles. She'd made the mistake of putting these in the center of the table only once and had saved Mandla from burning his finger by a split second. Now the candles were always placed high up on a shelf, where Mandla stared at them throughout the meal, mesmerized. Even Ebony, Monica's sixteen-year-old cat, received a special meal of sardines on Saturday nights.

After dinner, they settled on the sofa for the game Mandla had been promised. African jazz played softly in the background, and a gentle breeze teased the drawn curtains. If she ever needed reassurance that she'd made the right decision not to move to Italy with her parents, times like these provided it. But this was not what was on her mind right now; Zak was. She imagined him sitting across from her, counting out his moves on the board, putting a hand on Mandla's shoulder, whistling at Sipho's climb up the longest ladder, catching her eye and giving her an intimate smile. Zak would fit in perfectly with her little family.

"Your turn." Sipho looked at her quizzically, which made her think that this was not the first time he had spoken to her.

She thought of Zak as she'd seen him that afternoon, in jeans and a T-shirt, his usual serenity ruffled by Yolanda's behavior and being found out in his "accidental" stroll past her house. But what if she was mistaken and he was not interested in her? She pushed the thought aside as though it were a pile of dirty laundry she'd decided to leave for another day.

2

MONICA ARRIVED AT WORK ON MONDAY WEARING foundation, eye shadow and a new, darker shade of lipstick. All her attempts at rationalization over the weekend had failed to convince her that it was silly to be embarrassed about her disheveled appearance when she'd met Zak on her street, and this was her way to make up for it. Dudu, the receptionist, made no comment, but Monica could tell by the lift of the woman's eyebrows that she had gone too far, and so she decided to postpone her visit with Zak.

The next day her foundation was lighter, her lipstick paler. She wore a linen dress embroidered with small carnelian flowers and sandals with heels. A fine string of copper beads accentuated her delicate bone structure. Yesterday's makeover would have won her mother's approval; today's got a nod and the comment, "You look pretty," from Dudu. Monica's mother always nagged her to take more pride in her appearance, but for Monica the issue was her mother's interpretation of *pride*. To Monica, pride meant presenting yourself to the world in clean, neat clothes. Spending thousands of rands on imported designer clothes and hours each week in a beauty salon or poring over fashion magazines was vanity. Her mother would never see it that way.

Monica thanked Dudu for the compliment and went into her office, closing the door behind her. She did not want Dudu to hear her phoning the Department of Fisheries.

The young man who answered her call did not ask for her name. He told her that the season for abalone picking ran from December to April and that it had been reduced by five months because scientists worried that the supply was dwindling. He was happy to tell her the regulations. Anyone who picked abalone had to have a government-issued recreational or subsistence permit; the legal daily limit was four; and the abalone were not to be sold. Pickers were to carry a special U-shaped measuring tool so that they did not take undersize abalone, and the tool with which they picked abalone had to be a specially regulated iron with no sharp edges so as to minimize the chances of cutting off the abalone's foot. Abalone do not have a blood-clotting agent and if damaged will die before they can reattach to the rock. Diving for abalone with a snorkel was allowed, but scuba equipment was not and neither was the use of a boat.

Monica thanked the young man for his time, put down the telephone and got up from her desk to stare out the window at the morning pedestrian traffic on Main Street. Even if the ladies took only the legal limit of four abalone each day, they still sold them for personal gain, and Anna had said that they had been doing this for years. Monica presumed this meant they didn't stop when the legal picking season closed.

Monica was faced with a real problem. Knowing of this illegal activity in Lady Helen, it was her civic duty to report it to the police. And yet there was Anna's baby and the other ladies' young children to think about. If these mothers had to pay large fines, where would they get the money to feed their children?

Monica paced the length of her office. Max Andrews, the paper's former editor, had kept a long orange couch in here for times when his mind was in a twist and he couldn't sleep at home. What would he do in her place? He seemed to have an unlimited store of rules for improbable situations.

The women had not gone to the police, which proved that they knew what they were doing was illegal. Or did it? After decades of apartheid, when the police were often complicit in brutal crimes against anyone who opposed the white government, many people still distrusted the police. Sometimes attitudes took longer to change than reality.

Monica thought that it was time to be a troublesome thorn again, to give the ladies a push so they'd make the right decision for themselves. She enabled change, she did not force it.

She dialed Anna's number. It rang for a long time, and Monica was about to replace the receiver when she heard Anna's voice.

"Sorry, I was putting the baby down for his nap."

Monica asked if she could drop by to discuss the ladies' problem.

"Good, I was just about to make tea." Anna sounded pleased at the prospect of company.

Ten minutes later, Monica parked outside a small whitewashed cottage on the southern edge of town. Anna lived in one of the stone houses built by the slaves Lady Helen had freed almost two centuries ago. If Oscar's campaign succeeded, the houses would be declared part of a national monument by the end of the year. There was no need for the residents to move out when this happened, he said. The only stipulation would be that the residents would not be allowed to make any changes to the buildings, either inside or out.

The cottages were made of stones found in the area; their original straw roofs had been replaced with tin. Anna came out to greet Monica in a brightly colored apron.

"The tea's on the table."

Monica had to stoop as she entered the doorway. The house was divided into two rooms, one for living and cooking, another where the baby lay sleeping. Anna motioned for her guest to sit at a table covered with a blue gingham cloth, and Monica's mind went back to another first visit, when she'd found Ella ill in bed in her flat. Her bedroom curtains had been blue gingham, too.

In the corner of this room a small stove and a single sink were sectioned off by a bookshelf filled with dishes, pots and pans. The concrete floor was polished to a shine. A smell of lemon hung in the air.

When Monica and Anna's polite preliminary conversation about family and health was over, Anna asked, "What did you find out?"

Monica sighed. There was no other way to begin.

"Do you have a permit to pick abalone?"

Anna shook her head but seemed unperturbed. "We only take about six or seven each."

"The limit is four, and they are supposed to be for personal consumption."

"What's the difference if it's me or someone at the golf resort who eats them? Does this mean you're not going to help us?"

"The police would help if—"

Anna stood up and began rinsing their teacups noisily in the sink. Her baby cried in the next room. With a sigh, she wiped her hands on a towel and went to get him. She returned jiggling him on her hip.

"He has his father's smile," Anna said. "I'm so lucky I have a husband who has a job at Peg's Dairy. I don't know how my friend Innocentia manages it. If I were in her place, with no husband and two hungry mouths to feed, I'd pick more than six or seven abalone." She looked Monica straight in the eye to see if her point had been made.

"Thanks for the tea." There was no reason for Monica to stay.

"Anytime."

"I'll see what I can do about your problem."

Anna smiled. "Thanks."

If Monica had needed confirmation that she was no longer an outsider in Lady Helen, this was it: Anna had complete faith that Monica would not alert the police. Doreen, the librarian, had once told Monica that only an outsider could tell the truth. Did belonging take from her that important ability?

Monica arrived at her office to find Dudu in tears.

"What's the matter?"

"I think I did something terrible," sobbed Dudu.

"Sit down and I'll make us a nice cup of tea."

Dudu obliged, and when Monica handed her a cup, she stopped crying and sat cradling it as though warming her hands even though it was eighty degrees outside.

Monica sat down beside her. "Tell me what happened."

"A man called from Johannesburg and asked if we had any information on a new discovery of Bushmen—" she quickly corrected her use of the pejorative word "—I mean, San paintings."

"And what did you say?"

Sipho had not yet presented his project to his class, and besides Monica, Dudu and Oscar, no one knew of the rock art's existence.

Dudu began to cry again. "I said what I always hear people on TV say— 'No comment.'"

The fateful "No comment." Through overuse it had become the plainest expression of complicity or guilt imaginable.

"And what did he say?"

"He asked if we had any hotels in town."

Monica reached out and put a hand on her shoulder. "Don't worry, Dudu. It was bound to happen sooner or later. The paintings are a national treasure and must be studied. We just don't want people who might deface or damage them to know of their existence."

Monica had heard some landowners kept the existence of San paintings on their properties secret in order to protect them from vandals. She made a mental note to start work immediately on her newspaper story and to tell Sipho to ask permission to present his school project ahead of schedule.

Dudu sniffed. "You should put me to work filing in a back room."

"Don't be silly. I need you out front. You are the face of the *Lady Helen Herald*—and normally a smiling one."

Dudu made an attempt to look cheerful. "Thanks for the tea."

"I make an awful cup, don't I?"

An impish smile spread across Dudu's face. "No comment."

Once Monica had written her first draft of the story about the paintings, she announced that she was going to the hospital to meet Zak. There were a number of other jobs that needed her attention, but she couldn't concentrate on any of them. She hoped her eagerness wasn't obvious to her colleague.

"He's a good man." Dudu's comment came without a hint of mischievousness or irony.

"It's for a story." Monica regretted her defensive—and telltale—tone immediately and quickly added, "Lady Helen is fortunate to have a dedicated doctor."

"It's a shame his wife didn't realize how fortunate *she* was."

As Monica drove north toward the hospital, she realized that it no longer disturbed her that the cemetery was next door to the hospital. Now it seemed the natural place for it.

The main part of Lady Helen Hospital was in an old farmhouse, but it had outgrown the space, and a jumble of prefabricated additions sprouted behind it like wild mushrooms. Monica parked in the shade of a jackalberry tree and checked her face in the rearview mirror. She felt relieved that she had not visited Zak yesterday. He would have wondered what had come over her with all that makeup.

In the shade of the covered veranda, Sunny the cat lay sleeping on a riempie bench, its crisscrossed leather straps sagging from years of use. Sister Adelaide, the beautiful nurse Monica had interviewed for the story on the burn unit, rose to greet her from behind the front desk.

"Monica, it's good to see you."

As Adelaide hugged her, Monica felt the nurse's bracelets pressing into her back. Listening to Adelaide talk was like attending a music recital. Her mellifluous voice, combined with the soft tinkle of her bracelets, would, Monica imagined, calm even the most agitated patient.

"How was your visit home?"

Adelaide had recently spent three weeks with her family in Kimberley, a town known for its half-mile-deep hole where diamonds were once mined.

"My sister has another baby. That makes four. She says I won't find a husband because I'm too skinny."

Monica suppressed a smile. Adelaide was, as her boys' late mother, Ella, would have termed it, a stout woman, and her white nurse's uniform fit her as snugly as a latex glove. She was in her late thirties, and with her beauty and grace it was impossible that she had not had at least one proposal of marriage.

"Dr. Niemand is expecting you."

Monica had not fixed a time with him. Was *Adelaide* insinuating something? No. With her sweet and guileless nature, Adelaide would come straight out and say it.

Monica knew her way down the polished wooden passageway to Zak's office. She knocked lightly.

"Come in."

He lifted his head from a medical journal as she entered.

"Hi, Monica." He smiled at her and then a look of surprise lit his dark eyes.

Monica was mortified. Her makeup was obviously still too much. Now he would have the impression that she was trying to impress him.

He noticed the stiffness in her posture and tried to put her at ease by offering to make coffee. The kettle had just boiled, he said.

"Yes, please, but not too strong." She knew that he used three spoonfuls of instant granules in his own coffee.

From the cupboard behind his desk he took out a white cup and saucer for her and a chipped mug for himself and poured hot water into both.

"How's Yolanda?" This was the closest she would come to inquiring about his personal life.

He handed her the cup and saucer. "She doesn't deserve this."

He sounded bitter and Monica regretted her question.

He put down his mug and stood up. "Let's talk about the project. Please follow me."

She had not even tasted her coffee, but, sensing that he needed to move to escape his thoughts, she did as he asked. She heard the hollow echo of her heels on the hardwood floor as she followed him down the passage. He opened the door of the pediatric ward. Against the walls of the old farmhouse bedroom stood two baby cribs and six small cots—all empty.

"It needs a makeover. Some bright curtains, colorful murals and a box of toys. I'd like you to compose a call for volunteers."

"With all the artists in town, they'll probably have to form a committee and vote on what to paint."

She looked at him, expecting a polite laugh at her feeble attempt at humor, but his gaze had wandered to the view outside the window. The rocky koppies thrust up into the clear blue West Coast sky, catching the full force of the afternoon sun, which had not yet started its slow descent toward the ocean.

Monica imagined he was thinking of his daughter and how much of Yolanda's everyday life he would miss. Her regret at having brought a heavy note into their conversation was selfish; Zak was still grieving his loss. She tried to cheer him up.

"You can put Gift in charge. She'll keep everyone in check." The previous owner of Monica's house, an artist who wore bold caftans and colorful handmade jewelry, was known for her outspokenness. She had once told Monica that a newspaper story Monica had written about the library was as dry as toast.

He turned away from the window. "Thanks." His voice was flat.

"For?"

"Being a friend."

It took all her effort to smile at him. She wanted to be more than his friend.

"I'd better get started on my rounds." He held up his clipboard.

She had played this scene out in her mind on the way to the hospital, and it was not proceeding as she'd imagined. He had not mentioned their meeting outside her house on Saturday. He had not said that he'd like to see her again next weekend. The route of his walk had obviously been nothing more than a coincidence.

"And I have a newspaper to write." Her voice was too bright, but he did not seem to notice.

"Thanks for listening to my problems."

"That's what friends are for." There was a smile pasted across her face, yet, infuriatingly, she felt like crying.

He stopped at the door to the pediatric ward.

"I know my way out."

He was visibly relieved. "Thanks. The list is long today." He waved the clipboard at her.

Adelaide gave her a look of sympathy as she passed the front desk.

Had the nurse heard her conversation with Zak? Or was her bitter disappointment that obvious?

Zak was not interested in a romance with her—not yet, maybe not ever. She felt angry at herself for the stupid hope she had nurtured. She was the mother of two boys. Her thoughts should be only of them.

During the rest of the afternoon Monica wrote Zak's call for volunteers, answered letters to the editor and started laying out the next issue. The front-page story did not deserve its prominence, and Monica believed that this was not due to a lack of news in Lady Helen but to her inability to find it.

"There are stories—good stories—everywhere," Max had once told her. "Just allow yourself to be led."

This week she had not lived up to his expectations, and although she took full responsibility for the lapse, she found herself wishing that something big would happen in Lady Helen. She regretted it immediately because, as an experienced journalist, she knew that when something big happened it was more than likely bad. A whole year of smaller—she had once made the error of calling them *lightweight*—stories was better than one shocking story, at least to the residents of Lady Helen.

That evening Monica and the boys had been invited to dinner at the home of Miemps and Reginald Cloete in Sandpiper Drift. The tiny neighborhood lay a short distance inland from the Little Church of the Lagoon. Although worshippers had to wear boots to tramp across the mud from the parking lot to the church, there was no mud in Sandpiper Drift, only fine white sand that found its way into the houses every day, no matter how often the women swept. Sparse papery reeds and woody pincushion protea shrubs grew in clumps around low, whitewashed fishermen's cottages, the windows of which were all open this evening to catch the breeze floating across the lagoon from the ocean. The usual collection of overalls and cotton housedresses had already been taken down from the wash lines to be ironed. The house where Miemps and Reginald lived with their daughter, Daphne, was the last in the row on the left. It was identical to its fourteen neighbors except that it had window boxes filled with red, orange and yellow geraniums.

Reginald was sitting outside the front door, reading a newspaper, when Monica stopped her car in the dead-end street. Mandla bounded out of the car and ran straight into his arms.

"You're growing like a weed, son." Reginald hoisted Mandla onto his shoulders.

"This is for you." Monica handed her host a box of chocolates.

"They're my favorites. Your mother has such a good memory," said Reginald.

Mandla nodded, but Monica noticed a tightening of Sipho's mouth at Reginald's use of the word *mother*. Unaware of the awkward moment he had created, Reginald herded them inside with a wave of his newspaper.

"Daphne only has an hour for dinner," he said.

Their eyes needed time to adjust to the dim light inside the house. The aroma of roasting meat filled the small living room. Reginald led them to the kitchen to greet his wife and his daughter, who was dressed in her white nurse's uniform.

"We're so glad you could come," said Miemps, stirring a pot of gravy.

Ever since Monica had helped save the tiny neighborhood of Sandpiper Drift from the bulldozers, Miemps had treated her as though she were royalty. It was embarrassing, especially when it happened in front of other people, and that included her daughter, Daphne, who could be rather stern at times. Nobody would forget how Daphne had thrown her shoes at Mr. Yang, the golf course developer, when he'd arrived to order the women down from their roofs.

Miemps shooed everybody into the living room to sit at the round table behind the sofa, and as her husband carved the roast lamb, she told Monica about the new neighbors who had moved into Zukisa's old house.

Ten-year-old Zukisa and her mother had not moved back to Sandpiper Drift when the demolition was called off because Zukisa's father had a job at a pilchard-canning factory in Cape Town and they had wanted to be near him. Recently Monica had paid Zukisa a visit and found her caring for her sick mother. AIDS had already taken her father.

"The new neighbors have two boys," said Miemps. "One is fourteen, the other twelve." Miemps lowered her voice. "Their mother told me that she had to get them away from their old neighborhood in Cape Town because it's full of gangs."

"Have you met them at school?" Monica asked Sipho.

"Yes. Jake, the youngest one, is in my class."

"Their father used to be a fisherman on one of those deepwater trawlers," continued Miemps, "but now he has a job taking out divers with James."

Miemps was referring to the husband of one of Monica's dearest friends, Kitty, who ran the local bed-and-breakfast, called Abalone House.

"I'm sure that with a baby on the way Kitty's happy that her husband is going to be around more to help at Abalone House," said Monica, thinking that it had been too long since she and her friend had sat on the veranda drinking coffee together.

"Don't be sure of that," said Reginald. "I heard James has bought another boat."

Monica saw Sipho frown. Since the accident with the shark cage, when Sipho had been wrongly accused of tampering with the mechanism on the door, an uneasy truce had held between Sipho and James.

After dinner, they all moved to the floral sofa and chairs to drink their coffee.

"Why don't you take the plastic off?" Mandla asked Miemps.

Monica felt her face turn red.

"It protects them," explained Miemps, unfazed.

"But my legs get sweaty," said Mandla, who was wearing shorts.

Daphne laughed. "I have the same problem, little one, but this is an argument we will never win." She put a hand on her mother's knee. "The couch will still be covered when it's twenty years old."

"There's nothing wrong with taking care of your things," said Miemps defensively. "There's so much waste in today's world. Would you like a piece of cake, young man?"

Mandla nodded enthusiastically.

"Yes, please," Monica reminded him.

"Yes, please," repeated Mandla obediently.

Miemps handed him a plate with a large slice. "Now you can eat this without me fussing at you not to make a mess on the couch."

Mandla smiled. He was in favor of this idea, sweaty legs and all.

Daphne excused herself to go back to work at the hospital. After she left, Reginald suggested that he and the boys go outdoors to kick a soccer ball.

"Do you think you should be doing that at your age?" asked his wife.

"I'm not ancient."

It was six-thirty, but the sun was still high in the sky. As they stepped outside, their eyes had to adjust to the bright light again. Reginald kicked the ball to Mandla, who was surprisingly nimble footed for his age. Mandla kicked it to his brother.

"I don't feel like playing," said Sipho.

Ella had encouraged her eldest son to play soccer, but he had always preferred his nature programs and books.

"Aw, come on, Sipho," complained Mandla.

Knowing his brother could badger a person forever, Sipho gave the ball a halfhearted kick to Reginald.

A couple of boys came out of their house to watch the game. Reginald waved them over.

"Hi, Sipho," said the smaller of the two.

"These are the boys I was telling you about," Miemps explained to Monica. They had sat down on a bench to watch their menfolk.

The other boys were clearly seasoned soccer players, and Monica could tell that Sipho was embarrassed by his lack of skill. The eldest one kicked a hard shot that went flying past Sipho's legs. Monica did not like the way the boy chuckled. Sipho retrieved the ball and then sat down on the curb to remove a stone from his shoe. Monica wondered if it was imaginary.

She watched Mandla kick the ball a couple more times to Reginald and then called her sons to leave. Mandla complained, but the relief on Sipho's face was clear.

"Reg would have made a great grandfather," said Miemps sadly.

"Why did Daphne never marry?" As soon as the words were out of her mouth, Monica wondered if she had gone too far.

Miemps answered without hesitation. "She was engaged once, but the man broke her heart. I tried telling her that not all men were like her ex-fiancé—just look at her father—but she would not listen. Daphne is like my late mother-in-law—hardheaded."

Across the road a man came out of the house with a bag of garbage. He kept his head down and did not wave at his neighbors. Lionel DeVilliers might have escaped prison for his role in helping Mr. Yang trick the government into selling this land, but the residents of Sandpiper Drift had become his unofficial parole officers. They monitored his actions and did not allow any late-night visits from fellow gamblers. And to top it all, he had been forced to give up his mansion in Bloubergstrand and rebuild the house that had been destroyed by the bulldozers.

Monica assumed that DeVilliers's wife, Lizbet, had seen them sitting outside the house, but would not come out to share greetings. Lizbet had confessed her husband's crime to the people of Sandpiper Drift, and although she had not known of it until she'd dragged the truth from him, she was no longer comfortable among her old neighbors. Miemps had been her best friend, but their daily cup of tea together was a thing of the past.

"She'll get over it," said Monica.

Miemps nodded, understanding immediately that Monica was talking about her estranged friend.

The boys thanked Miemps for the meal and waved at Reginald, who wanted to continue the game with the newcomers.

"He won't be able to walk tomorrow," said Miemps.

Monica reversed down the road so that she would not disturb the soccer game. Mandla almost fell asleep in the car on the short ride home, but Monica managed to engage him in a game of I Spy using colors. He was too dirty to put to bed without a bath.

She had just turned on the bathwater when Sipho called her from the living room. She turned the water off and took Mandla with her. Sipho was crouched over Ebony.

"I think she's dead." His voice was unnaturally high.

The cat lay on her side, legs out straight. Monica felt for a pulse.

"You're right," she said quietly.

Sipho threw his arms around her neck. "I'm going to miss her," he sobbed.

"Me, too," she said.

Mandla studied Ebony from different angles. He did not cry.

The cat had adored Monica's late brother, and Luca had always asked after her in his letters home from the army.

Monica stroked Sipho's hair. "She had a long and happy life."

Her brother had not.

Monica wanted to bury Ebony straightaway.

"In the ground outside, all by herself?" Mandla started to cry.

Monica took him in her arms. "She'll always be close to us."

Over his head she saw Sipho's expression and wished she had not used those words. Ella's ashes were scattered in the Garden of Remembrance in Johannesburg, about nine hundred miles away.

"It doesn't matter where someone is buried," she added quietly, watching Sipho. "They'll always be in our hearts."

He nodded, but she wished she had thought before speaking.

"Was Ebony very old?" asked Mandla through his tears.

"Yes, sweetie."

"It's okay, then."

Monica turned away so he would not see her tears. A small boy should not be accustomed to the idea of people dying young.

She dug a hole under the tall syringa tree in the back garden. Mandla and Sipho took turns saying prayers as she lowered Ebony into it.

"Goodbye, little friend," she whispered, pulling a sheet of plastic over Ebony.

Mandla reached for Sipho's hand as she started to fill the hole. Once she had finished, she smoothed out the soil and laid a single gerbera daisy on the mound. Mandla hurried off and came back with a rose.

"We'll ask Oscar to make us a cross," she told the boys.

They both agreed that this was a good idea. Not wanting to leave Ebony alone just yet, they stayed outdoors until the sun slipped into the ocean and darkness descended on the garden.

3

FRANCINA SHABALALA STOOD ON HER BALCONY, watching the dark triangle of ocean at the end of the street turn flamingo-pink as the sun came up over the koppies. She had promised Sipho and Mandla that she would help them build a birdhouse this afternoon when they came home from school. Her boys. Monica would not be happy to hear her use these words, so she was careful never to say them out loud when Monica was near. But she had cared for them since they first came to live with Monica during their mother's illness and she could only think of them as hers.

Below, on Main Street, a boy pushed a newspaper through the mail slot of the gallery across the street and then skipped to the next door. It was not the *Lady Helen Herald* he was delivering but a Cape Town daily that included news of the capitol, the country and the rest of the world. Before long, Francina would go downstairs to collect the copy that had landed on the mat, and Hercules would read snatches from it to her while she served him pap and eggs. He was a teacher with a college degree; she was merely a housekeeper turned dress-maker, with a grade nine School Leaver's certificate obtained only last year. But despite the difference in their formal educations, Hercules shared his thoughts with Francina and he respected her opinions.

They'd met at a choir competition. Francina was singing with her choir from Johannesburg, Hercules conducting his from Dundee. Their relationship had developed slowly, as any good relationship should.

Francina's first marriage had ended more than twenty years ago when her husband, Winston, beat her so badly that the doctors had to remove her left eye. She was used to people staring at her while they tried to figure out what was different about her face. Sometimes she even acceded to children's requests to take out her glass eye so they could study it.

Winston had gone back to their village in the Valley of a Thousand Hills and claimed that his wife had been unfaithful. People believed him. He was the son of the chief. When he became chief, people con-tinued treating Francina as though she were a stray dog scrounging for food in the village.

Last week a check had arrived in the mail from her village elders. It was the first distribution of profits from Jabulani Lodge, the safari lodge that the village had set up on land given to them by the gov-ernment as part of its land redistribution program. The check had only been for a small amount, but she was satisfied because Winston could have excluded the sons and daughters who no longer lived in the village. Her threat last year to tell the villagers about his drinking and gambling in Johannesburg must have played heavily on his mind when he'd made this decision.

She heard Hercules opening the door to the balcony.

"Another beautiful day."

As he stooped to kiss her, she smelled the new shampoo she had bought from the store that sold only natural products. Who would have thought you could make shampoo with rooibos tea? His shirt looked as crisp as when she'd ironed it. He had taken her advice not to dress until he was completely dry after his shower.

"What's the occasion?" she asked, looking at his red tie.

"The school inspector's coming."

"You'd better eat your breakfast so you can be on time." She brushed a stray hair from his shoulders.

It was an unnecessary directive, since Hercules had not once been late for school, as a teacher or as a student, but she enjoyed this gentle bossing to which marriage entitled her.

Hercules sat down at the table, and Francina served him a bowl of steaming pap and a glass of freshly squeezed orange juice. Cat—or Kitty, as Francina had been instructed to call the young lady who ran Abalone House—was not the only one who could put on a breakfast spread.

Francina wondered which stories in the paper would catch her husband's attention today. He knew that she wasn't interested in politics unless it had to do with the fulfillment of the government's election promises. Grudgingly she admitted that the ANC government had made progress; her village now had a connection to the local power grid and a communal water faucet outside the elders' meeting hall. Running water in each house could not be far away.

Hercules liked stories of how other countries were run. In Francina's mind, it was pointless. She would never use a dress pattern printed in Europe for an African woman. It was better to make one after taking exact measurements.

Thank goodness her husband did not spend hours poring over the sports pages, the way other men did. He'd glance quickly at the scores if Bafana Bafana, the national team, was playing in a big competition such as the African Cup, but the sports pages were usually the first he discarded, and she used them to wrap up her vegetable peels.

Sometimes Hercules would cut out articles to read to his students at school. Francina felt warm all over when she saw the respectful way young people looked at him. He was not a teacher who relied on frivolous entertainment to capture the attention of his students but rather organization, steadiness and gentle wisdom. His lessons ended with a discussion of how the events of the past could lead to better decisions today.

But the esteemed teacher did not read her any tidbits from the newspaper this morning as she fried his eggs, and with wifely wisdom, Francina realized that he was nervous about the visit from the school inspector.

Francina cleared the table when he was finished, but instead of starting to wash the dishes and receiving a goodbye kiss at the sink, she accompanied her husband down the stairs. She held his briefcase as he put on the jacket that was unnecessary in everyone's mind except his own.

"Just be yourself, my love, and that will be more than enough."

He gave her a look of gratitude. He never said as much, but she knew that he was happier than he had been in years. One day, he might even be able to stop taking his little blue pills for depression.

She watched him through the window until he had disappeared from sight and then she hurried upstairs to clean the kitchen before starting work in the shop. There were no appointments in the book for at least two hours, and if she worked quickly, she might be able to finish Ingrid van Tonder's dress. Ingrid was the wife of the pastor of the Little Church of the Lagoon and had been Francina's first paying customer.

With the kitchen clean, Francina cut up a pineapple and ate a few slices standing at the sink. Then she put some on a plate for her mother-in-law and left it on the table with a glass of orange juice.

She inspected the small two-bedroom flat. Every surface gleamed. Hercules often offered to do the housework, but it was not a man's job and she enjoyed keeping her home in order. A home needed a woman's touch. Would a man put roses in his mother's bedroom every week? Would a man shine the faucets with vinegar? Would a man think to take down the curtains and wash them every now and then? Francina had heard that men were doing all sorts of women's jobs now, even nursing, but at forty-one, she considered herself part of the older generation and did not go in for such modern notions. Imagine if her father stopped tending his cattle and came and poked his nose in the cooking pots. Her mother would think he'd had too much sun and send him inside the house to rest. Francina had to be careful with what she taught Sipho and Mandla. Monica was modern and didn't want the boys growing up thinking they were little princes. Francina respected her wishes, but in her mind they *were* little princes.

With a cup of rooibos tea in her hand, she went downstairs to unlock the door of the shop. The large capital letters across the display window cast pale, spindly shadows on the shiny wooden floor. Hercules had insisted the sign writer use gold for the name of her shop. Jabulani Dressmakers. It was the name of her village and meant *happiness* in the Zulu language.

After half an hour of sewing, she heard heavy footsteps on the stairs.

"Good morning, daughter."

Her mother-in-law carried a large shopping bag for the morning's marketing. She thanked Francina for remembering that today was the first day of her diet.

"I'm going to buy milk, bread, apricot jam and apples. Anything else?"

"Tea, please. Are you sure you can manage all that?"

Although the list was short, the shopping expedition involved a walk up to Peg's Dairy Farm for the milk and then a walk back into town to the bakery, the general store and the market stall where the local produce farmers set up every Monday, Wednesday and Saturday.

"I'm getting used to this way of shopping. It's good exercise."

Francina knew that afterward her mother-in-law would stop in at her good friend Mama Dlamini's for a cup of coffee. She wondered if the cake of the day would put an end to the diet.

"I'll be back in time to make lunch," said her mother-in-law, waving as she stepped out onto the covered sidewalk.

Francina waved back. She enjoyed their time together at midday, when her mother-in-law related conversations from her morning in town. It was not surprising how fast news traveled here. This was just another way in which Lady Helen was similar to Francina's village. She had found out that Hercules had been offered the job at Green Block School before he'd arrived to tell her. The housekeeper across the street had met the cleaning lady from the school at the dry cleaner's. The grapevine was short in a small town.

After lunch, her mother-in-law would take over the shop, while Francina hurried to pick up the boys from school. Monica had hired someone to do the cleaning and only required Francina to supervise the boys, but Francina always found something to do that the other lady had missed. It was quite astonishing how nobody nowadays thought to dust light fittings, polish school shoes or water the garden.

When Francina had asked Hercules if he thought his mother would mind helping in the shop while she looked after the boys in the afternoon, she had not expected him to say no with so much enthusiasm. His mother had been shut away in her house for too long, he'd said, and would appreciate the activity of Main Street.

Hercules was a good son. Francina would not have married him if he was not. A man who treated his mother well was to be trusted. Another woman might be shocked if her fiancé announced that he'd invited his mother to move in with them, but not Francina. It was only right. She could not understand how people could put their elderly parents in homes to be looked after by strangers. It was not the Zulu way—or at least not the old Zulu way. She had heard sad stories of sons and daughters abandoning their parents at the hospital when they became difficult to care for.

Mrs. Shabalala's eagerness to help, however, was not matched by her skill, and Francina often had to rush out and buy new fabric when her mother-in-law cut out two fronts and no back or cut against the bias when she should have cut with it. Many a night Francina had stayed up late unpicking the hems her mother-in-law had sewn because they were untidy. While Monica and the boys were away in Italy this past Christmas, Francina had taken advantage of her free afternoons to teach her mother-in-law the right way to put together a dress. Her work had improved immensely, but Francina suspected that Mrs. Shabalala's main contribution to the shop would always be her friendly nature that made clients smile even when their dresses were delayed. Keeping the ladies of Lady Helen happy was half the battle of running a successful business.

As she sewed, Francina turned on the radio for company, but the channels were full of thumping music for teenagers or the wailing and sighing of soap operas. She turned the radio off and listened instead to the ticking of the grandfather clock, the only item that remained from the watchmaker's store that had once operated inside these walls.

Ingrid's dress was turning out to be beautiful. It was black chiffon, a color with which Francina used to have difficulty working. The clear, bright light of Lady Helen not only helped artists but enabled a one-eyed seamstress to expand her palette. The delicate sleeves would end halfway between Ingrid's elbow and wrist, which was fitting for the wife of a pastor.

As Francina cut the final thread, the bells of the front door tinkled. The postman normally shoved letters through the mail slot and gave her a wave, but this time he stood on her mat, a single letter in his hand and a serious look on his face.

"Good morning, Francina. I have a telegram for you."

She took the clipboard he offered and signed her name. He handed her the envelope, but instead of leaving, he waited, watching her face.

"I like to wait around," he said, noticing her puzzlement, "in case it's bad news."

Francina felt the tangled snake in her stomach stir. "Thank you for the offer, but I'm sure you have a lot of letters to deliver." She was surprised at the calmness of her voice.

"Sometimes people faint or are in such a state they can't pick up the phone to call their family."

Francina wondered why he could not see that his grave manner heightened a person's anxiety. After one more offer of moral support, he left reluctantly.

With blood pounding in her veins, she tore open the envelope. The first line was like a blow to her chest. Her father was sick and in hospital in Durban. The whole family was at his bedside, and he was still lucid enough to notice her absence.

There was no mention of the name of her father's disease, but it was clearly too serious for the community clinic near the village to handle. Francina did not feel faint, as the postman had predicted she might, and she thought she would be able to pick up the telephone to call Monica. What she could have done with at this moment, though, was help up the stairs so she could wait for her husband and mother-in-law out of sight of passersby on Main Street. Her legs felt leaden and her footsteps sounded heavier than her mother-in-law's. Out of breath, she reached the landing above and then realized that she had not locked the shop and hung the Closed sign. But it would not be necessary for her to make the trip again, because at that moment the bells tinkled and, a second later, the bewildered voice of her mother-in-law called for her. Francina never left the shop unattended.

"I'm upstairs, Mama," she called. "Please lock the door and hang the sign."

Her mother-in-law made it up the stairs quicker than she ever had.

"What's the matter?" she asked, panting from the exertion.

Francina held up the telegram.

"Oh, no." Her mother-in-law put her hand to her heart. "Somebody has passed."

"My father is ill. I must go to him."

"Oh, daughter, I'll get Hercules."

Francina did not wish to offend her mother-in-law, but Hercules would be home in an hour and she needed the time to pack her bag and telephone Monica.

"Please, save your energy, Mama—for the boys. Can you fetch them from school and watch them until Monica gets home from work?"

Her mother-in-law nodded, pleased at the prospect of being useful.

An hour later, when Hercules came up the stairs, sniffing the air to discover what his mother had cooked for lunch, Francina was sitting on the sofa, a suitcase at her feet, and Mrs. Shabalala was already at the school to pick up the boys.

"What's happened?" he asked.

"It's my father." She started to cry. "He's sick."

Hercules put both his arms around her, a gesture he normally reserved for the privacy of their bedroom.

"I'll come with you," he whispered.

She gave a loud sniff. "Thank you, but you cannot leave your students. You must come to KwaZulu if he…if he…" She put her head on his shoulder, unable to finish her sentence.

Hercules knew better than to reassure her with well-meaning but naive promises that her father would not die.

"It's a long way, Francina. We have some money saved. Let me buy you an airplane ticket."

Francina covered her forehead with both her hands. "Never," she said, and from the tone of her voice Hercules knew that he would not persuade his wife. "I will take a minibus taxi to Cape Town and then find a long-haul taxi to Durban."

Seeing the apprehension in her husband's eyes, she took his hand. "I used to travel alone before I met you," she told him gently.

He nodded. "But there should be no need for it now. Mr. D, the principal, will understand."

"This argument is one you will not win," she said, smiling because she knew already what his reply would be.

"Do I win any?"

She looked into his worried eyes and for a second was tempted to let him accompany her. But if God wanted to take her father, then Hercules would be needed for at least a week in her village for the funeral, and there was already a shortage of teachers at Green Block School.

Hercules picked up her suitcase and the plastic bag she had filled with sandwiches, apples and a flask of tea and followed her down the stairs, through the shop and out onto Main Street.

"No, Francina, this is not right." He put her suitcase down on the sidewalk. "Let me at least drive you to Cape Town."

She saw the pleading in his eyes and nodded. "Leave a note for Mama or she will worry."

He dashed back into the shop and up the stairs.

"Going away?" said a voice behind her. It was Mama Dlamini.

Francina nodded. "To Durban. My father is sick."

"Ah, that's bad. I'm sorry."

Francina knew that within an hour the whole of Lady Helen would have heard that she had left and why.

Mama Dlamini offered her help in any way it might be needed. She had one request of Francina.

"Please bring me a bottle of seawater."

"But if you walk to the end of this street, you can fill one yourself."

"Yes, but I want water from the ocean that rolls up the beach of my beloved KwaZulu-Natal. The Indian Ocean."

Francina told Mama Dlamini that she would bring her a bottle. She thought that she might bring one for her mother-in-law, too. Although Francina was not fond of drinking seawater, her mother-in-law firmly believed that it was necessary at least twice a year to cleanse the body.

Hercules came out of the store and greeted Mama Dlamini.

"Don't worry, Francina, I'll take care of him while you're away," said Mama Dlamini.

"His mother will still be here." Francina hoped her tone was not too abrupt, but she did not need another woman looking after her husband, especially not when she had only recently won him from the memory of his late wife.

If Mama Dlamini noticed the edge to Francina's voice, she did not show it. "Have a safe journey, my friend." She squeezed Francina's hand.

Feeling guilty for her thoughts, Francina waved wildly at Mama Dlamini as she set off again for the café. Hercules looked at his wife, confusion on his face. *Dear Hercules,* she thought, *you're a sensitive man, but you will never know the unspoken conversations that go on between women.*

As they drove up the winding road to the top of the koppie, Francina looked back at the town that lay under a blanket of bougainvillea.

"Nothing will change while you're gone," said Hercules.

Francina murmured in agreement, but she felt a strange premonition that he might be wrong. As they descended the other side of the koppie, the vegetation grew sparser and more muted in color. Low clumps of shrubs with delicate rolled leaves shivered in the fierce, warm wind that raced across the flat landscape and buffeted the car with such force that Hercules had to keep a firm hold of the steering wheel. Uneven white stones lay scattered like toys left out by a child.

"Keep an eye on my boys, please," said Francina, for although she trusted her mother-in-law's sense of responsibility, she did not trust the older woman's physical ability to keep up with Mandla.

"I will," said Hercules, and he knew better than to correct her on her use of the possessive pronoun.

They turned onto the main road that led to Cape Town. Francina had never seen the tortoises on this road that Sipho was always talking about. Her father had once caught a tortoise eating his spinach in the vegetable garden. Other men in the village would have used it to make soup, but her father had built a miniature wooden pen for it, a kraal, and fed it with leftover vegetables.

Francina was grateful for the mind's peculiar habit of preserving good memories and allowing bad ones to fade like old photographs. For five years her father had believed the story that she had not been a loyal wife.

As the car approached Cape Town, Francina stopped talking so Hercules could concentrate on the thickening traffic. She watched the strange flat-topped mountain that guarded this city on the tip of Africa and wondered what historic events had taken place on its slopes. She did not ask Hercules, as she was not in the mood for a lesson.

"There's no tablecloth of mist on the mountain today," he remarked.

Francina had never seen the mountain without it.

"What a sight for sore eyes it must have been for sailors," he continued. "The vegetable gardens and fruit orchards that Jan van Riebeeck planted to feed the men of the Dutch East India Company in 1652 exist to this day."

He could not help himself, and Francina imagined that after dropping her off he would not leave Cape Town without a visit to the Castle of Good Hope—the oldest building in South Africa—or one of the museums. He had expressed a desire to visit the District Six Museum, which commemorated the forced removal of sixty thousand people from a vibrant community of Cape Town to make way for a whites-only neighborhood.

Sandpiper Drift residents, Miemps and Reginald Cloete and their daughter, Daphne, had been among those evicted from their homes in 1966 and moved to an outlying, desolate area known as the Cape Flats. Their home, along with thousands more, had been flattened by bulldozers. The land had recently been returned to a group of people who'd submitted a claim to the government. Some planned to move back, others to take the cash settlement. Still more, like Miemps and Reg, had missed the cutoff date and were trying to win an extension, but it may be too late for them. Miemps had confided in Francina that she wouldn't be disappointed about losing out on the land because she didn't want to leave Lady Helen, which was in many ways a modern-day District Six, but the money, of course, would be welcome.

The taxi stand was in the center of the city, and Francina and Hercules had no choice but to endure the traffic bottlenecks that choked the main roads. By the time they arrived, Francina was exhausted—and she still had another one thousand miles to go.

Hercules lifted her suitcase out of the car and led her by the hand through the noisy throng of people. Young boys hawked cigarettes, sweets and cold drinks, while women with carts offered curry and rice, and men cut the hair of clients who sat on upturned cooking-oil drums. If she had so desired, Francina could have bought a dress, shoes, soap, music CDs and even a reconditioned muffler for their car.

She followed Hercules, realizing that she had not bothered to think about finding the correct place to wait for her taxi. As a woman who had lived on her own for more than twenty years, the division of labor that marriage offered was a relief and a delight. She could not understand women who insisted on controlling their own lives after marriage, as though they were still single.

"This is it." Hercules set her suitcase down on the sidewalk.

The short line consisted of four middle-aged women, a young mother with a baby tied to her back, two young men and one elderly gentleman who was standing dangerously close to the road.

"Come this way," said Francina, taking hold of his elbow and steering him to a safer place to wait. Minibus taxis sometimes arrived like runaway horses.

The man thanked her, but she had a feeling that he did not know why. How could a daughter allow her father to travel alone when his mind had already begun its slow journey back to infancy?

Hercules smiled at her. "You would have made a good mother."

It was said with kindness, but Francina was suddenly filled with rage.

"You should have married a younger woman," she snapped.

The hurt on his face made her realize that she had gone too far. But instead of apologizing for her harsh tone and words, she lashed out at him again because he was right.

"You and your mother are always making me feel bad that I'm too old to have babies."

It was not true. Neither of them had ever mentioned children.

"You're upset about your father," Hercules said quietly.

"Yes, I am, and that's all the more reason for you not to upset me even more."

With the racket going on around them, it would have been impossible for anyone to overhear their argument, but Hercules was clearly uncomfortable that she had raised her voice at him in public.

"We'll discuss this when you get home," he said, the gentle tone gone from his voice.

"There's nothing to discuss. You want a baby, your mother wants a grandchild—and I can't give either of you what you want." She was too filled with anger to cry. It was not her fault she had passed her time early.

"Francina, please. What is happening?"

"Let's not talk."

They were two solitary rocks in the swirling current of people, luggage, beeping horns and nauseating exhaust fumes. They stood slightly apart, in silence, until Francina's minibus taxi pulled up at the curb and there was a race for the window seats. Francina waited. A window seat or a center one, what did it matter? She and Hercules watched as the driver loaded her suitcase into the trunk. It was fortunate that the taxi was not yet full or her suitcase would have been strapped onto the roof. People were always reaching their destinations and discovering that the new clothes they had bought for their families, the sweets and tins of coffee, the toys from rummage sales, had flown off and lay scattered along the road, to be picked up eventually by a herd boy or a child returning from school.

"Please phone when you arrive so that I will know that you are safe," said Hercules.

Francina nodded. He took her hand, and for an instant she thought he was going to pull her toward him despite the eight pairs of eyes watching them from inside the taxi. He squeezed her hand.

She climbed on board and looked out at him from her seat between one of the middle-aged women and the elderly man. Hercules stood motionless as the taxi driver climbed in and revved the motor. When the taxi pulled away from the curb, Francina felt herself suddenly filled with regret and wished she could shout for the driver to stop. But she could not; her mother had told her to come as quickly as possible.

4

FRANCINA HAD NEVER APPROACHED KWAZULU-NATAL from the south before, and if she didn't have faith that the snake in her stomach would begin to coil restlessly when she crossed the border, she might have thought that the green hills and open spaces of the Eastern Cape were part of her province.

The highway the minibus had traveled since Cape Town, mostly inland but dipping back to the coast at large towns, had run through areas Francina had only read about in geography books. When she returned to Lady Helen, she'd suggest that Monica drive the boys to see the Whale Coast, where tourists from all over the world watched the whales from Antarctica calve and mate in the warm waters. Sipho, especially, would like that.

The air inside the minibus was warm and stale. Francina dozed, and when she woke, she saw shadowy trees pressed right up to the edge of the road like village children begging for sweets from passing motorists. She thought of the map of South Africa she had studied for her exams last year and decided that this had to be the Garden Route, an area of forests, lakes and lagoons and the home of the old president who had refused to testify before the Truth and Reconciliation Commission.

A few hours later the minibus left the coastal city of East London, South Africa's only river port. The road became desolate, and more than once the driver had to stop for mangy dogs crossing the road. Near the village of Qunu the driver woke everyone to see President Nelson Mandela's house.

"There it is," he said, pointing at a large walled redbrick house, clearly visible in the light of the full moon. "Our first president has built a tunnel under this highway to allow the village children to visit in safety."

Francina made a mental note to remember to tell Hercules; this was the sort of information he filed away in his brain like a computer.

She knew she was traveling along the area known as the Wild Coast, but the highway never got close enough to the ocean for her to determine whether it really was wild.

Early in the morning, crossing the border into KwaZulu-Natal, Francina did not feel the restless snake in her stomach because she was asleep. She woke with the sun warm on her face. The highway had taken another dip toward the ocean, and the minibus was passing through South Coast beach towns. These looked quiet and restful, and she wondered if Hercules might like to visit here with her. Suddenly she realized that the only reason Hercules would come up this way was if her father died. She began to wonder if it had been foolish not to accept her husband's offer of a plane ticket. *Please, God,* she prayed silently, *let me not be too late.*

There were many cars coming from Durban, but the minibus had a clear run into the city to which Francina had lived so close for sixteen years but had visited only once, one afternoon on a school trip. The elder of her two brothers had lived here since he was a teenager. She knew nothing of Sigidi's life now except that he was a bricklayer, earned good money and lived in a small flat near the beachfront with two other men. Sigidi was a man of the world. Whenever he went home to his village, he wore new clothes, expensive shoes and sunglasses. Their father worked outdoors, too, and he had done without sunglasses his entire life. Sometimes Francina had to stifle an uneasy feeling that her brother had other sources of income, most likely from the horse races for which Durban was famous.

"Anyone for South Beach?" asked the driver.

"Yes, please," said Francina. Hercules had looked up the address of the hospital and told her that it was right on the beach.

After wishing her fellow travelers well, she thanked the driver for delivering her safely to her destination and picked up the suitcase he had deposited on the pavement. The taxi took off before she crossed the road. Rising up before her were two tall brown buildings. The view alone, she thought, would lift the spirits of the patients. Francina wondered if her father was able to go to his window to see the ocean. The horizon he watched in the village every evening ended with the swell of another hill; here it stretched on forever.

She walked across the parking lot, hearing the palm trees rustling in the breeze, and found the main entrance. The receptionist gave her directions to her father's ward and reminded her that morning visiting hours ended in thirty minutes.

"The lifts are out of order," the lady added, shrugging as though this were a regular occurrence.

Francina wondered what would happen if a patient had to be rushed to surgery. Puffing as loudly as her mother-in-law, she reached the sixth floor and put down her suitcase to wipe the shine from her face before greeting her family.

She found her father's ward without having to disturb the nurses from their important work and knocked quietly. Quick footsteps approached. The door opened and there was her mother, wearing the dress Francina had made for her for special occasions.

"I knew it was you, Francina."

Her mother held her tightly. The embrace lasted so long Francina feared she had come too late.

"My father?" she whispered.

"Bad." Her mother's voice caught in a sob.

Francina felt a chill in her bones. Her mother only cried in the presence of death. The last time had been when her firstborn son had died in a mine accident in Johannesburg. Francina had been just nine years old.

"How much longer does he have?"

"He has been waiting for you, daughter."

Her mother ended the embrace and motioned for Francina to follow. Her sweet mother, with her tiny, delicate body that did not look strong enough to have given birth to four children, had the posture of a queen despite years of bending over a hoe in the family field.

Francina became aware of the presence of Sigidi and her younger brother, Dingane, his wife, Nokuthula, and their two teenage sons. In any other circumstances, she would have rushed to greet them, but now she walked solemnly toward the last bed in the ward—the one next to the window.

How small her father looked under the white blanket with the blue stripe. When she was growing up, Francina had believed her father was as strong as the Zulu kings who'd once ruled the province. He could wrestle a bull to the ground with his bare hands, dig giant boulders out of his field and swing a hammer bigger than her head. Only five years ago he had built the family's three-room house, consisting of a living room, kitchen and bathroom. Her father was only seventy-two. Without ever consciously thinking about it, she had assumed that he would be around for at least another twenty years.

The family made way for her next to his bed.

"Baba, it's me, Francina." She took his limp hand from on top of the blanket.

Her father opened his eyes, and she saw immediately that they were the eyes of a man in grotesque pain. The corners of his mouth twitched as though he were trying to smile. It was then that she noticed the mound of his belly under the blankets. Nobody had told her the name of the disease that was trying to take this man from the world, but it was not important. What would she, a simple seamstress, have done with the information? She knew that it was bad enough to make a grown man appear as small and weak as a child and that it hurt too much for him to smile. What more did she need to know? She trusted that the doctors had done their best and now it was up to God.

The skin of her father's fingers felt papery and dry, so different from the warm, slightly clammy hand that had rested briefly on hers before he'd escorted her down the aisle to meet Hercules. He had not hugged her then, as he had on the day she married Winston, nor told her that she'd made him proud.

He opened his mouth to speak, but no words came, only a grimace. Francina knew in her heart that he wanted to say the words she had been waiting to hear for more than twenty years. She bent down and whispered in his ear.

"It's okay, Baba, I forgive you."

His eyes filled with tears.

Her mother approached from the other side of the bed and took her husband's other hand. She did not speak, but Francina knew that her mother had longed for this simple ceremony of forgiveness between father and daughter.

He began to moan, at first softly and then so loudly that a nurse came running.

"Can you give him something for the pain?" asked Francina.

"We already gave him the best stuff we have. What he needs is morphine, but our hospital is on a waiting list for it."

Her father called out his dead mother's name.

"He's delirious," the nurse explained. "Death is close. Some of you might find it too upsetting." She looked at Dingane's sons. "We have a waiting room outside with a television."

But it was not the Zulu way to shield children from death, which was, after all, a natural part of life. The family huddled closer to the bed and watched as their father and grandfather thrashed about until he had kicked off the blanket.

"I can't bear it," said Francina's mother, sobbing.

Her words sent a shiver down Francina's spine. She had never heard her mother so much as grumble that her feet hurt.

Her father's gaze was fixed on a point above the heads of his family. He seemed to be watching something. He moaned, and the jagged line of his mouth told Francina that he did not like what he saw.

The nurse returned. "Hallucinations can be pleasant—of deceased family members or of times gone by. But they can also be like nightmares."

"Can we wake him? I think he's having the bad kind." Francina's mother would not usually have spoken in the presence of a stranger, but her husband's distress seemed too much for her to witness.

The nurse shook her head. "It's not the painkillers doing this. It's the process of death."

Francina saw her mother's eyes widen and went to put an arm around her shoulders. They felt as slight and bony as Sipho's.

"It's God's way," she whispered in her mother's ear.

Francina stayed close to her mother, ready to comfort her when the time came.

Her father pulled his lips back, baring his teeth.

"He's smiling, Mama," she whispered.

His eyes remained shut. Francina heard Dingane groan. Francina began to pray aloud. Sigidi gave her a sharp look, but then closed his eyes and bowed his head. Words flowed from her mouth. She begged God to make His presence known to her father so that he would not be frightened as he began his long journey home. She watched her father's face as she prayed. The donkey grin had stuck, just as her mother used to warn her children when they pulled a face at someone. The words stopped coming to Francina.

"In Jesus's name, amen," she finished.

Dingane squeezed her hand. There were shiny rivulets of tears on his cheeks. "That was beautiful, sister."

A gurgle came from their father's throat, and for an instant his eyes were luminous with fear. The donkey grin slid from his face.

"Baba?" Her mother put her hand on his forehead as though checking for fever, as she did to her grandchildren when they were sick and as she had done to her children when they were young.

A light of recognition passed briefly across her husband's face. She bent down and kissed him on the mouth. This was the first time Francina and her brothers had ever seen their parents kiss. Sigidi and Dingane looked at their feet, embarrassed. Francina put a hand on her mother's back.

When their mother pulled away from their father, they could see the change on his face. His lips were slack, his eyes unblinking. Their father had died in the brief moment of their mother's kiss.

Sigidi spoke first. "Is he...?"

Francina nodded.

Her mother let out a loud, keening wail. If her husband had passed away at home, she would have been joined by relatives and close friends, and the whole valley would have reverberated with their ululating cries.

Francina pulled her mother close, but that made her grieve even more loudly. Choking on her own tears, Francina patted her mother's head as though comforting a small child, the daughter taking the role of the parent.

"Shh, Mama," said Dingane, but before he could say any more, his wife tugged on his sleeve and gave him a disapproving look. His wife did not join in with the wailing, but Francina suspected Nokuthula would have if this were not a public hospital.

The nurse must have heard, but she waited—out of respect, Francina hoped—before coming to her father's ward.

"I'm sorry," she said, addressing Francina's mother.

Francina's mother continued to wail, but Francina knew by the way she tilted her head toward the nurse that she had heard. The nurse pulled the sheet up to her father's chin but did not, as Francina expected, cover his face. He lay there staring blankly at the spot above their heads that had captured his attention earlier, his lips slightly parted, a faint sheen of sweat on his forehead. The nurse put her hand over his face and closed his eyes. Now it looked as though he were in a deep, relaxing sleep.

On the way out of the ward the nurse took Francina aside.

"Your mother is going to upset the other patients."

Francina nodded and watched as the nurse closed the door behind her. She looked at her family gathered around the bed and felt a sudden painful stab of guilt. She hadn't been home in more than a year. There had been the wedding, her exams, her business. She wished that she'd gone home one more time after her confrontation with Winston, that she'd seen her father's face when Winston's men had started arriving with bales of hay to feed his cattle during the drought, that she'd sat on a lawn chair outside the hut with him, watching the sun slink down behind the hills and the valley fill with blue-black twilight as a million beetles started their brittle chafing.

The family waited until the porters came to wheel her father away. Sigidi spoke with the men in hushed tones. Francina knew that he was trying to find out where to collect his father's body. The porters shook their heads. They did not know or were not allowed to say. Francina saw an uphill battle ahead, but as the daughter, it was not her fight. Sigidi and Dingane followed their father out of the ward as the porters took him away on a gurney so narrow his arms fell over the sides, revealing his stiff fingers poking out from under the draped sheet.

Francina steered her mother to a chair. Her nephews leaned against the wall, their mouths set in tight lines, their eyes locked on the empty bed. The vulnerability of their age was betrayed by the quick, nervous movement of their hands and feet. Francina started to pack up her father's things. A comb. A box of snuff. Leftover *vetkoek* that nobody had been in the mood to finish—not even her brother's sons, who were usually as hungry as lions. She found her father's clothes and shoes in the bedside cabinet. The trousers were old but well cared for, the shirt a dazzling white, the shoes worn but shiny. He had dressed in his best church clothes to come to the hospital. Francina felt fresh tears on her lashes, but she did not allow herself to break down. Somebody had to take care of the practical matters that had been her mother's responsibility for more than fifty years of marriage.

Her brothers returned, their faces dark with rage.

"We were told his body can't be released until the necessary paperwork has been completed. It could take a day or two." Sigidi's voice was scornful.

The keening coming from the chair in the corner of the ward stopped.

"Tell them that my husband is a traditional man, and our Zulu custom says that the deceased head of a household must come home on a Thursday. If they won't let us take him home today, then we will wait here until next Thursday." Francina had never heard her mother speak so forcefully.

After trying in vain to get the family to move into the waiting room, the nurse complained to the matron, who, with good sense, did not try to exert her power over the family but went straight to the morgue herself to assist with the paperwork. By late afternoon it was done.

Dingane pulled his SUV up outside the morgue, and his sons slid the simple pine coffin into the vehicle. The end stuck out, but Dingane managed to secure the door with a length of rope.

Francina joined her mother in Sigidi's truck, and her nephews jumped into the back. As darkness descended, she could hear the boys pointing out cars to each other. Her mother sat in silence, watching the red taillights of Dingane's SUV.

Jabulani was in darkness as the sad convoy approached, but when it turned onto the rutted road that led through the heart of the village, torches began to appear—two, then another four, ten more from the compound on the right. Every person in the village had risen from his warm bed to greet the Zuma family. As the vehicles began a slow procession through the center of the village, a cry went up from the women, sharply pitched like the screech of chalk on a blackboard. Francina's mother bowed her head. In the back of the truck the boys grew silent. Deep male voices rose in song, and one by one the women joined in. Francina's mother was silent. Her eyes never left the car ahead of her.

The convoy reached its destination and came to a halt. The Zuma family's compound consisted of three traditional round huts with thatched roofs: one for Francina's parents, one for Dingane and Nokuthula and one for their sons. A three-roomed brick building in the center of the dirt yard housed a living room, bathroom and kitchen.

Francina laid her father's sleeping mat on the floor of the living room and watched as her brothers opened the coffin. The illness had taken its toll on their father; her brothers lifted him as though he weighed no more than a newborn calf and settled him lightly on the mat. Their mother hovered nearby with a blanket, which she put over her late husband and tucked under his chin. She stroked his forehead, as she must have done many times over the years. Fresh tears flowed down her face. Nobody said a word.

This was the room Francina used when she visited, but she did not wonder where she would sleep now. Her place was with her mother. Sigidi would have to sleep with his nephews or under the stars.

Nokuthula tried without success to get her mother-in-law to drink some tea and then slipped off into the darkness to go to her sleeping hut. Sigidi and Dingane hugged their mother before going to bed.

Francina slept on the floor next to her mother's bed. Dingane had bought the bed for their mother some years back, but their father had refused to give up his sleeping mat. A grass mat had been adequate for his father, he'd said, and he saw no reason to change. Her father's stubbornness in adapting to new ways was the main reason that his would be a traditional funeral. Young people nowadays might not do it this way, but it would be an insult to her father's memory to give him a quick funeral or a cremation, like so many white people. For Zulus, death was a communal affair, and like all communal affairs, a funeral required time if it was to be carried out properly.

5

MONICA SWATTED THE SNOOZE BUTTON ON THE ALARM clock with a heavy arm. It was five in the morning. Just as she'd dropped off to sleep last night, Hercules had telephoned with the news that Francina's father had passed away and he would be joining his wife in KwaZulu-Natal for the funeral. Francina would be away for twelve more days.

She had found it impossible to go back to sleep after Hercules's telephone call. At around eleven she'd put on her dressing gown and made a cup of rooibos tea, which she drank standing at the kitchen sink, looking out at the shadowy limbs of the syringa tree. The night air had been unusually still. This tree was not meant to be here, she'd thought. It was from Asia, and the South African government, in its bid to preserve water, was encouraging people to get rid of alien invaders. Now that Ebony lay buried under it, Monica knew that she could never chop it down. Where would Francina's father be buried? she'd wondered. She knew little about Zulu funerals, but she'd hoped that he, too, would find his final resting place close to his family in his beloved Valley of a Thousand Hills. She'd put the empty mug in the sink and headed back to bed. The hot tea had calmed her, and she'd drifted off to sleep praying that Francina would find peace in her heart as she bade her father farewell.

Her alarm clock beeped again. If she wanted to be in place before the abalone poachers arrived, she had to get up now. Groaning, she sat up in bed and stretched. As she pulled on jeans and a sweater, there was a light tap at the front door. Oscar, an early riser, had agreed to watch over the boys for an hour.

"I wish you would tell me what you're up to."

"I will, Oscar. Just not now."

After leaving him at the kitchen table with a fresh pot of coffee, she drove down to the beach south of town, parked her car on a side road and continued on foot until she came to an outcrop of rocks at the edge of the sand. As long as the abalone poachers didn't arrive from the north, the rocks would provide good cover. A low line of scrub bushes ran from the rocks to the road—more cover if she needed to make an escape.

To the east, a faint glow of crimson outlined the koppies. The light from the full moon filled the beach with plump shadows. Monica felt a shiver of fear run through her, but she shook it off, telling herself that the poachers were probably teenagers or old men supplementing their pensions. Fishermen wouldn't be dangerous.

Monica had never seen the ocean at this time of the morning. The dark swells rolling toward shore turned silver and then crashed onto the beach in a spray of luminous white. The ladies of the town could not gather abalone while the tide was high, but they were adamant the poachers did. Monica crossed her arms, wishing she'd worn a Windbreaker to ward off the chill coming from the ocean.

She heard a vehicle in the distance and crouched lower, trying to squeeze into the crevice between the rocks as though she were one of the crabs she had seen skittering across the sand. The sound grew louder and then stopped. She peered out from her hiding place and saw a truck parked a few hundred yards away. Five figures jumped out, four of them in black wet suits. These were not boys or old men. They went round to the back of the truck to pick up scuba tanks and then quickly, as though they had followed this schedule a hundred times, waded into the surf carrying burlap sacks. The remaining man hopped up onto the hood of the truck, leaned against the windshield and held up something to his eyes. In the moonlight Monica could make out the flash of a pair of lenses.

She wondered how long the men would be under the water. In an hour it would be dawn, and fishermen and early risers walking their dogs would be on the beach. Her left foot prickled with pins and needles. She wriggled it so she would be ready to leave—in a hurry, if necessary.

The surface of the ocean showed no sign of the divers down below, the bubbles from their tanks lost in the shimmering turbulence of crashing surf.

She checked her watch. Twenty minutes had gone by. The waves broke farther out now and ran up the beach meekly. From behind the koppies, a pale light seeped into the black sky, dimming the stars. A seagull alit on the rock next to Monica and let out a ragged squawk.

She could make out iridescent drops of ocean spray on its breast. If she tried to leave now, the man on the truck would spot her. She had waited too long.

After another ten minutes, the man jumped down to open the back of the truck, and the four divers waded out of the surf, dragging their burlap sacks. The lookout man emptied the contents of the sacks into a large chest on the back of the truck, while the divers took off their masks, unzipped their wet suits and peeled them down to their waists. Monica heard a clang, then a curse, as an oxygen tank dropped into the back of the truck. With sudden frightening clarity she realized that she would be caught in the sweep of the truck's head-lights if the driver drove on a few yards to turn around where the road widened. She crawled around the rocks to be more shielded from the road. The men climbed into the truck, three in the front, two in the back with the equipment.

In the distance, a solitary fisherman stood knee-deep in the water, his line cast out past the breakwater. There were other people about now; Monica was safe. It would be best, though, if the poachers did not know that they had been spotted. Then the unthinkable happened. A rock beneath her foot gave way, unleashing a cascade of pebbles.

"Who's there?" shouted a man's voice.

Too late, Monica realized that she should have waited until the driver had started his engine before making her move. There was a wild flash of binocular lenses in the early-dawn light. Monica knew she had been spotted when the lenses stopped moving. The man jumped out of the truck, shouting, and ran toward her. Two of the other men followed close behind. Monica took off as fast as she could over the rocks, praying that she would not lose her balance. At last she reached the level ground of the road and sprinted to her car. As she got in, she looked over her shoulder and saw the man climbing onto the road. He had a gun in his hand.

She trod heavily on the accelerator, sending a spray of gravel into the still morning air, and headed straight for the police station.

Lady Helen's two policemen, Mike and Dewald, lived in a house behind the station and could be called on at any time of the day or night. Mike came to the door holding a piece of buttered toast.

Monica skipped the pleasantries. "There's a man down on the beach with a gun."

"Did you hear that, Dewald?" he called into the gloomy interior of the house.

Dewald came to the front door, wiping his mouth with a square of paper towel.

"They're poachers," explained Monica. "I was watching them and they saw me."

The two officers looked at each other. Monica had written a story about them shortly after their arrival in Lady Helen for their twelve-month stint. Dewald came from a farming community in the Northern Province; Mike, like her, came from Johannesburg.

"What type of car were they driving?" Mike asked.

"A blue truck. I think it was Japanese. There were five men in it."

"Stay right here. We'll be back," said Dewald, hurrying inside. He returned with two revolvers and handed one to his partner.

"Lock yourself in," he shouted as they ran to the police vehicle parked in the driveway.

Monica watched as it reversed onto the road and then took off toward the beach. She looked at her watch. There was no time to wait around; the boys had to get ready for school. She would wait fifteen minutes, no longer.

She stepped inside the house, locked the door behind her and found herself in the living room. It was tidy, but the navy-blue sofa, matching armchairs and light wood coffee table showed the wear and tear of a succession of tenants. She went into the kitchen. Porridge was already hardening in bowls. A magazine lay open on the table. One of the officers had been reading a story about the best shark-diving spots on the southern African coast as he'd eaten his breakfast.

Ten minutes to go. She thought the policemen wouldn't mind if she poured herself a cup of coffee. It was not hot and she drank it quickly. She was tempted to have a look at the other rooms in the house, but that would not be polite, so she remained seated in the kitchen until she heard a car stop outside. She lifted the curtains. The policemen had returned. She quickly got up and unlocked the front door.

"We didn't see anything," said Dewald. "We drove right up to the top of the koppie but there was no sign of a blue truck."

"We'll need to take a statement from you," said Mike.

"Can I get my boys ready for school first?"

Dewald nodded. "There's no rush. They won't come back if they know they've been spotted."

Monica thanked the officers and got back into her car. As she drove home, she realized that she might be in for a long morning at the police station. All the policemen who came to Lady Helen needed rest after busy postings in large cities where the police force was often understaffed and thinly stretched. Some relished the quiet of the small West Coast town, but others felt sidelined and made more than was necessary out of little incidents in the day-to-day life of the town. Gift had told her that one year there had been a young officer who had taken it upon himself to sit outside Green Block School every morning and write down the names of children who were late. Monica would discover the true character of these two officers later in the morning.

Oscar was standing at the stove stirring porridge when she returned. Sipho and Mandla were still asleep. Monica considered telling Oscar what had happened but he would scold her for putting herself in danger, and she wouldn't have gone down to the beach if she had suspected that was what she was doing. How was she to have known that abalone poachers carried guns?

Oscar put two steaming bowls of porridge onto the kitchen table and motioned for her to sit. But there was no time. She had to wake the boys.

"You need a husband, young lady."

"What?"

"I'm not kidding. You're a single mother with a career, and if the one person you rely on goes out of town, you struggle."

He blew on a spoonful of porridge before putting it in his mouth.

"There are others who can help."

Oscar shook his head. "You know what I mean."

"I'll be okay," she said feebly.

"This is a small town. Dating will be difficult. But surely there's someone here that you could consider."

She nodded, but then she didn't want him to know that she already had someone in mind, so she added playfully, "I'll run through my list."

"Some of the chaps here might need a push. You're a famous television reporter. They're intimidated."

It was interesting, thought Monica, how people viewed things differently. She looked at her past career and saw failure because she had not been offered a permanent job at *In-Depth*.

Oscar ate his last spoonful of porridge and wiped his mouth.

"Thanks for the breakfast. I'd better get to work. Gift wants the skylights installed in her studio by the weekend."

"Thanks for watching the boys."

"Anytime." Oscar wagged a finger at her. "Think about what I said."

After he had left, she hurried to wake Sipho, who took longer to get moving in the morning than his brother. Mandla jumped out of bed ready to take on the world before his feet touched the floor.

While Sipho dressed, she went to rouse Mandla. Like her, he had struggled to fall asleep last night, and she wondered if Mrs. Shabalala had given him chocolate. Chocolate had a drastic effect on Mandla. She would tell Sipho to keep a lookout.

She arrived at the office late. Her friend Kitty had telephoned, Dudu told her. A professor from the university in Johannesburg had made reservations at Kitty's inn, Abalone House, for the following week. Kitty had no idea of the reason for his visit, but she always notified her friend of any visitors who might provide story leads for the newspaper. Monica's fear had been realized. Word had gotten out about the San paintings.

"Never mind, Dudu," said Monica when it became clear that the receptionist was on the verge of tears again. "Oscar can build a fence around the cave."

Around midmorning she went to the police station and Dewald

and Mike took her statement. Thankfully they didn't keep her there long or press her to reveal how she'd known that the abalone poachers would be on the beach that morning.

For the rest of the day she worked on the layout of the next issue. Requests for advertising spots were up, but she refused to increase the number available. The *Lady Helen Herald* was a serious newspaper, not a weekly advertorial.

She left the office a little earlier than usual to relieve Mrs. Shabalala of her babysitting duties and found the elderly woman sitting in a chair surrounded by what appeared to be every toy Mandla owned. There was no sign of him or his brother.

"Sipho has taken Mandla to the bathroom to wash the marker off his arms." Mrs. Shabalala sounded weary.

Monica felt guilty for having to impose on her and even more so that it would be necessary again next week.

"It's been a long time since I had little ones around," said Mrs. Shabalala. "I wanted to start dinner for you, but—"

"Thank you, but that's not necessary. I'm sorry that the boys—I mean Mandla—wore you out. Didn't Sipho keep him in check?"

"He was trying to do his homework. I think the baby is disturbed by the new arrangement."

"I'm not a baby, Gogo," shouted Mandla from the doorway, calling his elderly babysitter by the Zulu word for grandmother.

"Mandla! Don't speak to Mrs. Shabalala like that. Say you're sorry."

Mandla looked at the floor. "Sorry."

"I'll pick them up from school again on Monday." Mrs. Shabalala pulled herself to her feet.

On the way home Monica had decided that she would tell Mrs.

Shabalala it would be fine to take the boys to the shop if she wished to work while they played. Now it seemed that this might not be wise, and Monica felt awful that Jabulani Dressmakers had to be closed in the afternoons because of her. Perhaps Mandla's behavior would improve next week.

The boys were quiet during dinner and Monica did not force conversation. As she cleared away the plates, Mandla asked, "When's Francina coming back?"

"Another eleven days, sweetie."

He knew this. This morning she had told the boys that Francina's father had passed away.

Mandla insisted on six bedtime stories rather than his usual three. Realizing that he needed to control at least one thing in his life, Monica gave in. When she went into Sipho's bedroom to kiss him good-night, he had already fallen asleep. She picked up the novel that had slid to the floor beside him and placed it on his nightstand. The boys were unsettled; they were missing a member of their family. Against her will, her thoughts went to Zak. It was impossible for her to comprehend how he must feel with his family disrupted permanently. *A good friend.* The words felt like lead weights on her heart.

6

FRANCINA AWOKE THE DAY AFTER HER FATHER'S DEATH
to find her mother outside stoking a fire. Although there was elec-
tricity in the kitchen, her mother had never stopped using the outside
lapa for cooking, and today was no different. Her mother went to a
shelf lined with bottles that Nokuthula had filled at the communal
faucet outside the elders' meeting hall.

"I'm going to warm it up," said her mother.

Francina nodded. She knew that it would make no difference to her
father now whether the water her mother used to bathe him was hot
or cold, but Francina would never have thought of pointing this out.

Her mother put a second pot of water on the fire to cook their
morning pap. Francina watched the sunlight seep into the valley
below. In the distance, smoke from cooking fires in the next village
curled into the morning air like cold morning breath. She inhaled

deeply. This smell of burning wood had followed her to Lady Helen and taunted her daily from Mama Dlamini's Eating Establishment. The day would be warm by noon, but now she felt a chill in her bones and wrapped the blanket she had brought from her bed tightly around her shoulders.

Nokuthula emerged from the sleeping hut she shared with her husband, rubbing her eyes.

"Good morning, sister," she said and Francina returned the greeting.

"My boys were up till late last night listening to music and didn't want to get up this morning to let the cattle out the kraal. Dingane went. I'd better take him some breakfast."

Francina did not know why she didn't wake her sons to do that, but it was not her place to ask. If you allowed young men to lie around being idle, then that is what they would be.

"Their grandfather's death has upset them more than they show," said Nokuthula as though reading her sister-in-law's thoughts.

Francina wondered when she would stop treating Sipho and Mandla as little princes and allow them to start taking responsibility. Perhaps never, so she ought to reserve judgment on her nephews.

Nokuthula went into the kitchen and emerged with a basket of sandwiches and fruit for her husband. Francina wondered if her sister-in-law had felt strange making sandwiches with the dead body of her father-in-law lying a short distance away.

"I'll be back in thirty minutes," said Nokuthula. "Don't start without me."

Francina realized that her sister-in-law had spent more time with her father than she had; Nokuthula had seen the signs of his impending illness, the grimaces of pain that he'd tried to hide, his faltering appetite, the shadows around his eyes because he couldn't get comfortable to sleep. Francina felt a pain in her chest as she pictured herself laughing with Sipho and Mandla while her father had been suffering hundreds of miles away.

Francina and her mother ate their breakfast outside in silence. When it was this cool, they would normally have gone into the living room, but it didn't seem right to eat in the presence of her father. Her mother sat in her usual chair, a wooden stool that her husband had carved when they were newlyweds. Francina looked across the neatly swept dirt at the lawn chair in which her father had sat every evening as twilight descended on the valley. Somehow she could not bring herself to sit in his chair and so she went back into the *lapa* and fetched a plastic one. Together she and her mother watched the sun rise above the distant hill until they could feel its warmth on their faces. A line of ants crawled up the trunk of an umphafa tree, a tree her father had sat and dozed under after his lunch and a morning in the fields.

Francina washed the dishes in a tub, filled from one of Nokuthula's water bottles. She and her mother were pretending to wait for Nokuthula to return from taking food to Dingane, but actually they were putting off the inevitable.

As Francina emerged from the *lapa,* she saw Nokuthula coming up the track from the kraal.

"Would you like some pap?" asked Francina's mother when Nokuthula was near.

Nokuthula shook her head. "No, thank you, Mama. I ate with Dingane. He has selected the ox. It's a fat one—enough for the whole village."

Francina's mother picked up the pot of water she had warmed on the stove, and without another word the three women went into the living room to prepare the body for burial.

That afternoon, Francina heard a loud bellow from the kraal and knew that Dingane had killed the ox. A short while later, she heard a car coming slowly up the dirt track to the family's compound and rushed out to greet her husband. Hercules had driven straight through the night, stopping only to fill up with petrol. His eyes were bleary, his muscles aching. Sigidi was watching, but Francina could not hold back the words she wished she had said before climbing into the minibus taxi.

"I'm sorry for—"

"Shh," he whispered. "There's something I wish I'd told you before you left. It's true—I would have loved a child. But I love you even more."

She would have liked to put her arms around him, but she knew that would have made him uncomfortable with her brother looking on. She hoped he could see her love for him in her eyes.

As she watched him offer his condolences to her mother and brother, Francina realized that if she hadn't gone to live in Johannesburg, she would never have met Hercules, the perfect man from KwaZulu-Natal. God worked in mysterious ways.

Dingane had offered them a *rondavel*—or *round house*—at Jabulani Lodge, but Francina said she would stay with her mother. She knew her mother was grateful when the newly bereaved widow offered to sleep in the kitchen so that Francina and Hercules could have privacy.

When evening came, Dingane and Sigidi picked up their father and put him on a grass mat outside his sleeping hut. Then they gathered chairs, stools, empty paint tins and logs, arranged them in lines before the body and stuck torches into the ground to be lit later.

As the crickets took up their evening song, the villagers began arriving. They held the widow's hands and whispered into her ear before finding a place to sit. Soon the seats were all taken, but still the people kept coming. Nearly all the villagers were there and most of the congregation from the family's church in the next village. Winston had not arrived, and although Francina was indignant that he had not thought it necessary to pay his respects to her father, she was also relieved. He and Hercules had never met and she knew that people would be watching if that happened.

People sat on the floor, stood, or leaned against the umphafa tree. Children dressed in handmade sweaters grew tired of the hushed atmosphere and started to play hide-and-seek among the huts. Tonight they would be allowed to stay up late, and the shadows would turn an ordinary game into an adventure.

Dingane started the vigil by welcoming everyone.

"My father was a traditional man," he said. "He believed in family, he believed the community has a responsibility to each and every one of its members, he believed in and loved our God. I believe he is going to a better place."

There were murmurs of assent. Sigidi got up next and told everyone his father had set an example to his children that was difficult to live up to.

Francina wondered if her brother was feeling guilty about time and money wasted at the horse-racing track.

"When I was a child, I looked up to all the men of my village. Now, when I walk the streets of Durban, I see men of my father's age, but I realize that men like my father are hard to find. My father taught me about cattle, about living off the land, but the lesson I keep closest to my heart is the one he taught me about dignity." He addressed his father, and as he did, his voice broke. "Baba, I will try harder to be like you."

Sigidi sat back down next to his nephews, and Francina wished that he had a wife who would comfort him tonight.

Her uncles spoke next and two of her aunts. A cousin got up and told everyone how his uncle had come to his rescue and fed his family when he'd lost his job in Johannesburg. And then one by one the villagers got up and told of the things Francina's father had done for them. "He always helped me mend my fences."

"During the drought, he shared some of his food for the cattle."

"He lent me money when my son was in trouble."

"He helped me find my child when she had gone missing down at the river."

"He gave me advice on marriage."

"He helped me build my house."

The list went on.

The only ones in the family who had not yet stood up were Francina, her mother and Nokuthula. Francina knew in her heart that her mother would not say anything tonight in front of everybody but would slip into the house later tonight to say goodbye to her husband. Tears slid down her mother's cheeks as she listened to the stories about her husband, but she cried silently, head bowed, looking up only when it was a voice she did not recognize.

Nokuthula stood up. "My father-in-law was a kind man. He treated me like a daughter. He gave me my husband. I know that many of you think that there are not people like my father-in-law around anymore, but I want to tell you that there are. My husband is the same as his father. And I will always be grateful to my father-in-law for making him this way." She sat down and her husband put his arm around her shoulders.

The crowd grew quiet. Children had fallen asleep on their parents' laps. It was getting chilly and everyone needed to get home to rest. Francina knew that it was her turn.

She stood up and looked at the faces before her, faces that she had known growing up, faces that had hardened toward her and only recently softened. She felt her family's eyes upon her. They begged her silently to leave the past undisturbed.

"I have spent many years away from my family. There were often times I wanted to come back, but I couldn't."

In the flickering light of the torches, she saw Dingane's troubled expression. "I missed my mother and father."

From the dirt track leading to the family compound came the sound of deep voices. The crowd turned to determine the identity of the late arrivals. It was Winston and one of his bodyguards.

The crowd turned back to Francina to see what she would do. She looked at Dingane's pleading face, the silent misery in her mother's expression and the fear in Nokuthula's eyes. Only Hercules did not appear to be worried.

"Forgiveness is a gift from God," she said more loudly than she had intended. "It allows us to invite peace back into our hearts."

There were murmurs of "Amen."

She knew that Winston was not a believer and that he would be angry that she had hinted at the past in front of his people. Tomorrow she might awake to the sickening thought that she had said too much, but tonight she had said what was in her heart.

"I have always loved my father and I always will. He is going to meet our Lord with a pure heart. I will keep him in mine forever."

She sat down and Hercules took her hand. He and her family were the only ones present who knew that she was talking about forgiving her father; everyone else must have thought that they were finally hearing her ask Winston to forgive her for committing adultery. After her confrontation last year with Winston, he had ordered people to treat her with respect, but she was sure he hadn't admitted to lying about her alleged infidelity.

Winston walked to the front to speak. Francina knew that he would not say that her father was a man who could have taken revenge on him but chose to keep silent. He would not mention the ways he had tried to make it up to her father after Francina had threatened to expose Winston's past life of drinking and gambling. He would not mention the extra bales of hay during the drought. History books were filled with leaders who walked through the madness they had caused to emerge unscathed on the other side without a word of regret on their lips.

Winston's eyes rested briefly on Hercules. Then he looked at the villagers and people from the church he had never set foot inside.

"I have come to pay my respects to a man we should all strive to be like. He was not full of noise, he only spoke after thinking and he knew his place."

Francina felt her fingers trembling in Hercules's grip. More than anything, she wished she could get up and scream at Winston that her father had kept silent because of fear, nothing else. Nobody else perceived the insult. Francina listened to his speech about loyalty and obedience with a growing feeling of nausea. How dare Winston use this vigil for her father as a platform for a thinly veiled political speech?

At last, Winston stepped back into the shadows with his body-guard. The vigil had come to an end. Women got to their feet, cradling young children; men scooped up the older children who had fallen asleep leaning against their parents' legs. Everybody pulled their blankets tightly around themselves and headed back to their homes.

Sigidi and Dingane returned their father to the living room and the family went to their huts to rest.

At three o'clock on Saturday morning Francina heard a light tapping at the door.

"It's time," whispered her mother.

Francina rolled out of bed and left Hercules sleeping. He'd had a long journey, and the first part of this morning's activities belonged to the women.

Francina joined her mother in the living room. A pot of warm water waited next to her father's body. Francina was tired, but she realized that her mother had had even less sleep. They picked up fresh cloths and began to wash her father's body for a second time.

After they'd dried him, her mother sprayed Sigidi's cologne on her husband's chest, behind his ears, in the crooks of his elbows. Francina's father had never used cologne in his entire life, but circumstances made it necessary now. Francina saw that her mother had laid out her father's smartest clothing: navy-blue trousers and a white shirt. There was no jacket. Her father had never worn a suit in his life, said her mother, and there was no point in beginning now.

When her father was ready, Francina went to wake Hercules, her brothers and nephews. They came to the living room, wiping sleep from their eyes, and gathered around the body. One by one they nodded, as though in approval of the job the women had done. Dingane took up his position at his father's head, Sigidi at his feet. On Dingane's count of three, they lifted their father into the coffin. Then the family took turns kneeling at the side of the coffin.

"I love you, Baba," Francina whispered when it was her turn.

She stepped back to allow her mother to take the last look. Her mother knelt beside her husband and touched his cheek.

"This is not goodbye, my love. We will meet again in the presence of our Lord."

"Amen," said Francina and Hercules in one voice.

Her mother took two steps backward and watched her youngest son close the lid of the coffin.

"There are three pots of water boiling on the fire," she said. "The men can bathe first. Please return the pots to me when you are finished so I can fill them up for the rest of us."

By six o'clock they had all bathed and dressed, their mother in the black skirt and blouse she had worn to her son's funeral so long ago, Francina and Nokuthula in the black skirts and red jackets that were their church uniforms, the men in black trousers and white shirts. Sigidi wore a tie and dark sunglasses.

They had a cold breakfast of ham and bread, washed down with hot tea.

Three cousins arrived carrying poles and a large sheet of plastic.

Dingane indicated a spot and they began to dig holes. Then they inserted the poles and spread the plastic over the top. When the corners of the plastic had been secured, Dingane, his sons and Sigidi brought the coffin outside and placed it under the tent.

Reverend Ngubane arrived and spoke quietly to the widow while waiting for the villagers and church members. Francina knew him only from her annual Christmas trips to her village, but her mother had once told her, as they'd washed dishes together, that he was sweeter than pumpkin fritters with brown sugar.

Nearly everybody who had been at the vigil the night before arrived for the service. Only those on duty at Jabulani Lodge did not turn up, but they were excused because a bus of British tourists was expected later that morning. Winston was not among the crowd. Some of the women went to work in the kitchen.

Reverend Ngubane had a gentle voice, and Francina soon found herself feeling sleepy in the warm morning sun. Nobody was invited to speak, but the voices were strong in songs that lifted their spirits up to the heavens.

"Let us remember our duty to this fine man's widow in the year to come," said the reverend.

After the prayer, Dingane, his sons and Sigidi took their places around the coffin.

"Please join us, brother," said Dingane, looking at Hercules.

Francina felt a surge of pride as she watched her husband move toward the coffin of the man he had met only once, at their wedding. Her father would have grown to love Hercules if he'd been granted the time.

The assembled crowd heard a whistle and knew that the herd boy who watched the cattle when Dingane's sons were at school was on his way. Since her father was the head of the household, his coffin could not be taken to the cemetery until his cattle had come back to the kraal.

The men fell into step behind the coffin and followed it to the kraal. A few of the women took the children back to the family compound. Nobody under the age of eighteen was allowed at the graveside ceremony. When the rest of the women reached the kraal, the men had all gone inside. The women found rocks and patches of grass to sit on and, through gaps in the kraal fence, watched the men settle themselves in a semicircle around the coffin. Dingane's strong baritone voice rang out, and with cows lowing and shuffling in accompaniment, the men joined in the traditional song of remembrance for their ancestors.

After four songs and a prayer by Dingane, the men came out of the kraal. The skin of the ox that had been killed the day before was draped over the coffin. The women took up their places in the rear, and the procession slowly made its way to the Zuma family cemetery on a hill behind their home.

Three young men took off their sweaters and began to dig a hole in the dirt. Sigidi placed a grass mat at the bottom of the shallow hole and then the pallbearers placed the coffin on the mat. One of the young men measured the coffin with his hands and gave instructions to his friends to start digging the burial hole alongside the coffin.

When the hole was about six feet deep, Sigidi spread a grass mat at the bottom. Even in its final place of rest the coffin was not permitted to touch the ground. Reverend Ngubane began a hymn of farewell, and the men and women joined in as the coffin was lowered into the ground. The young men placed another grass mat over the ox skin and wooden planks over the grass mat. Winston arrived as they were arranging a sheet of corrugated iron over the planks. Finally they packed earth on top of the iron.

At the head of the grave Dingane piled stones young boys had collected the day before in the village. Sigidi had made a small white cross and, with tears in his eyes, stuck it into the ground.

Winston cleared his throat. "Thank you for helping to bury our dear brother. It is solidarity like this that makes us strong and keeps us together when so many villages are shrinking and disappearing."

Wisely Winston stopped here and allowed the son of the deceased to speak next. Dingane thanked everybody for helping to bury his father and invited them to his home to share a late lunch.

The women who had stayed behind had prepared basins of water with ash floating on the surface, and everyone who had been present at the cemetery waited their turn to wash their hands and face.

The slaughtered ox was served as a rich stew with *stamp mielies*. People sat wherever they could find a place.

Winston had returned to his compound after the funeral, citing urgent business that required his attention, and now reappeared when most people were almost finished their meal. If Francina's father had been alive, her mother would have rushed to get Winston a plate of food, but now she looked at him and looked away. One of his three wives brought him a plate, and he sat down with the other men to eat.

Out of the corner of her eye Francina saw Hercules watching Winston. Hercules was not a violent man, but it was not an everyday occurrence to be confronted by the man who had beaten your wife. She watched him put down his plate half-full.

"Don't you like it?"

"I'm not hungry anymore."

"It's in the past, Hercules. I have dealt with it."

"It galls me that a man can get away with such evil."

"One day he will have to face his maker."

"Sometimes, God forgive me, I wish I was one of those men who sort things out with their fists."

Francina put her hand on his arm. "One of the things I love about you is that you're not." She looked up and saw Winston watching her.

After lunch, a few of the older men fell asleep where they were sitting. As the others made preparations to leave, Francina's mother stood near the gate to the compound, flanked by her two sons, to thank everyone for coming. After a few minutes, Francina joined them. She saw Winston's eyes follow Hercules as he picked up plates. A small smile played at the corners of Winston's mouth. When Hercules took the pile of plates inside, Winston got to his feet and came to say goodbye to the family.

"Your husband was a good man," he said to Francina's mother.

The widow pursed her lips and nodded.

Dingane saw that his mother had no intention of saying a word to their chief.

"My mother is tired," he said. "Thank you for coming."

Francina's mother looked out across the valley. Francina knew that she was more than tired; she was exhausted from the pretense of many years. And now no more. There was nothing Winston could do to her. He would not throw an old widow off her land, he would not assault her. The weight of her years would protect her.

Winston stopped in front of Francina.

"You look better than the last time I saw you."

Dingane moved closer to hear their conversation, but at that moment a large family came to say goodbye to him and he had to turn away.

"Come with me," Winston instructed Francina.

He grabbed her hand and pulled her behind her father's sleeping hut.

"If you touch me, I will scream."

"I want to talk."

"Make it quick. My husband will be looking for me."

Winston frowned, and for an instant Francina thought she saw pain in his eyes.

"You could have chosen a man, not a mama's boy," he scoffed. "Picking up plates like a woman."

Francina felt her ears burning and an overwhelming urge to slap Winston's face.

God, give me patience, she prayed silently. "Hercules is more of a man than you will ever be," she said in a controlled voice.

"Oh, yes? How many children does he have?"

Francina knew then that she had to get away from Winston before she did something she'd regret.

"You do not measure a man that way. A man is— Oh, what's the point? You will never understand."

"I'll show you a man. Come here and give me a kiss."

"Is everything okay?" Hercules stepped into view.

A showdown was not what Francina wanted.

"Ah, Francina's new man." Winston dragged out the word *man*.

Hercules came to stand next to Francina. He put an arm around her shoulders. Winston looked at this and shook his head, snickering. He would never show affection to any of his wives in front of another person.

"You're welcome to her," said Winston. "I had enough of her years ago."

Francina felt Hercules begin to tremble beside her and knew that his natural instinct for peace was being tried.

"If you ever come near my wife again, you will be sorry," said Hercules in a voice Francina had never heard before.

Winston spat on the ground at Hercules's feet. "We'll see about that."

He walked off laughing, as though he had just heard the best joke in years.

"Did he hurt you?" asked Hercules.

Francina shook her head. She smiled. "You were great."

"The man walked off hee-hawing like a hyena."

"You were great because you didn't try and fight him."

"I could have."

"I know, but I'm proud that you didn't."

He looked around to make sure that nobody was near and kissed her lightly on the forehead. "Your mother is exhausted."

"I'll put her to bed now for a nap. And then I'll take you to see my father's land."

"I wish I'd known him better."

"Me, too."

The next morning, Francina helped her mother and Nokuthula wash her father's blankets. The widow wore a simple black dress.

When Francina arrived home in Lady Helen, she would make a wardrobe of black clothing for her mother's year of mourning. Jabulani Dressmakers seemed a world away.

7

ON MONDAY MORNING, AFTER THE WEEKEND OF Francina's father's funeral, Monica sat in her office unable to concentrate on her story about the fancy new milking machine at Peg's Dairy Farm. When the machine had finished with each cow, an automated voice wished the cow a good day. This caused the cows to kick the walls of their stalls, but Peg could not find a way to silence the voice.

The telephone on Monica's desk rang, and she looked at it as though she, too, were searching for a way to silence it. This shrill sound had been the herald of nothing but bad news in the past few days.

"Monica?" She recognized Zak's voice. He sounded agitated.

"Is everything okay?"

"Not really."

She was right. Fresh bad news was on its way.

"I've just heard from Yolanda's mother." Monica noticed that he did not refer to Jacqueline as his ex-wife or use her name. "Yolanda's school has been closed until the end of the week because of an infestation of lice. Her mother doesn't have anyone to watch Yolanda while she's at work, so she asked me."

Monica wondered why he was telling her this.

"I'm about to start emergency surgery here and may not be out until late this afternoon."

Monica looked at her calendar. She didn't have any appointments for the rest of the day.

"I'll go and get her."

She could almost hear the smile in his voice. "I owe you one."

"What are friends for?" The disappointment had not gone, but she meant it.

As he was giving her the address, she heard Daphne calling him to the operating room.

Monica looked at the notepad. Yolanda lived in a good neighborhood of Cape Town. Monica's assumption had been correct; the new man in Zak's ex-wife's life had money. For weeks Monica had been meaning to visit Zukisa—the little girl who had moved away from Sandpiper Drift—and today was the perfect opportunity. Monica would collect Yolanda and then drive down to the docks to check on her young friend who was now caring for her sick mother.

Dudu popped her head in and asked if Monica wanted a cup of tea.

"No, thanks. I'm off to Cape Town."

Dudu looked puzzled. The receptionist knew which stories Monica was working on, and none required a trip out of Lady Helen.

"I'm doing Zak a favor. He needs me to pick up his daughter." Monica noticed the lift of Dudu's eyebrows.

"He has an emergency at the hospital." She sounded defensive. What would Dudu think now?

"He's a good man." Dudu's phrase was becoming a mantra.

"Call me on my cell phone if you need me," said Monica, hurrying out the door. If she continued the conversation about Zak, she was sure that her feelings would be obvious, even to someone half-asleep—and Dudu was one of the sharpest people Monica knew.

The drive into Cape Town always lifted her spirits, but this time there was no need. She felt strangely hopeful. Zak might think of her as only a friend, but he would not ask anyone but a *close* friend to collect his daughter. Unlike this drive south, the journey from close friend to girlfriend was ridiculously short.

She found the house easily with Zak's directions. It was in an old part of the city that had recently become fashionable. Like its neighbors, Yolanda's house was a Victorian with an ornate wrought-iron balcony that was covered with feathery green ferns. The houses at each end of the block had been converted into restaurants, the patios of which were filled with diners enjoying lunch in the shade of flower-covered arbors.

Monica parked her car and stepped onto the veranda of Yolanda's house. Two chairs were arranged around a small table that held a vase with a single rose. Someone had enjoyed a romantic dinner here. Monica wondered where Yolanda had been when this dinner for two took place. Was the girl getting used to spending time with a stranger? Sipho and Mandla had done it, but for them there had been no other option.

Monica pressed the doorbell. A few seconds later, she heard the click of heels on a wooden floor. The door opened.

"Yes?" said Zak's ex-wife.

"I'm Monica." Jacqueline Niemand's face was blank. "Monica Brunetti. Zak asked me to pick up Yolanda."

They had once exchanged pleasantries at a school concert; why was Jacqueline so confused? Then it dawned on Monica.

"Zak didn't tell you?"

Jacqueline shook her head, and the smooth dark ponytail that hung to her shoulder blades whipped from side to side. Zak's mind had been on the surgery. He had probably walked straight into his surgical gown without a thought of calling his ex-wife.

Jacqueline looked at her watch. "I have to get back to the office." She called for her daughter.

Yolanda appeared at the top of the stairs.

"Monica has come to take you to your dad's."

Yolanda stared at Monica, silent and unsmiling.

Jacqueline clapped her hands. "Come on, chop-chop. I have a meeting."

Yolanda disappeared for a few seconds, and when she returned carrying a backpack, her sulky pout was gone. For an instant she looked bewildered, a lost little girl. Monica felt suddenly ashamed of her feelings for Zak. This child's life had been torn apart; romantic desires at this moment seemed out of place.

Jacqueline kissed her daughter lightly on the forehead. "Daddy will bring you back on Sunday evening. I'll phone tomorrow to check on you."

Yolanda nodded, but Monica could see that she had no faith in her mother's words. Had Jacqueline broken promises to her daughter before?

Yolanda followed Monica across the veranda, down the steps and through the wrought-iron gate that squeaked noisily as it swung shut behind them.

Monica noticed Yolanda looking back as they drove away, but her mother had already hurried inside. Monica tried to break the stiff silence in the car.

"The lice must have been bad."

Yolanda did not answer.

"I had lice once. It took my mother three hours to get the nits out of my hair with a special comb. My father kept telling her it would be easier to shave my head." Monica remembered clearly the scornful look her mother had shot her father.

She saw that Yolanda's head was turned toward the window, her eyes trained on the squat blocks of flats that had replaced the elegant houses about a mile back. Monica knew that the girl was not taking anything in. She had seen that blank stare on Sipho in the months after his mother's death.

Yolanda said nothing, not even when Monica stopped outside a grocery store and held the door open for her.

"We won't be long."

Yolanda sighed as though it took great effort to climb out of the car. Inside the store, Monica filled her shopping cart with tea, sugar, milk, bread, fruit, vegetables and biltong. She did not know if Zukisa and her mother ate the salted dried meat, but it was worth a try since it was protein Zukisa wouldn't have to cook. Finally Monica stopped in the biscuit aisle and selected a few packs, some plain, some chocolate. She had no idea if Zukisa's ailing mother was even capable of eating solid food. Yolanda walked alongside her in silence, preoccupied and absent.

While Monica loaded the groceries into the car, Yolanda climbed into the backseat without offering to help.

Monica had never approached Zukisa's neighborhood from this direction and hoped that she had the right road. Colorful graffiti covered the walls of tiny convenience stores, liquor outlets and secondhand furniture dealers. It was a weekday, yet groups of young men congregated on street corners—little knots of bluster and bravado listening to blaring music. Empty cartons of *magau*—a fermented drink made from maize—lay discarded at their feet. It would be foolish to stop and ask directions. If she had known what it would be like approaching Zukisa's house from this direction, she might have made a big detour to take the more familiar route.

Monica imagined Zukisa slipping through her front gate in one of her colorful dresses, head bowed so as not to invite attention, an empty shopping bag flapping against her legs. She imagined the little girl pushing her way into one of these shops, scanning the shelves for food that her mother would be able to swallow, offering crumpled notes to an indifferent shopkeeper. Ten years old and she was the head of her household.

Yolanda moved around restlessly in the backseat.

"I need to check on Zukisa," said Monica, answering the question Yolanda would not permit herself to ask.

Again there was no response from Yolanda, but Monica knew that she must remember the girl from Green Block School.

The houses in Zukisa's street were in better condition than the rest of the neighborhood, the tiny squares of front lawn neatly mowed, all of the windows still intact. Monica drove to the end of the dead-end street and pulled up outside Zukisa's small block house.

It needed to be painted, but Monica knew that this would not happen, not until new owners moved in. She climbed out of the car to open the gate, drove up the short driveway and closed the gate again. Her car might still be stolen, but at least she would have made an effort.

Monica opened Yolanda's door.

"Please, come with me."

Yolanda pulled a face, but Monica knew that she would not have the courage to remain alone in the car.

Monica knocked on the front door of the house. Silence. She sensed the little girl on the other side of the door, listening fearfully.

"Zukisa, it's Monica."

She heard a succession of clicks—locks being slid open.

Zukisa opened the door, smiling broadly. Her dress was the color of a summer sky, its collar edged with clouds of white lace.

"Hello," she said. Her smile dimmed when she saw that Monica was not alone.

"Do you remember Yolanda?"

Zukisa nodded nervously. "Hi, Yolanda."

Monica prayed that Yolanda would manage more than her usual silent response.

"Hi." It was more a grunt than a greeting, but Zukisa accepted it with a smile.

"Come in. Would you like some tea?"

Monica thought of the girl's burns that were only visible if she lifted her skirt. She had tripped while making pap for her family's evening meal, and the pot of boiling water had scalded her all the way from her neck to her knees. Zak had given her skin grafts, which had healed remarkably well.

"No, thank you," said Monica.

Zukisa looked disappointed. "We don't have any juice."

"Water will be great," said Monica. It was rude to refuse an offer from this girl who had so little. She thought of the bags of groceries in the car. They would spoil in the heat if she didn't bring them in soon.

Zukisa hurried to the kitchen and returned with two glasses set on saucers, like milk shakes at a roadhouse.

Monica took a sip of the tepid water. "How is your mother?"

The bright smile brought on by this surprise break in routine slid from Zukisa's face.

"She has fevers and a lot of pain. The doctor gave her pills, but they don't work."

"She went to the hospital?" Monica was encouraged by the news that Zukisa's mother was able to travel.

Zukisa shook her head. "No, I took a bus on my own. I waited six hours before I saw the doctor. He said he wasn't allowed to give me the pills. But he was so sorry about my wait he slipped them to me in a brown paper bag."

Zukisa smiled, remembering the kindness of this stranger. Monica knew that Zak would like to hear about the compassion of one of his colleagues.

"I have a few things for you," said Monica, getting to her feet. "I'll only be a minute."

As she hurried out to her car, she wondered whether the girls would speak to each other. After three trips, she had unloaded the bags and placed them in the hallway. It would be rude to search for the kitchen and start unpacking them.

She returned to an uncomfortable silence in the living room.

Yolanda was staring at her hands in her lap, Zukisa looking around as though hoping that a topic of conversation would reveal itself in the threadbare contents of the room.

"Some things need to be kept cold," said Monica.

Zukisa hurried out, and seconds later she came rushing back into the living room. "Thank you," she said breathlessly. She wandered closer, and Monica thought that she might be coming to give her a hug, but the girl stopped short, obviously feeling shy.

"Anytime," said Monica. "Now put the milk in the fridge or it'll go sour."

The minutes ticked by as Monica and Yolanda waited for Zukisa to return. Yolanda had completed her study of her hands and was now gazing out window at colorful dresses fluttering in the breeze on a circular wash line. This was the work Zukisa had been doing when she should have been at school.

Zukisa returned, grinning broadly. "Thank you. It's hard for me to carry more than a few things at once when I go to the shop."

Monica wished she could do more. But what?

"Mother will be happy to see both of you."

Yolanda pulled her gaze from outside and looked directly at Monica. The soft skin between her eyes was furrowed with worry.

"Maybe just one of us," said Monica. "We don't want to tire her." She saw the relief on Yolanda's face.

"Come with me." Zukisa led the way down the small hallway and pushed open the first door. "She's awake."

"Are you sure your mother won't mind?"

Zukisa looked puzzled. "Mind? She'll be happy to see someone at last."

"Doesn't she have any other visitors?"

Zukisa shook her head. "She doesn't have any family and all her friends are afraid. My father's sister is all we have. Come in."

Monica followed Zukisa into a small square room. Heavy curtains were drawn across the window that faced the street. Zukisa's mother lay on one side of a double bed, staring at the wall, a blanket of multicolored crocheted squares pulled up to her chin.

"You have a visitor," said Zukisa so loudly that Monica wondered if the poor woman had lost her hearing.

Zukisa's mother did not turn her head toward them.

"Sometimes she dreams when she's awake," explained Zukisa. "She sees her own mother."

The woman's cheekbones were accentuated by the sagging hollows beneath them, and there were dark weeping blisters all over her head and neck. Monica remembered seeing Themba for the last time in the hospital. His teeth had also seemed too large for his face.

Monica approached the bed and smiled tentatively.

"I'll do whatever I can to help," she said loudly, her words intended for the little girl who hovered at the foot of the bed.

"She knows you're here," said Zukisa.

Monica had not seen anything to make her believe Zukisa, but she nodded and gave the girl a watery smile.

"We can go now," said Zukisa.

Monica wondered if the girl sensed her discomfort, her feeling of utter helplessness.

"When I take Mother her milk, I'll tell her that you brought it." Zukisa smiled, and in that moment Monica knew that the little girl was trying to make *her* feel better.

Though she had spoken loudly to her mother, Zukisa closed the door quietly behind them.

"Where is your aunt?" asked Monica. Zukisa needed the help of an adult.

"She has a lot to do," said Zukisa, her eyes bright as she defended her father's sister.

"I'd like to speak to her. Do you have her telephone number?"

Zukisa nodded, her eyes filled with confusion. "Am I not taking good care of Mother?"

Monica placed a hand on the little girl's bony shoulder. She regretted having made Zukisa feel this way. "You're an excellent nurse. I'd just like to find out a few things."

Zukisa opened up a lined schoolbook. On the first page were three telephone numbers—her aunt's, the police and the hospital. Monica punched the first number into her cell phone.

"I'll get better reception outside." She didn't want Zukisa to hear her conversation.

With the door closed behind her, she waited while the phone on the other end rang.

"Hello?" The irritation in the woman's voice was obvious.

Monica introduced herself, wondering what she had interrupted. "I'd like to talk about Zukisa."

"She isn't in trouble, is she?"

Monica wondered where the girl would find the time, even if she had the inclination.

"No, I'm worried about her looking after her mother on her own." Immediately Monica wished that she had phrased it differently.

This sounded like an accusation. She anticipated the bristling response of Zukisa's aunt.

"Children all over the country are doing it," said the aunt, her tone no longer antagonistic but weary. "Zukisa is no different."

Monica would have liked to tell her that the girl should be in school, but she knew the response she would get to that comment. School could be caught up. A dying parent needed to be fed, bathed, watched.

"She's a big girl. She can do it," said the aunt in a firm tone. Then she softened a little. "I'd like to help more, but I'm looking after three grandchildren. The youngest is still in nappies."

"I want to give you my telephone number."

"I don't have a pen with me." The irritation had returned. "I'll remember it and write it down as soon as I have a free moment." She stressed the word *free,* as though reminding Monica that this call was holding her up.

Monica gave Zukisa's aunt her number and thanked her for her time.

"My pleasure," replied the woman. The words were fat with sarcasm.

Monica said goodbye and ended the call. She didn't like Zukisa's aunt's attitude, but she understood it. A call from a stranger, albeit well-meaning, was worth nothing. Monica knew then what she had to do. She dialed the third number in Zukisa's schoolbook.

"Clinic," said a sharp voice.

"I'd like to speak to a doctor, please."

"You and seven hundred others." The woman on the other end chuckled at her own quick reply.

Monica took a deep breath. It would be of no use to throw her weight around. Patience and humility would be more effective. She told the receptionist about Zukisa's mother.

"I'll put you through to a nurse." There was a click and the line began to crackle.

"Outpatient clinic," said a new voice.

Monica had hoped that her call would be transferred to someone on one of the inpatient wards. Zukisa's mother needed admission. Again she explained the predicament of the dying single mother.

"Bring her in tomorrow," said the nurse. "Come early. The line will be long. Four in the morning will be a good time."

"And then you'll admit her?" asked Monica, feeling that she had made progress.

The nurse clicked her tongue a few times and Monica imagined her shaking her head.

"There are no beds left."

"But what—"

"We can give her painkillers. That's all. Even if she was admitted, there's not much more we can do for her. She's better off at home."

"She's got painkillers. It's not enough."

"*Ai,* you can say that again," said the nurse, the frustration that she had masked with impatience coming through. "It's never enough. Don't forget—four o'clock."

Monica thanked her out of politeness more than genuine appreciation. As she pushed the front door open, she wondered if Zak might return the favors she had granted him whenever he'd wanted a story in the *Lady Helen Herald.* She knew that Zukisa's mother did not live in the right area for the Lady Helen Hospital, but she had once been a resident. When Monica returned home, she would ask him. Zukisa could live with her and the boys while her mother received treatment. And then what? It was impossible at this late stage for any medicine to cure Zukisa's mother; the best that could be hoped for was effective palliative care. Whether the woman died in pain at home or in comfort at the hospital in Lady Helen, Zukisa would still be an orphan.

When Monica walked back into the living room, the girls were sitting on opposite ends of the sofa, Yolanda showing continued interest in the wash line outside, Zukisa staring straight ahead. Monica wondered if a single word had been exchanged in her absence.

"We'd better go now," she told Yolanda.

The girl jumped to her feet.

Zukisa's shoulders sagged as though she had been passed a heavy load.

"I'll come again soon," Monica told her.

"Thank you." Zukisa watched her guests walk to their car and opened the gate.

"Go inside now," said Monica. "I'll close the gate."

Zukisa gave a polite wave in Yolanda's direction and went to stand in the doorway. There was nobody else on the street, but Monica saw a curtain move in a window next door. Zukisa had not mentioned any help from neighbors, but Monica hoped they would be useful in an emergency.

Zukisa waved wildly from the doorway as the car pulled away from the curb. Monica tried to imagine the little girl's feelings as she closed the door and returned to her house of illness, but she knew that even though she told Mandla and Sipho to put themselves in other people's shoes, this was one case where she could not follow her own advice.

She did not say a word to Yolanda as she navigated her way out of Zukisa's neighborhood and found the road north to Lady Helen. Yolanda had resumed her silent watch of the flashing scenery. The traffic thinned. Low scrub bush lined the road on either side, their narrow rolled leaves muted green. Wispy white clouds looked lost in the wide arc of stark blue sky.

"What will happen to Zukisa when her mother dies?"

The question startled Monica. She looked in the rearview mirror and saw Yolanda leaning forward to catch her answer.

"She'll live with her aunt."

Yolanda nodded, pleased with the answer. "You know, my father has some medicine locked away at home."

Monica took her eyes off the road for a second to look back at Yolanda. "You must never tell anyone what you've just told me."

"I was only trying to help."

Monica's tone softened. "I know, and it's a wonderful idea, but—"

"I know. My father could get into a lot of trouble. Mother said he might even be suspended. She wanted him to flush the pills down the toilet."

Jacqueline Niemand had loved her husband enough to want to protect him. Or maybe she had wanted to protect her lifestyle.

"One day the president will come to his senses and these antiretrovirals will be available to everyone who needs them. But until then—"

"My mouth is zipped."

"What's your new school like?" Monica wanted to prevent the girl from slipping back into sulky silence.

Yolanda's face darkened. "There are more than a thousand pupils."

Monica whistled, relieved that Yolanda had not clammed up again.

"At first I was happy to be away from Green Block School, where everybody knew my business."

Monica knew what business she was referring to. It couldn't have been easy for Yolanda to go to school after the news of her mother's affair became public.

"I liked the fact that nobody knew me, nobody cared about my parents. But now I find it lonely—and scary."

Monica understood. She had left Johannesburg to come to Lady Helen for this very reason.

"It'll get easier over time," she said, but Yolanda's scowl made her regret her words. Yolanda did not deserve trite responses.

Monica saw a scattering of bumps in the road and slowed down, happy for the distraction of a common sight along this stretch of road.

"Look, Yolanda—tortoises."

Sipho and Mandla held competitions to see who would be the first to spot them on the way to Cape Town. Monica always held her breath. Large shards of cracked shells were sometimes all that remained of the plodding travelers, and then she would have to comfort Mandla in his angry sadness. She had asked around and still did not know why the tortoises made the dangerous journey across the road.

Monica had slowed her car to a crawl and kept checking the rearview mirror to make sure another car was not barreling toward them.

"Look, look," said Yolanda, sounding as excited as Mandla did when he spotted the tortoises.

"They're wonderful, aren't they?"

"No, not the tortoises. Over there, between those bushes."

A car was approaching at speed from behind, and Monica pulled off the road onto the sandy shoulder.

"There." Yolanda pointed in the direction of a lone protea bush, its dusty pink flowers as large as the heads of babies.

Monica saw a lump covered in khaki fabric.

"It's probably a shirt or something that fell out of a suitcase on top of a taxi," she said.

Yolanda opened the door.

"Wait!"

"We have to check."

"Let me," said Monica. Her heart had begun to thud furiously in her chest. She had noticed a shoe where the khaki fabric ended. If this was a dead body, she did not want Yolanda to be anywhere near.

She approached silently, like a hunter tracking an impala. When she was closer, she stopped to see if she could make out any more details from this new angle. The shoe moved and a scream escaped her lips.

"What is it?" shouted Yolanda from the car.

"Stay there!"

A groan came from the shade under the protea bush. Monica craned her neck to get a better look and saw the sharp contour of a shoulder. The man was lying on his side, his face hidden under his arm.

"Are you okay?"

Suddenly a cold shiver ran down her back. This was a familiar ploy of carjackers. They would stage an accident or emergency and pounce on the concerned motorist who stopped to help. She had fallen for it and left Yolanda, alone and vulnerable, in the car. She looked back. Yolanda's long, skinny legs hung out the open car door, the toes of her brown school shoes resting lightly on the gravel, ready to run as soon as Monica said it was safe to join her. There was nobody else in sight.

The man groaned again, and this time it sounded as though he'd said, "Water."

"Yolanda, please bring me the water on the passenger seat."

Yolanda sprang into action, happy to be playing a role at last. She raced toward Monica and handed her the bottle. Monica lifted the man's head and held the bottle to his lips. He drank thirstily. His head felt hot in her hand. When he had finished drinking, she laid his head down again and his eyes closed. He wrapped his arms across his chest as though he were cold and began to shiver.

"We'd better get him to a hospital."

"I'll phone my dad."

Monica wondered if it would be best to return to Cape Town or to go on to Lady Helen. They were about halfway between both towns. She remembered the difficulties she'd had with the nurse earlier and made the decision to take the man straight to Zak.

"Let's get him in the car first, and then we'll call your father."

The man was slightly built, but they struggled to lift him. After attempting a few different positions, they realized that the only way to move him was for them each to take a shoulder and let his feet drag. Lifting him into the backseat of the car was even more difficult. Monica went around to the far side of the car and pulled his arms while Yolanda pushed his feet. He was breathing but had lost consciousness.

Yolanda climbed into the passenger seat.

"Can I phone my dad now?"

Monica nodded. It was illegal to use a cell phone while driving, so Yolanda would have to give her father the details.

Yolanda must have dialed her father's cell phone number, because she got him on the line without talking to anyone else first.

"Dad, we found a sick man at the edge of the road and we're bringing him to you."

Yolanda listened to his response.

"Yes, he's breathing," she told him. "He's hot to touch, but he seemed to feel cold. He's lost consciousness."

She listened again to her father.

"No, no sign of a wound."

Nodding, she listened to her father for a minute more and then said goodbye.

"He says we have to do CPR if he stops breathing. Do you know how to do that?" Her eyes pleaded with Monica.

"Yes, don't worry. I'll do it if it comes to that. You just watch the rise and fall of his chest."

Yolanda swiveled around in the passenger seat and sat cross-legged with the seat belt stretched across her back.

Monica took the turnoff to Lady Helen. Mandla always gave a shout when he saw the ocean, and she'd fork over his five-rand prize while Sipho looked on indulgently. One day Mandla would realize that his brother always let him win.

The man groaned again.

"His eyes are open," whispered Yolanda. "It's okay, you're safe," she told him. "We're taking you to the hospital." She sounded just like her father when he addressed a patient.

"Water," the man whispered.

Yolanda put the bottle to his lips and he drained it with eager gulps. He closed his eyes again. Beads of sweat slid down his face. Yolanda found another bottle of water in her backpack and soaked one of the T-shirts she had brought with her. The man stirred as she wiped his forehead, but he did not open his eyes.

They reached the top of the koppie. Monica hardly noticed Lady Helen waiting below. Her focus was on getting down the koppie as fast as she could without putting her passengers in danger. Yolanda phoned her father again and warned him that they were about to arrive at the hospital.

He was waiting on the veranda when Monica pulled up.

"Hi," he said to both of them and gave his daughter a quick hug. Then he squatted down next to the man and felt his pulse.

Adelaide had left the front desk and appeared with a porter and a gurney. Between the two of them, the man was transported as though he weighed no more than a bag of flour.

"Thank you for fetching Yolanda," said Zak over his shoulder as he followed the gurney to the front door of the hospital.

Yolanda grabbed her backpack and took the stairs in one leap.

"Yes, thank you, Monica," she said, waving.

It was the first time she had addressed Monica by name.

"You're welcome."

As the front door of the hospital closed behind them, Monica prayed for the man's swift recovery. She went back to her car and found an old towel in the trunk to dry the pool of sweat on the backseat. One of the man's shoes lay next to the car. Monica picked it up. The sole was worn, but it was obviously an expensive leather dress shoe. She wondered what had led the man to be alone in the bush; he was not dressed for hiking, and there were no signs of trauma, so he had not been carjacked. It was a mystery—one for Zak to solve. She felt ashamed of her happiness at having an excuse to contact Zak again. But it was not the only reason she had to call him; she had to find out if he would admit Zukisa's mother to the hospital.

She drove away from the hospital, looking forward to feeling Mandla's small arms around her neck and Sipho's soft kiss on her cheek.

She could hear Mandla's voice inside the house before she opened the front door, and when she did, he was too busy whizzing around the room, airplane in hand, to notice her arrival. Mrs. Shabalala smiled broadly at her.

"Thank you so much," Monica said, catching hold of Mandla's hand. "I'll ask my friend Kitty to watch the boys tomorrow. I don't want you to lose clients at the shop because of me."

Relief washed over Mrs. Shabalala's face. "There *is* a lot of work waiting for me there."

After Monica had driven Mrs. Shabalala home, she opened the freezer and took out one of the meals she had made last week in a burst of energy. The boys both loved lasagna, but they ate in silence, as though it were an effort. Mrs. Shabalala was not the only one who was exhausted. Monica put them to bed around eight and carried the telephone to the bathroom so she would hear if Zak called, while she was taking a shower, to update her on the mystery patient's condition.

That night she dreamed of driving the long, flat ribbon of highway between Johannesburg and Pretoria. There was a small blond boy in the car with her. She put her arm out to touch his face and he shrank back in horror. "Luca, it's me," she told him. Her brother grabbed the door handle. She saw what was coming and reached across, but he escaped her grip and jumped out. Without waking, she knew that she was crying.

8

FORTY ARTISTS ARRIVED ON SATURDAY MORNING TO HELP decorate the pediatric ward. Monica heard Zak asking Oscar to go out and buy more paint and brushes. He was up to something.

Ten names were drawn from a hat for the job of brightening the ward, and the others were told that they would be painting the exterior of the hospital, as well as the kitchen and front waiting room. This group did not look as eager at the prospect of their task; they had come to paint murals of dishes running away with spoons, cows jumping over the moon and cheeky rabbits dressed in little blue jackets.

On Tuesday, the day after Monica had fetched Yolanda from Cape Town, Zak had called to tell Monica that the mystery patient she and Yolanda had found in the bush was suffering from malaria. Time would tell if it was the drug-resistant kind. Zak had said that the patient kept muttering in a language that he did not recognize.

Daphne thought it was Shona, the language of Zimbabwe, but it was strange that a man from Zimbabwe would be wandering around in the bush down here.

After Zak had hung up, Monica had called the police station to find out if Dewald and Mike were continuing to search for the poachers. Dewald had told her that he thought it strange that she had been alone on the beach at dawn looking for poachers.

"Somebody told me about them," she said quietly. "I'm sorry, I can't tell you who right now."

She couldn't let him find out about the abalone ladies, not until she'd managed to persuade them to give up their illegal activity.

She'd heard the restraint in Dewald's voice when he told her he could bring her in for questioning if he wanted. He'd said he'd check the beach one more time.

Zak had taken Monica's suggestion seriously and put Gift in charge of the murals. Gift immediately set about outlining a square where Sipho, Mandla and Yolanda could work. A day of Mandla and paint. This could only turn out badly.

On her way to check on the volunteers outside, Monica walked past an open ward and saw Daphne holding a cup of water to a patient's lips. She motioned for Monica to come inside.

"This is Silas Ncube, the man you rescued from the side of the road."

Daphne had propped him up with pillows. He smiled warmly at Monica as they shook hands.

"I don't know how to thank you."

She thought of the taxi driver who had found her lying on the side of the road after her carjacking. He'd wrapped her in a sheepskin seat cover and rushed her to the nearest hospital. Monica's father had tried to give him money to have his taxi cleaned, but he would not take a penny.

"We had slowed down to look at the tortoises," explained Monica. "Dr. Niemand's daughter has sharp eyes."

"A good girl," he said softly.

"Yolanda has been reading to him," added Daphne. "Silas is a long way from his home in Zimbabwe and has no visitors."

In Daphne's eyes Monica saw a new tenderness that had not been there before, even when she'd held newborn babies.

"You came a long way south," said Monica.

Most immigrants from north of the Limpopo River—legal and illegal—ended up in Johannesburg.

Daphne answered for him. "He thought he'd have a better chance finding a job in Cape Town. But the trucker he hitched a ride with threw him out in the middle of the night somewhere near Beaufort West."

Beaufort West was almost two hundred miles away. Surely he had not walked this far.

"He got lost," said Daphne, seeing the question in Monica's eyes. "He was delirious."

She explained that Silas had been a journalist in Zimbabwe. He had been imprisoned for writing a story that took a stand against President Mugabe, and when he was released, his newspaper had been shut down and there were no other jobs. Together with an ex-colleague, he had printed news onto letter-size paper and distributed the impromptu newsletters by hand. It was important, he felt, for the people of Zimbabwe to know what was really going on, but with no money coming in, he was forced to abandon his underground press and come to South Africa to find a job to support his elderly parents and widowed sister.

"I'm sorry about what happened to you," said Monica.

This man was one of her colleagues. In the old days in South Africa, journalists lost their jobs or were imprisoned for quoting the banned African National Congress. Things had changed since then, and she was proud now of South Africa's free press.

"If you need help of any kind, please ask Daphne to contact me."

Outside the open window, Monica saw Gift's husband, David, on a ladder, painting the walls of the burn unit. Daphne bustled around Silas, removing pillows from behind his back, pulling the sheets up to his chin. He fell asleep as she was taking his pulse. After writing in his chart, she indicated for Monica to follow her and closed the door behind them.

"He won't let me turn off the light at night. I hear him crying in his sleep. Something terrible happened when he was in prison."

"Torture?"

"That's what I suspect, but I don't want to ask him." As Daphne hurried off to attend to her next patient, she called over her shoulder, "Tell those artists not to paint any wild animals on the walls or the children will have nightmares."

Monica returned to the children's ward and found the artists hard at work, each in charge of a small section of the room, each painting a wild animal in bright colors. She was relieved to see that there were no wolves. Mandla's nightmares, on the rare occasions he had them, were always about wolves, and more than a few fairy tales had been removed from his list of bedtime stories.

Monica photographed the artists at work and then went outside to photograph the other volunteers. David flashed her a wry grin.

The work outside had gone quickly with so many helping, and the once-faded walls were now a dazzling white.

Monica saw Anna walking toward her.

"Your oldest boy told me where to find you." The baby on her back began to fuss, and she swayed from side to side to calm him. "I wanted to thank you."

This was turning out to be a day for thank-yous.

"The poachers have never come back and we're able to earn money again."

Monica wondered how Anna could apply the label to the men and yet not see that it belonged to her, too.

"They might come back," cautioned Monica. "You must get a permit."

"Me?" Anna looked aghast. "There are only a few permits, and they are always given to friends of the government officials or people who slip an envelope under the table."

"What about finding a job?"

Anna looked over her shoulder at the baby who had fallen asleep. "And what do I do with him when I'm at this job?"

Monica did not have a ready answer. "I don't want you to be caught."

Anna gave a brittle laugh. "If the police come to the beach, we'll throw the abalone back into the water. It won't be difficult to get rid of the small number we collect."

Anna stressed the word *small,* and Monica knew it was a challenge for her to pursue an issue that in Anna's mind was of no consequence. But it was more than a matter of the law; one day there would be no abalone left if poaching continued unchecked.

Monica stroked the sleeping baby's cheek. She hadn't seen Sipho and Mandla when they were infants. Sipho, she imagined, had been all big eyes, Mandla all fat rolls and dimples. What would they think if they one day had a baby sister or brother?

The volunteers had started to pack up and leave. Monica found Sipho, Mandla and Yolanda in the pediatric ward, admiring the finished work. Sipho's majestic elephant was quite realistic; Yolanda's butterfly had long eyelashes and full pink lips; Mandla had painted a flash of yellow lightning on his car's roof.

"I told him everybody was painting animals," said Sipho, shaking his head.

Zak arrived to praise their efforts. "Who's hungry?" he asked.

"Me, me," shouted Mandla, jumping up and down.

"Why don't we go into my office? Yolanda and I have prepared a picnic."

"Are you sure you have enough?" Monica asked.

"We were counting on you joining us." There was a shy, hesitant look in his eyes.

Her heart began to pound in her chest.

"Please, please, can we stay?" begged Mandla.

"Of course we can," she said quietly.

The corners of Zak's mouth crinkled into a smile.

When they reached Zak's office, Yolanda took Mandla by the hand and led him to a globe that was a new addition to the jumble of paraphernalia.

"Look," she told him, "that's Earth."

"Here's Italy," added Sipho, not to be outdone in the education of his younger brother. "That's where Nonno and Nonna live."

Monica and Zak watched the children in silence. Zak was the first to speak.

"Daphne's always telling me to take more time off. I don't see the point when Yolanda's not here."

Monica prided herself on her ability to give people a push in the right direction, yet she had never used this skill to her own advantage. Now was the perfect time.

"But you probably have more social invitations than you can cope with." She almost could not bear to look at him.

Zak laughed and the children's heads turned in their direction. But their distraction was only momentary.

"Japan," said Sipho. It seemed that there was a competition on between Sipho and Yolanda to be the first one to find a country on the globe.

"If you could only see me, Monica," said Zak. "I get home late, make myself a sandwich, watch the news and fall asleep on the couch."

She ignored her inner voice telling her to be careful, to let him make the first move. "Would you like to join us for dinner one night? The boys would love to have you over." She meant that *she* would love to have him over.

He looked at the children and saw that they were not listening.

"I would like that very much, but I was wondering if…" He looked nervous, but there was also a resolute quality to his expression, as though he'd made a decision to dive into an icy ocean and could not go back on it. "I was wondering if I could take you out for dinner one night. I know of this great place on the beach."

She thought her heart might leap out of her chest. Later she would look back at her response with embarrassment. She did not say yes but nodded over and over again like a toy dog.

"Let me know when…" He trailed off.

The competition between Sipho and Yolanda had ended and they were listening to the conversation.

Zak was right to be cautious in front of the children. If the blood had not been pounding in her ears, she, too, might have been able to think straight.

Their eyes met as he laid out the sandwiches, potato salad and apples on his desk. Neither of them spoke. Then Mandla tripped over a chair in his rush toward the food, and the moment passed, but she was sure that in Zak's eyes she had seen the same feeling that kept her awake at night.

After lunch, Zak asked Sipho if he wanted to tour the hospital.

"Yes, please," said Sipho.

For the next hour Monica and Zak were like awkward teenagers as they toured the empty burn unit, the intensive-care unit and all the other wards. Sipho wanted to see everything, including the store-rooms where the medicines and supplies were kept. Monica and Zak were overly polite when navigating narrow passageways, each waiting for the other to go first. In the dark confines of the linen closet, she felt his eyes on her.

Sipho and Mandla listened to Zak's commentary in silence and asked questions at appropriate moments. Mandla did not run, fiddle or find a hundred and one places to hide. He was on his best behavior, as though he knew something was happening between Monica and Zak and that if he acted up, the fragile threads that were beginning to be woven would snap. Or else he was just growing up.

Zak ended the tour in the reception area, where Adelaide produced lollipops for the children from behind her desk.

Monica's car was the only one left in the parking lot.

Zak leaned in her window. "Thanks for coming today."

If they had been alone, she felt sure he would have kissed her.

"I wouldn't have missed it for the world." She held his gaze until Mandla moaned at her to start the car.

When they arrived home, she found that Mandla had drawn all over his car seat straps with a marker. She was irritated to be brought back to Earth this way.

"Where did you get that?" she asked.

"Look at the cross little mommy," said Mandla, waggling his finger in front of Monica's face.

"She's not our mommy," snapped Sipho.

Monica froze. He had always expressed his displeasure at Mandla's use of this name for Monica but never in words.

"Yes, she is," argued Mandla. "Our real mommy's dead and Monica's our new mommy." His eyes were defiant, but Monica could see from his trembling lip that he was close to tears.

"It doesn't matter what either of you choose to call me," she said, trying to sound cheerful when what she really wanted to do was beat the steering wheel in frustration. "What you need to remember is that there is nothing more important to me in life than the two of you. So you can call me auntie, if it makes you feel more comfortable, or you can call me Monica or you can call me what my brother used to call me when he was small, and that's Minky."

Mandla screeched with laughter. "It sounds like *monkey*." He became serious. "No, I'm still going to call you Mommy."

She pulled them both into an embrace. Mandla rested his head on her shoulder. Sipho was stiff, but he did not pull away.

Monica could hear the concern in Zak's voice when he telephoned her the next day. He had visited Zukisa's mother on his way to take Yolanda home.

"I tried to bring her back with me so that I can admit her to this hospital, but she wants to die in her own bed. The only thing I could do was give her more pills to help with the pain."

"How much longer do you think she has?"

"It's hard to tell."

"I'll drive down there and see if I can change her mind. Zukisa's just a child. She shouldn't have this responsibility."

For a moment they were both silent. Neither brought up what had happened between them the previous day at the hospital. Monica felt her face growing warm. Finally Zak spoke.

"The place I was telling you about is on the beach, ten miles north of Lady Helen. Does Friday evening suit you?"

Monica tried to keep her voice steady. "Francina will be back by then. I'll ask her if she can babysit the boys."

Zak's beeper went off and he had to end their call. Monica looked at herself in the mirror. Her cheeks were flushed, her eyes shone and she had a ridiculous grin on her face. She bounced onto her bed, buried her face in her pillow and laughed hysterically. Mandla came into her room and pounced on top of her.

"Why are you laughing, Mom?"

"Because I'm happy."

"Me, too." He began to chuckle.

She tickled him, first in the soft hollow above his collarbone and then his sides, and he surrendered, laughing and squealing and begging her to stop.

9

FRANCINA STRETCHED HER LEGS OUT IN FRONT OF HER,
trying to chase away the ache that had settled on her like a docile cat.
It was a tiring journey, but at least it was in a car with her husband
and not in a crowded taxi. At one point, she had hopped into the
backseat to sleep, but since she could not help Hercules with the
driving she felt too guilty to steal more than two hours.

For ten days Francina's mother had not been permitted to leave
the family compound. Francina and her sister-in-law had cooked
meals, cleaned, swept the ground outside the huts and tended the
vegetable garden.

When the work for the day was finished, Hercules had driven
Francina to Jabulani Lodge. Watching Dingane make small talk with
guests, issue orders to employees and take phone calls from prospec-
tive tour companies, she'd realized she had never seen him looking so

at ease. Gone were the days when he had to pick up empty drink cans and wine bottles after driving safari guests to watering holes at sundown.

Francina had wondered if Sipho and Mandla missed her, and more than once she'd told Hercules that he should return to his students. Mr. D was teaching his class for him, and she knew that secretly Hercules worried that his students would think the school principal superior in comparison. But Hercules would not think of allowing her to take a taxi back alone.

Two days before the end of the widow's seclusion, Sigidi had asked Francina to accompany him on a walk to their father's grave. As they'd stared at the handwritten letters of their father's name on the little white cross, Sigidi had made an announcement. He had a white girlfriend in Durban whom he wanted to marry.

Francina had been shocked. It didn't offend her that her brother's girlfriend was white, but she had never imagined that a white woman would one day be a part of her family.

"You know you have to wait until the year of mourning is up," she'd told him.

His mouth had twisted into a grimace.

"It's tradition."

She was happy for this rule that helped her evade giving him a real opinion.

When the ten days were up, Reverend Ngubane had arrived for the blessing ceremony. He'd blessed the bowl of water Francina's mother had filled, and then, using a small grass brush, had sprinkled water on the widow's head, face, hands and feet. Next he'd sprinkled water on each sleeping hut and the central kitchen and living room.

That night in bed, Francina had held Hercules tight.

"Are you unhappy about leaving?" he'd asked.

She'd answered his question with one of her own. "Will you come back with me after the year of mourning is up?"

His voice in the darkness had been filled with emotion. "You know I will do anything for you."

Hercules tired as they approached Port Elizabeth, but he did not want to waste money on a hotel room. In the end, he agreed to stop, but in the parking lot of a busy shopping center. In the dappled shade of a black monkey thorn tree, the car windows open for fresh air and his wife watching over him, Hercules slept peacefully. The unofficial security guard sidled over to solicit a tip, but Francina shooed him away, saying, "Don't be so cheeky. We're sitting in our car and can protect it ourselves."

After three hours, Hercules awoke refreshed and as hungry as a boy after a day in the fields watching the cattle. They found a restaurant inside the mall, and when they returned to their car, the security guard stepped out from behind a truck with his hand out. Hercules took five rands out of his wallet and the guard accepted it with a nod.

"Highway robbery," said Francina as they watched the guard approach the next shopper. "If someone wanted to take our car, that man would not have put his life at risk."

"Extortion it might be," said Hercules in the calm voice he always managed when his wife was being what he called feisty, "but it's the way things are."

Francina thought of other things that people accepted that they shouldn't. Zulu women allowed their husbands to make the rules when it came to lovemaking because that was the way it had always been. And because of this, many of her sisters were infected with the deadly disease that was changing the face of the African continent. Her sisters were dying because they could not assume the right to demand that their husbands take care in matters of love.

They drove on, Hercules squinting in the relentless light of an afternoon sun, too low in the sky to be blocked out by the visor.

The alarm on Hercules's watch had gone off at four o'clock this morning, and with the car packed, the goodbyes said, all they'd had to do was brush their teeth and slip out quietly. But when they'd stepped into the cold morning air, the whole family had been there to see them off. Every parting from her family was difficult for Francina, but this one had been especially painful. Not only had her father's worried face been absent from the group, but she had been gripped by a sudden fear that this might be the last time she saw her mother.

Choking on tears, she'd hugged her mother until Hercules had whispered in her ear that they had to leave if they wanted to make it home before midnight.

Francina appreciated the beauty of the Garden Route on the return journey more than she had in the taxi. Without the constant chatter of her traveling companions and the stale air of too many bodies pressed into a small space, she was able to stare in silence at the dense forests that leaned in onto the road and the cliffs that tumbled down to the ocean.

She considered herself fortunate to have seen so much of the country on this short trip away from Lady Helen, even if the reason for it made her heart heavy. Her father had never been anywhere except Durban and the capital of the province, Pietermaritzburg. He hadn't seen firsthand the marked differences from one province to another. South Africa was a small country, yet it contained so much: two oceans, wide clean beaches, graceful mountains, grasslands where wild animals roamed, deep canyons, hardwood forests, wetlands that went on for miles.

Her father had seen but a fraction of it and yet he had been content with his small parcel of land and horizon that ended just across the valley with the swell of another hill almost identical to the one on which his village stood. There was something to be learned from the quiet satisfaction of her father's life. People traveled around the world to find peace in the beautiful spots of God's creation, but here was a man who had found it on the gentle slope of a hill, too far from the ocean to even smell the salt air.

"My mother would enjoy this," remarked Hercules as they came upon a dramatic view of two massive headlands guarding a bay.

"We could stop on our next trip."

"You'd better sell a lot of dresses," laughed Hercules. "Hotels around here cost a fortune."

Francina wondered whether Mrs. Shabalala had managed to complete any of the orders that were left half-done. Perhaps not, but her mother-in-law's cheerful manner would be like chamomile lotion on a mosquito bite if any of the clients were peeved at not having their dresses on time.

Hercules wanted to get as much distance as possible behind them before the sun went down.

"My mother will have food waiting for us when we get home. There's no need to stop again."

Francina peeled a banana and handed it to him before peeling another for herself. She had a box of leftovers from their lunch at the mall—enough to keep them going till they reached home.

At eleven that night they were ascending the familiar road up the koppie that guarded Lady Helen. Francina sighed as she saw the sleeping town below.

"Aren't you happy to be home?" asked Hercules.

"I've just realized that this place feels more like home to me now than my own village."

"I understand," he told her. "But you need not feel guilty about it. Your family wishes only for your happiness."

"Thank you."

"For what?" Hercules did not take his eyes off the road, but his tone told her that he was surprised.

"For coming to my father's funeral. For being the best husband a woman could want."

It was dark in the car, but Francina knew, as only a wife knows, that her husband was smiling broadly.

They didn't silence the bells when they opened the front door because a light was on in their flat upstairs.

"Don't," said Hercules as Francina moved toward the counter where she kept her order book. "The work will be waiting for you in the morning."

"That's what I'm worried about," she grumbled, following her husband through the shop in the dim light cast by the streetlamp outside. A delicious smell of roasted meat drifted down the stairwell.

Hercules took the stairs two at a time and Francina was not far behind. They were both hungry.

Mrs. Shabalala was asleep on the couch, a red evening dress draped over her lap. Francina crossed the room and removed the sewing needle from her mother-in-law's fingers. Things must have gone badly; only someone who is truly exhausted would fall asleep while hemming a dress.

Hercules lifted the lid of a casserole dish sitting on top of the stove.

"Roast pork," he whispered.

Mrs. Shabalala's eyes fluttered.

"You're back," she said, straightening her skirt. "I'm sorry about your father, my dear." She held out her arms and Francina went to her like a child. "He was a good man. An old-fashioned man."

Francina did not try to extricate herself from her mother-in-law's embrace.

"You must be hungry."

Francina wondered if her mother-in-law had heard her stomach rumbling.

"Sit down and I'll bring the food. But first let me show you something." She moved away from Francina and held her arms out at her sides, as Mandla did when playing airplanes. "Can't you see it?" she asked when Francina did not respond. "I've lost ten pounds."

"Congratulations, Mama," said Francina.

"It wasn't me. It was those boys. They wore me out. I didn't have a chance to eat or sit when they were around. Mandla is like a spinning top." She brought the casserole dish to the table and then took a salad from the refrigerator.

Francina was grateful to come home to her mother-in-law. It would have been awful to come home to a dark house and scratch around for a bite to eat at this hour. Other women might bristle at the thought of their mother-in-law sharing their kitchen, but for Francina it seemed right.

Mrs. Shabalala would not say that Mandla had been naughty, but as she gave Francina a progress report on the outstanding orders, her flustered expression said what her kind heart would not allow her to. She had only managed to complete one dress, and the client had brought it back to be hemmed again because it was longer than she'd requested.

"Didn't Sipho help with Mandla?" Francina wanted to know.

"The poor little soul tried. I think his homework has suffered. I don't know what got into Mandla. He's a lively boy but not usually so…" She still would not say the word.

Could it be, wondered Francina, that Mandla was upset by her absence? Did he believe that she'd gone for good, just like his mother? She put the question to Hercules, who, after all, was an expert in children.

"It's quite possible," he said. "Mandla is very close to you."

Not as close as I'd like him to be, thought Francina, but she kept this to herself. Nobody was to know that she was jealous of Monica for having the boys.

"I'll go there first thing tomorrow morning and set things straight," said Francina.

Just before seven the next morning, Francina used her key to enter Monica's kitchen and called out, "Good morning. I'm back."

She heard quick footsteps on the wooden floor, and then Mandla barreled around the corner like a truck that had lost its brakes, almost colliding into her legs. He put his arms up for her to lift him.

He was getting too heavy to be carried like a baby, but neither of them wanted to stop.

"How's my boy?"

He pulled back and looked at her solemnly. "You didn't say goodbye."

"I'm sorry, my baby," she said, rocking him as though he were an infant. "Were you scared I wouldn't come back?"

He nodded solemnly.

"I thought I heard your voice." Monica was dressed for work. She hugged Francina and Mandla together. "I'm sorry about your father."

"He brought four children into the world. His life was a good one."

Francina wondered if Monica could detect the wistful note in her voice, but Mandla had distracted her with a request for juice. Sipho came into the kitchen, and when he saw Francina his face lit up.

"I'm happy you're back," he said. "Someone—" he gave his brother a pointed stare "—has been impossible while you were away."

"*Gogo* said I could play with the empty rolls." Mandla pulled a face at his brother.

"That's right, the empty ones." Sipho turned to address Francina. "He unwound all the fabric you have in the shop and—"

"I used it to make a nest."

Judging by his confused expression, he had not been scolded immediately after his offense and the news now was a shock to him.

"It's okay, my little one. *Gogo* is not angry." *Exhausted, more like it,* thought Francina.

She watched Monica move around the kitchen, stirring the porridge, taking out the bowls, setting the table with fluid movements. When she'd first adopted the boys, Monica had been like a new daughter-in-law: well-meaning but clueless. Watching the scene that was also, at this very moment, taking place in millions of other homes across the country, Francina felt her throat tighten. If she hadn't spent her childbearing years cowering away from men because of the beating Winston once gave her, she would have a child. But it was too late now.

"I'll pick you up after school," she told the boys.

"Yay, we can play in the garden again!" shouted Mandla.

Francina nodded. Her mother-in-law had not had an easy time. In retrospect, she should have told her not to worry about the dress orders.

When she returned home, her mother-in-law had still not emerged from her bedroom.

"She needs her rest," Francina told Hercules.

In his wife's absence, he had prepared his own porridge.

"Here, let me help you with that." She took the wooden spoon from him to ladle the porridge into his bowl.

He sat down and opened the newspaper she had brought up with her.

"A thousand illegal immigrants are deported from South Africa every month." He whistled under his breath. "And those are only the ones who get caught."

"Well, South Africa is the most prosperous country on the continent."

Of course, Hercules knew that already, but Francina was always glad that he listened to her observations as though they came from the mouth of a university professor.

"Nevertheless," she continued, thinking that this particular word made her sound like a professor, "forty percent of our own people are unemployed."

"If we remember the parable of the Good Samaritan, these people are our neighbors and need our help."

Francina poured a glass of juice for him. She did not know the answer and she had to admit that the problem seemed removed from their lives in Lady Helen. Her only problem now was finding enough hours in the day to wade through the backlog of orders.

Later that morning, after Hercules had gone to school and her mother-in-law had finally gotten up and left to do the marketing, Francina sat in the shop, staring at the order book. It appeared that her mother-in-law had not worked in a methodical order. Dresses that Francina had left with only their hems undone had not been touched, and yet her mother-in-law had cut fabric for the most recent orders, which could have easily been put aside. The dress that had been returned to be rehemmed was in a paper bag under the counter.

Francina worked quickly, not stopping even to turn on the radio for company. Her business depended on a quick rescue mission. Her thoughts drifted to her brother Sigidi, who by now would have returned to his girlfriend in Durban. Would he tell this woman that they had to wait to get married or would he, like so many young Zulus nowadays, brush tradition aside as easily as if it were beach sand on a blanket? Francina would write to offer her brother support and express her desire to meet his girl, but she would once again warn her brother not to upset their mother.

* * *

Later, as Francina measured the wife of Lady Helen's banker for a dress, she wondered how she would place her. Every person who walked through the door of Jabulani Dressmakers found a place in one of two groups. Would Jane, like most women in Lady Helen and the world over, be offended if Francina was truthful about the fabric she had chosen for the dress she wanted to wear to her sister's wedding? Or would she be in Francina's favorite group, the one whose members appreciated an objective opinion?

"A plain color or fine vertical stripes would be more slimming," ventured Francina.

"Are you saying I'm fat?"

Group number one it was, then, for Jane.

"Not at all," replied Francina, embarking on her routine defense. "But for evening wear, strong, healthy women like you and I need to choose carefully."

Jane's eyes widened, and too late Francina remembered that white women were not interested in looking strong and healthy. Would Jane take her roll of fabric and try to find another dressmaker, one in Cape Town perhaps?

Jane sighed. "I ate too much over the Christmas holidays."

"Join the club. But, unlike me, you'll lose it. I still think you should go for a plain color. Blue to match your pretty eyes perhaps?"

Jane smiled, Francina's unintended insult forgotten. She fingered the fabric that Francina placed in front of her. "People say you're a magician. Please work your magic on me. My sister is superskinny."

Francina shook her head. She did not understand the logic of a world where some women starved themselves and others were plain starving.

"Let's draw a design for you."

An hour later Jane walked out of the shop in high spirits.

Another satisfied customer, thought Francina. People said that men were predictable, but she found women easier to understand. They required only three things to be happy: to feel needed, to feel loved and to feel attractive. Every woman harbored a degree of vanity in her heart. This was not immoral. In fact, there were some women who could do with a larger helping of it. Take, for example, Monica's good friend Cat. She actually went to the hairdresser and asked for that boyish haircut. And now that she was pregnant, her wardrobe had become even sloppier. Francina clicked her tongue. But she didn't try to fool herself; half of her disapproval of Cat stemmed from jealousy of her pregnancy. Monica would have a baby in a couple of years, too. Francina had not been the least surprised when she had been asked to sit with the boys tomorrow night so Monica could go on a date with Zak.

"I just want to know why he took so long to ask you," she'd told Monica.

In spite of her backlog of orders, she'd offered to make Monica a dress for the evening. But Monica had said she would find something in her closet. Francina thought of Monica's straight skirts, khaki pants and loose shirts and gave a little shudder. Francina imagined that the girl who had attracted Sigidi's eye wore high heels and feminine dresses. When he was a teenager, her brother had pored over the color pictures in magazines of white television and film stars. Jabulani had never been enough for him. He had told Francina that his girlfriend worked in the men's department of a large clothing store. Girls with obvious attractiveness were posted in the men's department. Women didn't want to feel self-conscious when trying on clothes, and nothing could do that more than a shop assistant who looked like a beauty queen. Men, however, would purchase the most expensive suits in the shop to impress a pretty girl.

"Oh, my brother," said Francina under her breath. "I hope you'll do the right thing."

Mama Dlamini came in at tea time with a chocolate cake. "I'm sorry about your father."

Francina thanked her and put the cake on the counter.

"Hercules loves that one," said Mama Dlamini.

Francina felt a prickle of irritation. Her husband was not fond of cake.

"He came into the café while you were away. Didn't you think he looked heavier when he arrived at your village?"

"No, and he's perfectly fine as he is."

"He's so skinny a strong wind could blow him out to sea."

Francina had worried about his health when she'd first met him because he was so thin, but there was no need. And one thing she would not stand for was another woman saying that she could do a better job of taking care of her husband. Why had Hercules not mentioned that he'd visited Mama Dlamini at the café? She wished her interfering friend would leave and take the cake with her.

"I'd better get back to work." Whether she had achieved her goal of upsetting Francina or simply realized that this was what she had done, Mama Dlamini knew that it was in her interest to leave now.

"Thanks for the cake." Francina could not manage more than a tight smile.

She watched Mama Dlamini walk down the sidewalk and stop to

talk to Oscar—probably about how well she had fed Francina's husband while his wife was away.

"Ouch." Francina never pricked her finger with a needle.

As she sucked the drop of blood, she saw Mama Dlamini move on and Oscar turn to stare at her. Realizing how odd she must look sitting there with her finger in her mouth, she felt herself blushing.

Oscar walked past her shop and waved every day, but this time he opened the door.

"I'm sorry about your father."

She thanked him for his condolences and inquired after his health.

"Fine, fine. You look busy."

She showed him the list of outstanding orders.

"I've seen ladies wearing your dresses. They're very pretty."

Francina wondered if he was referring to the dresses or the ladies.

"I'm proud of you."

She blushed again. This was their first normal conversation since that awful confrontation between him and Hercules. She'd had no idea that Oscar was in love with her. She had apologized for Hercules's behavior and thanked Oscar for helping her pass her exams, but after that she got the impression that he went out of his way not to talk to her.

"What about the rest of high school?" he asked.

Francina frowned. It had been her goal to finish the final three years. "I have too much else to do."

"That's a shame, because you owe it to yourself."

She didn't think of his words until later that night, when she was lying in a hot bath to soothe the tight muscles in her neck. Monica had finished high school. So had Gift. So had Mama Dlamini. All

Francina's irritation came rushing back at the thought of her friend. She would have to find a way to ask Hercules about his visits to the café without sounding as though she were accusing him of something. Men could be so touchy.

He was standing on the balcony when she came out of the bathroom in her pajamas.

"The air smells different here," he said.

She slipped her arm around his waist, and for an instant he was surprised. Then he turned back to look at the ocean.

"The place wasn't the same while you were away."

This was her opportunity. "It's lucky for you that we have some of our own people here." She watched his face. "Mama Dlamini said that she kept you company."

He said nothing, but she saw an almost imperceptible grimace.

"I didn't know you liked cake."

"Francina, you're completely wrong, so please stop."

"You do like cake?"

He turned to face her, and in the pool of light from the bedroom she could see that he was angry.

"My mother was with me both times I went there. *She* ordered the cake for me, even though I didn't want it. It was the only way she could get a few bites without feeling guilty about her diet. I am disappointed in you, Francina."

"It's just that—"

"I know what you were thinking. Don't you know that if there's anyone in the world you can trust, it's me?"

Francina felt miserable. She had hurt his feelings, and all over a piece of cake.

"I'm sorry," she whispered.

He squeezed her hand in reply. Francina was amazed; he had known exactly what was on her mind. And she had believed all along that her husband was not wise to the ways of women. The discovery pleased her. Her tall history teacher was a man of surprises.

"Can we start my lessons again?"

He turned to face her with a smile. "I thought you'd never ask."

10

MONICA HAD CHOSEN A BLACK SLEEVELESS DRESS splattered with red roses and strappy black sandals for her first date with Zak. The only thing Zak had told her about the restaurant was that it was on the beach, but this dress would be fine anywhere. For some reason, Zak wanted to go out early for dinner.

She gave her reflection in the mirror a final inspection. The lipstick was too dark. She rubbed it off and applied a shade lighter than the roses on her dress.

"You look pretty," said Mandla when she walked into the living room, where the boys were sitting with Francina and Hercules.

"Thank you, kind sir."

"I've never seen that dress before," said Francina.

"Never had an occasion to wear it."

"Why can't we come?" asked Mandla. "I like Dr. Zak."

"Dr. Zak and I have something important to discuss, sweetie."

She saw Sipho watching her, a tiny smile on his lips. This was what she had feared when she'd told the children she was going out with Zak. Sipho approved—no, he more than approved. He was ecstatic—but what if it didn't work out? He would be devastated.

With a helpless look at Francina and Hercules, she hurried to the kitchen and came back with a tray of strawberries and melted chocolate. Mandla selected the largest strawberry and dipped it into the chocolate till the tips of his fingers were submerged. Sipho chose a small strawberry.

"They're the sweetest," he explained.

"You should let me make you a dress," said Francina.

"Is there something wrong with this one?"

Francina pulled her mouth. "It'll last for a season. That's how they make clothes these days. I just thought you might need more dresses now that you and Zak are going out."

"Shh, Francina."

Mandla had licked the chocolate off his strawberry and was about to dunk it again when Sipho caught his wrist.

Francina gave Monica a meaningful look. "One day I'll make your most special dress."

Monica rolled her eyes. Francina could be exasperating.

"As soon as you leave, we're going to switch to speaking Sotho. Aren't we, boys?" said Francina.

Sipho nodded. "I don't know if he remembers any words." He thumbed in the direction of his younger brother.

"We'll soon change that. My Sotho is not perfect, but Hercules is fluent."

Monica had asked Zak not to pick her up at her house. If one of her neighbors saw her getting into his car, the whole town would know before sunrise. She felt oddly uncomfortable closing the door on her family to go out for the evening. Married parents did it all the time, but this seemed like sneaking around.

The sun hung low in the sky, partly obscured by streaks of pale clouds that had banded together above the horizon. She hoped that S.W. would not come outside to fill his birdbath before she had made her getaway.

Zak was not waiting in his car outside the hospital, as arranged. She parked her car next to his and turned off the engine, wondering how long she would have to sit here. It was only a couple of minutes before the front door of the hospital opened and he strode across the veranda and took all three stairs at once. He wore jeans and a polo shirt. She felt a flutter of panic. This dress made her appear eager, too eager, about their first date.

"You look nice," said Zak.

"I'm overdressed, aren't I?"

"My mother says there's no such thing."

He held the door for her, and she climbed into the passenger seat of his small sedan. A man like Zak would never have a showy, expensive car.

He drove north, past the imposing entrance of the golf resort, where the guard had been instructed to bar her from ever entering the premises again. As the road veered inland, Zak pointed to a section of the high wall that encircled the resort.

"Remember that?"

Monica nodded. It was where Daphne had led them over the wall to confront Mr. Yang, the owner of the resort.

Beyond the golf resort, the road straightened before intersecting with the main road. Cape Town was an hour and a half south. Zak turned left to go north.

"It's quite a way," he said apologetically.

Monica was relieved that he left what was in both of their minds unsaid. Neither of them wanted to be spotted by anyone from Lady Helen.

They rolled down the windows and breathed in the scent of wild rosemary. Monica's hair—that she had spent thirty minutes styling—blew every which way, but she did not care. She had a curious feeling that she had lived this experience before, perhaps in a dream. With the noise of the road and the car and the rushing air, it was impossible to make conversation. And there was no need to. She wished the journey would never end.

Just before Velddrif, Zak slowed the car as they neared what appeared to be the top half of a small wooden boat sticking up out of the ground. From it hung a rough wooden sign that read Lambert's Fish Shack. Plastic red crabs and pink lobsters clung to a fishing net draped over the top of the hull.

"I know it's cheesy," said Zak. "But you'll see why I love this place."

She wondered if he'd ever brought his wife here. Suddenly she found herself smoothing her hair and checking her reflection in the mirror. Was this how it would always be? Wondering if he had been to a place with his wife, eaten the same meal, said the same words? At one time he would have believed that he could never love another woman as much as he loved his wife, that he would never share a connection as strong as theirs with anyone else. How was Monica to compete with fourteen years of memories? Or was she not supposed to try? Francina would be the one to answer that question. After a disastrous beginning, she seemed to be managing Hercules's past without difficulty.

Zak parked in the gravel lot, which was surprisingly full this early in the evening.

"They come for the sunset," he said, answering her unspoken question.

The path to the wooden restaurant was lined with oars, cracked sailing masts, splintered wood, driftwood—anything and everything that could possibly wash up on a beach. Every few feet a faded and peeling plastic mermaid sat atop a pedestal like a vestal virgin in the Roman Forum. Whoever owned the place had a sense of humor.

A young woman in a sarong and tank top greeted Zak at the door. "Table for two, Dr. Niemand?"

Her glance at Monica was brief but long enough for Monica to see the question in her eyes. This was the confirmation Monica needed that he had brought his wife here.

The restaurant was completely open to the beach on the coastal side. Low tables and benches were arranged around a large fire pit tended by two men in aprons. Fairy lights hung from the tarpaulin ceiling.

The young woman led them to a table with a clear view of the ocean, which had turned a deep shade of violet as the sun slipped in the sky. Feeling conspicuous among the other diners dressed in shorts and T-shirts, Monica kicked off her shoes. The sand was surprisingly cool on her toes. A smell of garlic and grilling fish drifted over in a cloud of smoke from the fire pit.

There was no menu, Zak told her, and dinner could take up to three hours. She thought about the boys and wondered if it would have been better if they'd stayed over at Francina's house.

Zak saw the concern on her face. "We don't have to stay that long if you need to get back. Not once have I had room for dessert anyway."

A middle-aged lady announced to the diners that the first course was ready.

"You're going to love this," said Zak.

As he led her to the buffet table, she noticed that he was barefoot, too. Steaming loaves of bread and homemade jams—apricot, blackberry, tomato and watermelon—were spread out on tin platters.

Monica had never tasted anything like this and found herself licking the dripping jam from her fingers. An elderly man with a guitar walked up from the beach and began strumming a melancholy tune Monica had never heard before.

Seagulls swooped overhead, waiting for the remains of the snoek that diners had begun to fetch from the grill. Zak filled her plate and brought it to her. On his instructions, she daubed the salty fish with apricot jam, which melted quickly and pooled on her plate. The sun had begun to dip into the ocean.

Zak ate with obvious enjoyment, and Monica found herself thinking of him alone in his house with a sandwich for dinner in front of the television. She tried not to think of the woman who had walked out on him, but it was difficult. Even the smallest details, like the song he hummed along to with the guitarist, made her wonder if he'd heard it before when he'd been here with his wife.

"Why did you become a doctor?" she asked, in the hope that they could talk about a time before he'd met his wife.

"My father was one." A shadow passed over his face. "He had to give up his practice in Cape Town when I was fifteen. Multiple sclerosis."

"I'm sorry."

"He died five years later while I was in medical school." Zak looked at the waves that had begun to creep closer. "He always hoped I would take over his practice, but after medical school, I had to go in the army for two years and then I wanted to see the world. I spent three years doing short-term jobs in England and taking quick weekend trips to other European countries. One gray, oppressive day, I'd had enough and booked my ticket back to Cape Town."

He'd gone to work at Groote-Schuur—the hospital where Chris Barnard performed the world's first heart transplant in 1967—and furthered his training in intensive care. He and his wife moved to Lady Helen when Yolanda was five because they wanted to raise her in a small town. Monica was grateful that he didn't mention meeting or marrying his wife.

"And now Yolanda spends her weeks in a big city and only her weekends in a small town," he said.

The guitar player wandered over to their table, sat down on the bench opposite them and started to sing a ballad about a woman who promises herself that if she ever sees her soldier husband's smile again, she will never let it disappear. When the song ended, the man looked first at Zak and then at Monica.

"Ah, to be young and in love again," he said.

Monica wished the hole she had been digging with her toe in the sand was big enough to hide in. Zak looked at her, and on his face she did not see embarrassment but humor.

"He says that to everyone."

Monica felt even more embarrassed then because of her reaction and could have hugged the restaurant owner when she announced that the next course—grilled prawns—was available at the fire pit.

After filling their plates, Monica and Zak sat down, but she could not get the song out of her head.

"My brother went away to a war."

Zak was quiet, as though he knew what she was about to say.

She did not usually discuss her brother's death with anyone, and if she did, she wound up feeling inexplicably guilty, even sordid. But Zak had been a conscript, too. If anyone could understand the futility of her brother's death, it would be him. She felt the weight of a familiar sense of sorrow that appeared on special days: Luca's birthday, Christmas, the anniversary of his death.

She told Zak how a military policeman, not much more than a teenager himself, had come to tell her parents that their nineteen-year-old son had stepped on a land mine and been killed.

Zak reached for her hand.

"My father took a match and burned the letter in front of him."

Looking back, it was easy to pinpoint that moment as the time her parent's marriage fell apart, but then, as a teenager who had never needed to contemplate the strength of her family, she'd believed without thinking that they would comfort each other, that they would survive. Despite her parents' daily squabbles—the ongoing attrition that wore them all down—her parents had never parted, perhaps to punish each other, perhaps because they didn't know what they would do without each other, perhaps, as Monica liked to think, because deep down they needed each other.

"I was on the border, too," Zak said quietly. "As a medic."

"You weren't the one...?" She let the sentence hang in the air.

"No. I was never called for anything like that."

She nodded. It would have been a macabre coincidence.

Zak had not let go of her hand while she'd been talking. Now they sat in silence, watching the sun bleed into the ocean and the waves turn pink. Zak offered his sympathy as people usually did on the rare occasions she shared this story, but he did not say, as some had the gall to, that her brother had died a noble death in the service of his country. He held her hand and was quiet. Zak knew firsthand the banality of war. A feeling of ease came over her as the sun disappeared into the dark water.

They had finished five courses—the last, of course, was crayfish—and had been promised that dessert would be served in the next few minutes.

"Do you want some?" asked Zak.

Monica shook her head. "I can't eat another thing."

"Shall we take a walk?"

She nodded. He did not let go of her hand until they reached the cash register to pay. On the beach he took her hand again. They walked north, into the wind that had started to pick up. The moon was not quite full, and yet they could see clearly enough to make their way over the rocks. A lone seagull wheeled above them, squawking loudly.

"Maybe he couldn't get close at dinnertime," said Zak.

One of the restaurant's staff had scattered the leftover fish up the beach, away from the diners. All that was left now were the bones and scales, which were being picked over by crabs.

They had walked about a quarter of a mile up the beach when Zak stopped.

"Do you think we should turn back?" Monica asked.

He took her other hand. "Monica, I…" He shook his head as though the words had not come out right.

She thought of things she could say to make him feel at ease but chose to remain silent. Her heart beat so wildly as she met his gaze that he might have heard it if not for the wind and the thundering of the waves on the beach. They both knew what was coming but just not how it would happen.

He pulled her toward him. And then he leaned in and kissed her.

She did not close her eyes. She wanted to remember every detail of this moment.

When they finally pulled apart, he said, "I've wanted to do that ever since I climbed onto the roof of Daphne's house during the protest sit-in to check on her fever. You looked so peaceful up there."

"It was a beautiful evening. Like tonight."

"When the guitar started up that night, I wanted to put my arms around you and sit there with you until the sun came up. But it—"

"I know," she said softly. She put her arms around his neck and kissed him. No explanations were necessary now. That was all part of the past.

11

IT HAD BEEN DEBATED, VOTED ON AND APPROVED. ALL
that remained now was for Monica and the boys to make the offer.
When they arrived at the hospital midmorning on Saturday, Monica
was surprised to see Zak's car in the parking lot. He wasn't expecting her and she'd thought he'd be away, collecting Yolanda in Cape
Town.

All of a sudden she was assailed by doubt. Perhaps the morning after
their date was too soon to show up at his place of work unannounced;
he might think she was crowding him. She pushed aside the thought.
Zak did not play games; everything he did was after lengthy consideration. It had showed in the way he'd waited until he had come to terms
with the breakup of his marriage before going out with another woman.

What Monica and the boys had come to do this morning at the

hospital was important; Daphne had told them that Silas was ready to be discharged.

They met Zak and Yolanda in the corridor on the way to Silas's ward. Zak *was* surprised to see her, but his smile told her that he was pleased, as well.

"We've come to see Silas," she said, feeling as though she had to explain herself. "Hi, Yolanda." The girl returned her greeting with a sweet smile.

"I was just on my way to see him myself," said Zak. "How are you, young men?"

He shook Mandla's hand. Sipho waited his turn and then shook Zak's hand with extra vigor. Zak looked into Monica's eyes as he knocked on Silas's door, and she felt her stomach do a nervous flip.

As they entered, Daphne jumped to her feet. There was a book in her hand.

"My shift is over. I've been reading to Silas." Blushing deeply, she realized that her explanation had placed her in a difficult position.

Monica came to her rescue. "Poetry should be recommended reading for all journalists."

Silas nodded in agreement. "Poets use few words to say so much, and we journalists use many, sometimes to say nothing at all."

Mandla's high-pitched laughter broke the tension in the room, and Daphne started bustling around, tidying Silas's nightstand, straightening his sheets. She was his nurse again, in charge and formidable.

Zak and Monica looked at each other. They had unwittingly barged in on a tender moment, and the realization made them smile in complicity. It seemed to be the season for falling in love.

Thank goodness for the impatience of small children.

"When are you going to leave the hospital?" Mandla wanted to know of Silas.

Daphne stopped tidying to stare at Zak.

"That's a good question, son," said Silas. "Doctor?"

"The medication has done its job, but you need to build up your strength. Normally I would send you home now to rest, but—" he looked at Daphne "—the journey to—"

"He can't go back to Zimbabwe." Daphne's chin jutted forward slightly. She crossed her arms.

Zak took off his glasses and rubbed his eyes. "If the police find out you are here—"

"None of the nurses or hospital workers will tell them." Daphne stared at Monica and Zak, her eyes challenging.

"I am not bound by law to report anyone who is in the country illegally," said Zak. "Everyone in this hospital is equal."

"Thank you," said Silas.

Monica felt the heavy weight of yet another secret she had to keep. If this man were sent back to Zimbabwe, he would not find work, he would not be able to help his family and he might end up in prison again. He had survived torture once, but what if the next time the prison guards and police officers did not know when to stop? She would not have a moment's peace if she caused this man to be deported to an uncertain future in a country teetering on the brink of disaster. It was time for her to make the offer that she and the boys had decided on.

"I can offer you a place to recuperate," she said.

"In the Old Garage," added Mandla, almost shouting in his excitement. "But it doesn't have cars or tools or junk in it. It's nice."

"It has been converted into a studio flat," Monica explained.

Offering this man sanctuary was risky, but did Jesus not preach to clothe the naked, feed the hungry and welcome the stranger?

"My nonna's coming in one month," warned Mandla.

"My mother will be visiting from Italy, but she can stay in the house with us if one month is not enough," explained Monica.

Silas and Daphne smiled at each other.

"It will be more than enough," said Daphne. "Thank you."

They left Daphne and Silas alone to make plans and, at Zak's suggestion, went outside onto the veranda to get some fresh air. Yolanda, thank goodness, was unaware of her father's ploy to stretch out his time with Monica. Monica, however, kept picturing their kiss on the beach the previous night and was sure that her face betrayed every emotion she was feeling. Sunny the cat was not impressed with the company and left his usual spot on the riempie bench to slink off through the oleander bushes at the edge of the property.

While Yolanda and the boys examined a spider's web that had been spun overnight between the roof's eave and a bottlebrush, Zak took Monica's arm and steered her out of their earshot.

"I haven't stopped thinking about you since last night."

She felt a flush of heat in her body. "Me, too."

"When can I see you again?"

Monica looked at the children. It was Saturday, but she could not leave the boys with Francina again. And what about Yolanda? She had come from Cape Town to see her father, not to be alone at home with a babysitter. Then suddenly, Monica had an idea.

"What about lunch tomorrow? You and Yolanda."

He smiled. "A family date."

"Exactly. And if everyone's happy, we can go for a walk on the beach afterward."

His eyes were filled with amusement. "Like last night?"

She knew that her face had turned red, but she didn't mind. "Could you settle for a scavenger hunt? Mandla loves them."

He brushed her cheek with back of his fingers.

"I'd dig ditches to be with you."

Monica remembered that Hercules had once said this to Francina and she had been ashamed at how jealous it had made her feel.

"We'd better not keep you from your patients."

"I only have two more to see and then I'm taking Yolanda out for lunch. She's sick of my sandwiches."

Driving away, Monica looked in her rearview mirror and saw Zak put his hand on Yolanda's shoulder. A small action but one which made Monica realize that it was not possible to be in love with Zak without loving his daughter, as well. Yolanda had warmed to Monica, but what would the young girl think if she knew her father was falling in love?

Francina stood back to allow the afternoon sunlight to fall on the canvas. She had spent Saturday morning in the shop and the past two hours cleaning the flat. She was tired. Last night, after she and Hercules had returned home after babysitting the boys, she had stayed up late, trying to master a tricky section in the math curriculum. At midnight Hercules had declared that their brains had already gone to bed and they should follow.

Now she was ready for a nice long soak in her bath. If she had one regret about leaving the Old Garage it was that she could no longer lie in the tub and watch television through the open door. Not only was it logistically impossible in this flat, but her mother-in-law would fall over from shock.

Francina had been urging Hercules to take up painting for months. Before he started teaching at Green Block School he had gone every day to the galleries in town and read all the books on art in the library. Gift had offered him use of her studio when she was not painting, which was between three and five in the afternoon, when she and David took their daily walk on the beach, but Hercules was too shy to accept. Gift would see his work, and he did not want anyone besides his wife and mother to glimpse his efforts.

Francina took one step to the left. The painting might look different from another angle. How can I lie to my husband? she thought miserably. And how can I not lie?

The only reason she recognized Lady Helen was because of the palm trees and bougainvillea. Francina thought of the landscapes she had seen at the school's art exhibit. Hercules's painting would not look out of place among those of the fifth grade.

A crease appeared on Hercules's forehead as he watched her face for a reaction. Her delayed response had been noticed.

Think, think, think, Francina. Say something good about it. Anything.

"The colors are very vivid."

"*Vivid* is not an adjective normally used to describe watercolors."

"But the real colors of Lady Helen are vivid and I think you've captured that well." If nothing else, the painting *was* colorful.

Hercules picked up the canvas and returned it to its place under their bed. Francina hoped that her tepid compliment had been enough for him, but she realized it was possible that he simply did not want her to shatter his illusions any further. *I hope he doesn't show me his progress next weekend,* she thought, *or I'll run out of neutral adjectives.* She wondered briefly if she should ask Gift to give him some pointers. No, that would be a bad move; he would be humiliated if he ever found out. And besides, talent could not be taught. And maybe that was the ingredient he was missing. Everybody had their own special talent. His was teaching; Hercules could listen to a child as though nothing else mattered in the world. She felt a stab of pain in her chest as though someone had punched her. That was it! Children! Hercules had none, and on the days he did not teach he needed something else to satisfy him. His awful painting was a direct result of her not being able to bear him a child. Why had she not seen this before? A wave of nausea came over her.

The smell of frying onions wafted from the kitchen where Mrs. Shabalala was preparing the evening meal. Francina's nausea worsened. She shut herself in the bathroom and ran the water in the tub. When it was full and scalding-hot, she climbed in and settled back to read a dressmaking magazine. The words of the feature on bridal gowns began to swim in front of her as tears ran down her cheeks and slid silently into the water.

12

MONICA SAW THE PUZZLED EXPRESSION ON MANDLA'S face every time she dashed to the fridge in search of a called-for ingredient from her cookbook. He was right; she should have chosen a recipe yesterday and gone to the grocery store with a list. Zak and Yolanda would arrive in an hour. It was such a rush to come up with a special meal after church. Poor Mandla couldn't concentrate on his picture of a killer whale with all the groaning going on.

Finally she settled on a recipe for goulash, one she had not made before but for which she at least had all the ingredients.

"Why don't you just make lasagna? Everybody loves your lasagna."

Monica thought about this for a moment. Lasagna was her old standard, the dish she could make with her eyes closed. What on earth was she thinking wanting to try out a new recipe on guests— and not just any guest, on Zak?

"Good idea," she said, stooping to give him a kiss.

"You're never like this when Oscar comes over or Francina and Hercules. Is Zak your boyfriend?"

She and Zak had meant to keep their relationship a secret for a while, but she could not lie to Mandla.

"Yes, he's my boyfriend." Saying the words brought on a strange fluttering sensation in her belly.

"And when he's finished being your boyfriend will he be your husband?"

"I don't know. We'll have to wait and see. Right now we're getting to know each other."

Mandla was so young when his father and mother split up that he didn't recall them living together at all. His only experience of a relationship between a man and woman had been with Francina and Hercules.

"How long will it take?"

"Before we know each other?"

He nodded.

"I don't know, sweetie. But I don't want you to worry about it. Nothing is going to change around here."

He went back to his coloring, satisfied with her explanation and content that the groaning had stopped.

Sipho came in from the dining room holding a fish knife.

"Where do these go?" His big eyes were filled with anxiety.

"We won't be needing those, just the regular knives and forks."

He dashed back into the dining room, and she could hear the clang of the fish knives being returned to the cutlery box.

She hurriedly prepared the meat sauce, put the béchamel on low and went to check on Sipho. The sight of the table made her catch her breath. Sipho had folded the paper napkins into swans—a technique learned at school, where the art class had recently been introduced to origami—and a vase in the center was filled with freshly cut daisies from the garden. He hadn't managed to find the good tablecloth, but he had placed the side plates strategically to cover the stains on the everyday one. There was enough cutlery at each setting for a three-course meal.

"It's beautiful, Sipho."

"How long before they get here?"

"Thirty minutes."

"I hope Mandla behaves."

Monica placed a hand on Sipho's shoulder. "You know, Zak really likes you. You and Mandla don't have to do anything but act normally."

Sipho looked at her with a weary expression, as though she were a child who was slow to learn.

"I know. It's just that I want him to…" He let the sentence hang, but Monica knew what he'd intended to say.

"Relationships can't be forced, Sipho. Let's just all be ourselves and see how it goes."

He nodded and then went to straighten a fork.

Zak asked for a second helping of lasagna and Sipho jumped up to get it for him. Yolanda ate slowly. When prompted by Mandla, she said that the lasagna was good. Throughout the meal Mandla kept trying to get Yolanda's attention, but her interest was centered on what her father and Monica had to say. Monica became so self-conscious under the scrutiny that she found herself looking at her plate or at the boys, not at Zak, whenever she addressed him directly. She could not follow her own advice to Sipho. At one stage, she felt Zak's leg brush against hers under the table. Blushing, she met his gaze, and his expression told her that she should relax. He was right; Yolanda was a child, not a rival.

After fruit salad and ice cream, Monica suggested a walk on the beach. The boys were enthusiastic, but Yolanda gave her father a look that said, *I thought we were just coming for lunch.*

"Yes, let's go," said Zak, returning his daughter's look with an expression of warning. Something had changed in Yolanda since yesterday.

Since the day was not too warm, they decided to walk to the beach. The children raced ahead, but every now and then Yolanda would wait for the adults to catch up. Then she'd take her father's arm. Sipho, with an insight beyond his years, tried to engage Yolanda in a conversation about her old classmates at Green Block School. It seemed unsuccessful at first, but her interest was finally piqued when he mentioned that one of the girls had won a modeling competition in Cape Town.

Zak briefly put his arm around Monica's waist.

"I'm trying to behave in front of the children," he said, "but I want to take you in my arms and kiss—"

"Shh. They'll hear." She gave him a look that said she wanted the same thing.

"Do you think you can manage to get away one evening this week after work? I want to take you up past the golf resort to see the shipwreck. At low tide you can walk out to it."

"I'll ask Francina if she'll watch the boys. I just feel badly because

I know she studies at night. Maybe Mrs. Shabalala can be enticed to watch them if I promise that Mandla won't be as wild as he was when Francina was away."

"We're not twenty-one anymore," Zak replied. "We have responsibilities. But somehow we'll make this work. There's nothing more I want in this world."

Monica looked into his eyes, saw tenderness and felt an unexpected urge to cry. Her feelings for her previous boyfriend, Anton, seemed stunted in comparison, a flimsy gossamer imitation.

There was only one reason a woman would be so attentive to the weight of words, so observant of fleeting expressions; there was only one reason why a usually composed woman would feel so off balance: she was in love. When Anton had proposed to her, she'd needed time to think. If Zak got down on one knee this afternoon, she would say yes. What recklessness! It was too soon to be thinking about marriage. But she'd never felt like this before. Her mouth was dry, her hands trembled and, yet, deep inside she felt a curious peace.

They had reached the beach and Zak set to work helping the boys build a sand fort. Yolanda stood by, obviously bored but unwilling to leave her father.

Monica, wondering if the girl felt excluded, tried to start a conversation with her.

"How's Silas?" she asked. Unlike Zak, Silas was someone they held in common, with equal shares of interest in his well-being.

"He's happy about coming to live in your Old Garage." Yolanda smiled for the first time that day. "I think Daphne's going to do double-duty nursing at the hospital and at your house."

"She's a strong lady."

Yolanda nodded in agreement. "Have you seen Zukisa lately?"

"Yes, this week. Her mother isn't responding anymore, but Zukisa is sure that she wants to die at home."

Yolanda dug a hole in the sand with her toe. "Whenever I think of Zukisa caring for her mother, I feel guilty for worrying about stupid stuff in my own life."

Monica wanted to reach out and touch Yolanda, but she didn't want to shatter the fragile connection between them. The girl was clearly unnerved by her father's blossoming relationship with Monica. How should she reassure Yolanda? To say bluntly that she didn't want to come between the girl and her father might set off a spark of irritation for its presumption. In the end, Monica decided that a less obvious approach would be better. *Be natural, befriend Yolanda and everything would work out,* she told herself.

"What are you girls talking about?" asked Zak. The fort was almost complete. Sipho and Mandla had gone off to gather sticks, shells and bits of seaweed to serve as catapults, ladders and flags.

"Nothing," said Monica teasingly.

"I'm going to swim," said Yolanda. She stripped off her T-shirt and shorts to reveal a school swim team bathing suit.

"Don't go in farther than waist-high," Zak instructed. He watched Yolanda skip down to the water's edge. "She seems happy."

"I don't know, Zak. There's something I can't put my finger on. I hope she doesn't think I'm going to come between the two of you."

"I don't see why she should. My relationship with you is different from the one I have with her."

Monica's stomach did a flip at his use of the word *relationship.*

He checked that the boys and Yolanda were not looking and pulled her close. "I've been wanting to do this all day," he said and leaned in to kiss her.

"Me, too. I feel like a teenager sneaking about when my parents aren't watching."

"It will change."

"I didn't say I didn't like it."

He laughed and kissed her again. When he pulled away, he had a serious look on his face. "I love you, Monica."

She thought her legs might give way beneath her.

"You probably think it's too soon for me to be saying something like that." He had interpreted her silence as doubt. "But it's true. I'm in love with you."

"I love you, too."

Their kiss this time lasted longer, and when they pulled apart, Monica saw Mandla looking at them.

"Have the teenagers been spotted?" asked Zak, laughing.

"I'm afraid so."

"Well, let's talk of something ordinary then. What does your week hold for you? Besides a romantic walk on the beach with your boyfriend."

Her stomach flipped again. "The usual—a difficult decision on what to do with information I wish I didn't have in my possession." She swore him to secrecy and then told him about the abalone ladies.

His immediate concern was for her safety. "Please don't go hunting poachers alone again."

"I won't. I've alerted the police to poaching in our area, but now I'm worried that the abalone ladies are the ones who are going to be caught."

"They know the risks. And Anna's right—they can just throw their catch back in the water. An ice chest full of abalone would be much more difficult to dispose of in a hurry."

"Are you saying that a little catch doesn't matter? Do you think I should back off and let them do what they've been doing for years?"

"It's sad that the greed of some has made an activity that many in these parts have been doing for years illegal." He smiled at her. "That was a very selfless offer you made to Silas yesterday. I'm sure you'll do the right thing by your abalone ladies."

Your abalone ladies. He had not cast any further light on the path she should follow, but now it came to her in a flash: the person she should ask for advice about the abalone ladies was the man who had once been in her position—Max.

The boys had returned, Sipho with his hands full, Mandla with a collection in the pouch he'd created by lifting the end of his T-shirt.

"Back to work," said Zak, giving her a wink.

That evening as she was getting into bed, the phone rang. It was Zak, wanting to say good-night and to repeat the words he had spoken on the beach. *I love you.* She drifted off to sleep thinking of the tender look in his eyes when he'd pulled her close.

13

WITH DAPHNE HOVERING OVER HIM LIKE AN ANXIOUS mother, Silas moved into the Old Garage, and the two of them soon fell into something of a routine. Daphne stopped by before work in the morning to give him breakfast, at noon to give him lunch and after her shift to give him dinner and keep him company.

At the same time, Zak and Monica settled into a routine of their own. One evening during the week they'd go for an early dinner and she would be back to tuck the boys in bed. On Friday nights they went on dates that could last longer since Francina, an enthusiastic champion of their relationship, offered to bring her tutor over to Monica's house and stay there until midnight if need be. Monica and Zak did not sit together at church, preferring to keep their relationship private for as long as possible.

"A month at the most is all that's possible in this town," Zak had joked.

But they sent each other lovelorn looks across the aisle, both counting the minutes till their families could get together for lunch and then walk on the beach or climb the koppies or watch a movie, which was always about horses when it was Yolanda's turn to choose. Sometimes Monica dropped in at the hospital for lunch, always armed with an excuse for a story in case Adelaide or Daphne intercepted her on her way to Zak's office. The rest of the time they relied on the telephone and e-mail messages. In truth, there wasn't much time for them to be alone together, but Monica was satisfied with the balance they had achieved between their responsibilities to their children and their deepening relationship.

They had been seeing each other for a little over a month when the air turned cool. Monica put extra blankets on the boys' beds and stopped using the ceiling fans. On Sundays, when they went to church, the birds seemed louder than usual. Mandla said it was all the mother birds telling their children to calm down while they were packing. Sipho prayed they would choose a Sunday to depart for the long journey up Africa to spend the summer in Europe; he wanted to see it with his own eyes.

One night, the long-billed whimbrels disappeared, and Sipho was crestfallen. They had been the last to leave the previous year. The curlews, bartailed godwits and greenshanks remained, eating, resting and making languid flights to the beach and back as though committing to memory the topography of this corner of the earth.

One afternoon after work, as Monica sat on the back step with a cup of tea watching the boys make piles of the dead leaves from the syringa tree, she heard Mandla ask his brother if he thought the young birds would manage.

"They've grown up now. Birds and animals develop quicker than humans," said Sipho.

"Do you think you'll go away when you grow up?"

Monica strained to catch Sipho's reply.

"Probably not."

Sipho noticed Monica watching and led Mandla by the hand around the other side of the tree to where he thought they were out of earshot. "Monica is going to marry Zak, and when I've finished medical school I'm going to work in the hospital with him."

"Is Monica getting married?" Mandla's voice was shrill. "What about us?"

She wanted to rush to him, put her arms around him and tell him that he and his brother would always be her first priority, but a part of her wanted to hear Sipho's thoughts.

"If we're good, nothing will change."

She felt an icy grip on her heart. Did Sipho really believe that she might abandon them as though they were pets that had turned out to be unsuitable? Or was he just trying to scare his brother? Even so, she was disturbed that the idea had even entered his head.

That night as she tucked Mandla in bed, she whispered in his ear, "You'll always be my boy, no matter what."

"Even if I'm not good?"

"Even if you're wicked."

She kissed him on the top of his head and he smiled sleepily at her.

* * *

The birds were not to disappoint Sipho. In church the following Sunday, as Reverend van Tonder discussed the importance of self-control in times of stress, the congregation heard a loud prolonged squawk from a single bird. And then it was as though all the other birds replied in unison. Sipho scrambled over Monica's legs and dashed to the window.

"Last year the birds waited until the closing hymn," said Reverend van Tonder. "I wonder if God's telling me something about my sermon."

There was polite laughter in the pews.

"Oh, go on, all of you." Reverend van Tonder flapped his arms as though he were one of the birds about to take off.

There was a rush to the windows, but some, like Sipho, ran outside to be able to experience the spectacle in full. Monica was caught in the squeeze at the door. Outside, the air was filled with the sound of furious flapping as the birds headed straight up before leveling off to allow the stragglers to get into formation.

Monica joined Sipho as the flock closed ranks. A large shadow fell across their faces.

"Godspeed," shouted Sipho. He added quietly, "Don't forget to come back to us."

She waited as the noise receded into the distance and the congregation made its way back into the church to hear the rest of the sermon. Zak was not in church this morning because his ex-wife wanted to see him urgently. Monica thought it strange that Jacqueline couldn't wait until he dropped off Yolanda later that afternoon.

When Monica and Sipho were finally alone, she said to him, "You might also go away one day."

He seemed panicked.

"To university in Cape Town," she explained further.

"Oh, yes."

"But I hope you'll come back, because I will always be here for you, for the rest of my life."

His eyes filled with tears. "Just like my mom."

She had meant to reassure him, and yet he had been reminded that people died young these days. The right words to say now eluded her, and so she tried to hug him instead.

"No, Mom, there are people watching from the windows."

It was the first time he had called her Mom. As they walked back into the church, Monica wiped her eyes.

Later that day, as the wind whipped the waves into a froth, Anna appeared, alone, at Monica's front door. She did not want to come in. She had to get back to her husband and baby, she said. Then she added, "The poachers have come back."

Monica nodded. "I'll see what I can do."

"Thank you. My regards to your family."

Monica watched her walk away, hunched against the wind. What was she supposed to do now? She couldn't go to the police after refusing to tell them how she'd found out about the poachers. Mike and Dewald had not persisted in questioning her because the problem had gone away, but they would not be as generous again.

She saw Silas returning to the Old Garage on foot from his Sunday lunch at Daphne's house. She waved to him and he shouted a greeting, but his words were lost in the roar of the wind. He had been living in the Old Garage for over a month now, and, with Daphne's nursing, had recovered from his illness. Monica had told him that he could stay on. Her mother had postponed her visit because Monica's father had cut his hand with a power tool and needed surgery. He was on the mend, but it was too late for nice weather in Lady Helen. Monica wanted her mother to be swept off her feet by the beauty of the town, not by the strong southeaster.

Now that Silas was well, Daphne no longer came to visit him in the Old Garage, but Zak said he saw them each day eating lunch together in a secluded sunny spot at the back of the hospital. Silas had started doing odd jobs for Zak. He was a whiz at fixing things, thanks to all those years of dealing with temperamental old computers—even typewriters—and having to improvise when they broke down because there weren't any replacement parts.

Thinking of Zak made her feel an annoying stab of jealousy. At one time he had been happy with his wife, Jacqueline; together they'd brought a child into the world. This was a tie that would bind them together forever.

But there was more than one reason Monica couldn't wait for Zak to get back this evening. Zak had agreed to make one final attempt to get Zukisa's mother to Lady Helen.

The afternoon dragged by with no call from Zak. The boys made kites, but when they took them outside into the garden, the wind shredded them within minutes.

At around six Monica made dinner for the boys and put a plate aside for Zak, who had said he would come straight to her house. Clouds had begun to bank over the ocean. It was a little early in the year for rain, but the sky looked promising. If the wildflowers were to appear in spring, a winter of plentiful rain was required.

Monica and the boys were eating dinner when a car pulled up outside the house. Mandla turned to the window.

"It's Dr. Zak!" He slid off his chair.

"Not so fast, young man." Monica caught him with two hands. "You have to finish your food."

She left to answer the doorbell and heard Mandla telling Sipho that the chicken tasted like hippo food.

She opened the door and saw immediately that something was wrong. Zak's face was grim.

"Come in. It's cold."

He shook his head. "I don't want the boys to hear this."

She closed the door behind her, and the wind went straight through her thin sweater. If they weren't so visible to the street, she would have hugged him—for warmth, she told herself, but she really wanted him to put his arms around her and tell her that everything was okay, that nothing had changed.

"There was nobody at Zukisa's house."

Monica knew immediately what that meant.

He nodded, confirming her conclusion. "Zukisa's mother passed away ten days ago. A neighbor told me that Zukisa went to live with her aunt. Fortunately the lady had the address."

Zak had gone to the aunt's two-bedroom flat and found Zukisa cooking food for her aunt's three grandchildren. Zukisa had told him that her mother had fallen asleep with her eyes open.

Monica no longer noticed the cold. She tried to imagine Zukisa's face, but all she could see was the lost look on Sipho's and Mandla's faces in the days after their mother's death.

"Let's go inside," she said, opening the door.

Zak did not move. "I have to go to the hospital."

"A new patient?"

There was a strange, guarded expression on his face.

"There's some stuff I have to do. I'll speak to you tomorrow."

He leaned in to give her a kiss and then withdrew, as though he'd suddenly realized that the neighbors might be watching.

She shut the front door without waving as she normally did, partly because the telephone was ringing inside, but mostly because she was angry and confused. There was not a new patient, nor, she suspected, any *stuff* waiting for him.

Mandla had picked up the telephone before she got to it.

"Why didn't Dr. Zak come in?" he asked her. "Hello, Mandla's house."

He smiled as he listened to the caller and then handed the telephone to Monica. "It's Miemps."

As they exchanged greetings, Monica could hear that her friend was too anxious to even ask what Mandla had meant about Zak.

"Daphne's in love and I'm so worried she's going to get hurt again."

Miemps was afraid that Silas would return to Zimbabwe without Daphne—or, even worse, take her with him. Her fear was not unfounded; one word from someone in town to the police and Silas would be deported.

"He seems nice, but we know nothing about him." Miemps dropped her voice to a whisper. "What if he's planning to ask her to marry him so that he can stay in the country? For all we know, he could have a wife back home."

Monica tried to reassure Miemps that her daughter was no longer the girl whose heart had been broken but a woman who knew her mind and would ask the necessary questions.

"Oh, Monica, it doesn't matter how old a person is. When you're in love, you close your eyes to things you do not want to see."

Monica heard the sigh in her friend's voice as they said goodbye. People said she had a talent for solving problems, but it eluded her this miserable afternoon, perhaps because all she could think about was how she wished Miemps's words were true for her, too. But they were not. She could not close her eyes to the fact that something in her relationship with Zak had gone seriously wrong, and the reason lay in the words that had passed between him and his ex-wife this afternoon in Cape Town.

He did not call that night. She would have liked to have heard more about his visit to Zukisa. Was the little girl's aunt helping her cope with her grief? Was Zukisa back at school? Had the aunt given Zak any indication that visitors were welcome? If not, how long should Monica wait before paying a visit? And when she did, what could she offer in the way of help? She thought of Zukisa in her trademark colorful dresses and of the smile she'd worn when she'd been a normal little girl living in Sandpiper Drift, the smile she'd worn before she'd become an orphan.

14

MAX LIVED WITH HIS SON AND DAUGHTER-IN-LAW IN A house within walking distance of his old office. Although he had never told anybody, this was one of the reasons he had agreed without a fight to sell his house and move when his son had suggested it. In Max's disciplined mind, he had envisaged taking daily walks to the newspaper to make sure that his successor was performing her duties with the same dedication he had for ten years.

That was before his body had let him down. He had been using a cane to walk for a couple of years now, but in the past year his joints had become so painful he could go no farther than the garden gate to fetch the mail.

Monica thought he sounded delighted when she called early this morning to ask if she could come by for a visit.

Max's daughter-in-law was leaving as she arrived.

"He's waiting for you in the living room."

His interference in the newspaper and all-knowing attitude had once bothered Monica, but some days, especially one such as this, she missed having him around to confide in.

He started to get up as she entered the room, and she quickly waved at him to remain seated. On the coffee table before them Max's daughter-in-law had left a pot of tea and a plate of scones topped with apricot jam and clotted cream.

"She's always baking," complained Max. "Look at how much weight I've put on."

Monica could not see it in his sagging cheeks and bony shoulders, but she smiled as though she agreed. With his clear blue eyes and strong jawline, Max had once been handsome, she was sure. The tufts of gray hair above his ears had been woolly when she'd first met him, but now they were closely cropped, a testament to his daughter-in-law's care.

He fingered the pearl inlay in the handle of his cane. "I take it this is not a social call."

Monica did not disagree.

"I know you can handle everything, so my guess is that this is about an ethical dilemma," he speculated.

Max's body had let him down, but his mind was as sharp as ever. She knew it was unnecessary to swear him to secrecy. He was always discreet. He listened in silence as she told him about Anna and the abalone ladies. When she finished, she braced herself for what she knew would come first—criticism for going to the beach alone to watch for the poachers.

"Well, Monica, I'm not sure you need my advice. You managed to save Sandpiper Drift without my help," he said, surprising her.

Monica felt her face redden. "I meant to edit that part out of the story."

When he nodded, she felt irritation rise in her. Why did he still have the power to make her feel like a teenager at her first summer job?

He rolled his cane with both hands as though he were making a fire. "I think that part of the story was closer to the truth than any of us knows. Any of us beside Lizbet, that is." He looked her directly in the eye.

She had never divulged her real role in the rescue of the neighborhood. And that was why she was furious with herself for not having cut the offending sentence from her article. What was the point of doing good things in secret if you were going to sound your own trumpet afterward?

When he saw that she was not about to take his bait, he settled on pouring the tea. The teapot shook in his hands, but Monica knew better than to take it from him. She did, however, reach over and take her cup from the tray before he had time to pass it to her.

"It's that horrible rooibos tea," he said. "Did you know it's not even made from a proper tea plant? It's from the legume family of plants. And it's green when it's picked and only turns red after fermentation."

Max drank his tea with lots of milk and downed it in three gulps. He poured himself another cup.

Monica planned to take the boys sometime to see the tea farms in the Cedarberg region of the Western Cape, northeast of Lady Helen. Rooibos was the country's hot new export.

She did not press Max for advice about the abalone ladies. A consummate chess player, he would not be coerced into making his opening move before he had the subsequent ones mapped out.

Finally he broke the silence. "The government has a crisis on its hands with the way fishing licenses are distributed."

In the past, he went on to explain, most of the licenses for abalone were given to whites, and now the same people who had been turned away because of their skin color were being turned away because the government scientists said there were not enough abalone to go around.

"They're frustrated and resentful and so they ignore the quotas and restrictions. Did you know that poachers can earn four thousand dollars for a night's catch of eighty abalone?"

Monica caught her breath. No wonder the men on the beach had been armed; abalone was a profitable business.

Max continued to tell her that many organized-crime syndicates, from the Far East especially, paid locals in drugs for abalone. Gangs in the Cape Flats now fought over abalone turf.

"I advise you not to go out there alone again."

"And the abalone ladies?"

He shrugged. "Do you sacrifice the small fish in order to catch the large ones? Fishermen do it all the time."

Monica smiled, but she was angry. She had come to hear his advice, and here he was using fishing analogies and rhetorical questions to toy with her. She knew it would be polite to inquire about his memoirs, but all she wanted to do was leave. This visit had been a mistake. Zak hadn't helped her figure out what to do and neither had Max.

Leaning heavily on his cane, he pulled himself up to show her out. As she walked down the garden path, she turned and saw him watching her. She wondered if he'd had any visitors this week. Not long ago, Max had been a man with his shirtsleeves rolled up, thoroughly involved in the everyday world. Now he would shut the door and return to his computer alone in a silent house.

She adjusted her bag on her shoulder and then purposefully strode back up the path, as though trying to trample her irritation.

"I forgot to ask about your memoirs."

"Oh, those." Max waved a hand at her dismissively, but there was a new light in his eyes.

"If you ever need a reader, you know where to find me," she said.

"Thanks."

She turned to leave again.

"Monica?"

She stopped.

"I've always used cornmeal, never live bait."

She smiled. Max, it seemed, would never lose his uncanny ability to read people. She'd never been keen on fishing, and now was not the time to start. It had not been a mistake to come here after all.

Monica went back to the office and began writing her story about Lady Helen's latest hero, Justice—David and Gift's eldest son, who had been awarded a Rhodes scholarship to study at Oxford University in England. Halfway through the first paragraph, she found herself staring at the telephone. Zak would normally have called her by now.

She marshaled her thoughts back to her story. Justice planned to pursue a master's degree in developmental economics to prepare for his long-term goal, which was a job with the African Development Bank. Monica had interviewed him over the telephone and would take a photograph when he came to Lady Helen this weekend to attend the celebration his parents had planned.

Monica read through her first draft. It needed a quote from Justice about his thoughts on leaving South Africa, but that could be added after the party on Sunday.

Teatime, she decided, would come early today. She found Dudu in the storeroom sorting old issues of the newspaper into chronological order.

"How far back do they go?" Monica waved away the dust.

"Ten years or so, but the oldest look like lace if you hold them up to the light."

"Fish moths?"

Dudu nodded.

Monica remembered the legion of filing cabinets that Max had kept in his office. He was a hoarder; that was clear.

"What shall I do with all this?" asked Dudu.

"Send it off for recycling."

Dudu, it seemed, did not have enough work to fill her time. Organizing was useful, but before long everything would have a place. Dudu had quickly mastered the modern switchboard system at the *Lady Helen Herald* and had a natural affinity for computers, which, unlike her children, she said, responded to her first command.

"What would you say if I sent you to take a course in newspaper graphics? You could learn to lay out our pages."

Dudu wiped the dust from her face with the back of her hand. "Why? You always make the newspaper look so pretty."

Monica smiled. Dudu was frequently complimentary.

"Thanks, but you could be better. You have an eye for symmetry and balance. Just look at you straightening out the chaos of the storeroom."

"It's irritated me since I arrived."

"Well, there you have it. You like order and that's exactly what layout entails. I'll look into the courses available. Don't worry. It'll be during office hours and I'll make sure you're home by five."

"Thank you."

"And now, since you're busy, should I make the tea?"

"No, no," said Dudu with a mock look of fear on her face. "I'll wash my hands and put the kettle on."

As they sat drinking tea together, Dudu updated Monica on her youngest child's progress at school. It seemed that Phutole was a lively boy and always in trouble for not sitting still.

"Why don't you try taking him to school early so that he can work off some energy playing outdoors before classes start?"

"I never thought of that." Dudu's voice was filled with hope. "You really are a problem solver."

Monica felt a shiver run up her spine. The abalone ladies had called her this and it had almost landed her in serious trouble. And she had failed to get them to give up poaching. Last year she had managed to help save Sandpiper Drift, but this year she didn't seem capable of accomplishing anything. One of the recent sorrows that she might never shake was that a little girl she'd grown to love had nursed her mother to the bitter end entirely on her own and Monica had not been able to help at all.

15

THE NEXT DAY, FEELING BETTER BECAUSE ZAK HAD CALLED late last night sounding more like his old self, Monica took Dudu to lunch at Mama Dlamini's to show her the brochure for the design course. Zak had told her he was tired, and she had begun to regret not being more understanding when he'd shown up at her house obviously upset after what had probably been a petty domestic squabble with his ex-wife. During their conversation last night she'd suppressed the urge to ask him about it.

Now, in the mood for a little celebration, Monica decided to order slices of lemon meringue pie for herself and Dudu. But when Dudu asked about Zukisa, Monica lost her appetite thinking of the little girl in mourning for her mother. She took her slice away with her for the boys.

Leaving the café, Monica and Dudu saw a crowd gathered on the other side of the street outside a gallery run by a woman from Durban. Nalini, wearing a bright yellow sari and a green cardigan, had been sitting at the table next to them in the café.

"Let's go and see what's happening," said Monica.

A Lady Helen patrol car arrived while they were crossing the road, and the crowd cleared to allow Dewald and Mike through. Gift was in the crowd.

"Somebody broke into Nalini's gallery and emptied the cash register," she explained. "It's the first robbery in Lady Helen in ten years."

Monica caught snatches of conversations around her. "This is what happens when we have foreigners living here." She heard the hoarsely whispered comment but could not see who had made it.

"Illegal immigrants."

"We don't need them."

"Something should be done."

Suddenly it dawned on her that the crowd was talking about Silas. They were blaming him for the robbery. She saw the events that would unfold as clearly as if they had already taken place. When the police had finished taking fingerprints inside, they would step into the crowd and an indignant, fearful voice would tell them about Silas.

"I'm going back to the office," she told Dudu. Her car keys were in her desk drawer.

"Don't you want to hear what the police have to say?"

Dudu was obviously surprised. Crime never happened in Lady Helen, and now that it had, the town's sole reporter was leaving the scene.

"They won't say anything of importance now," said Monica. It was true—but, of course, Dudu was also right.

Dudu nodded, accepting her boss's judgment in this matter.

Monica handed Dudu her tape recorder. "If the police have anything to say, record it."

Dudu's eyes lit up. "Like a real reporter."

"Exactly."

Monica ran back to her office, grabbed her keys and drove to the hospital as fast as she could.

She burst into the waiting room.

"Where's Silas?"

Adelaide looked up in surprise from the form she was filling in for a young mother. "I don't know. Why?"

"I'll tell you later."

She ran down the passage to the ICU and found Daphne checking equipment.

"Do you know where Silas is?"

"Hello to you, too," said Daphne rather curtly.

"You have to tell me where Silas is."

"In the storeroom working on the hot-water geyser."

Monica took off running.

"What's wrong?" yelled Daphne.

Monica heard Daphne's quick footsteps behind her and then she heard the sound of metal against metal coming from the storeroom.

"Silas," she called.

He came to the door, wiping his hands on his overalls.

"The police are going to come looking for you. There has been a robbery on Main Street."

"A robbery?" said Daphne. "In Lady Helen? But what's it got to do with Silas?"

"I heard people in the crowd talking about an illegal immigrant. If one of them decides to share their suspicions with the police..."

"This is just ridiculous. Silas hasn't robbed anyone. I'll tell them he's been in the hospital all morning," Daphne said indignantly.

Silas grimaced.

"We'll just tell them the truth," said Daphne, eyes flashing.

"The truth is I'm here illegally."

"Not for long," replied Daphne, smiling. "We're getting married, Monica. But don't tell my parents, because they don't know yet."

Silas took off his tool belt. He looked at Daphne. "I'm sorry."

"Please, Silas. This is not Zimbabwe. The police are not going to—" She could not finish.

When he kissed her cheek, she grabbed his shoulders.

"Don't go, Silas. I'll explain to the police that you didn't rob anyone. We can get married today and then they can't deport you. Please, Silas, this is not a police state."

He stared at her face as though trying to memorize her features. Then he turned and ran out of the hospital.

Daphne slid down the wall, sobbing. She shrugged off the hand Monica placed on her shoulder.

"He can come back when the crime has been solved," said Monica. "And then the two of you can get married. Congratulations."

"Congratulations?" Daphne spat the word out as though it were bitter. "For what? Being jilted?"

"Please, Daphne, don't be angry. He had no choice."

"It's not him I'm angry with." Her voice was quiet and resolute.

"I'm angry with God. Twice in my life I've found love, and He's taken it away both times."

Monica knew Daphne didn't mean what she said; it was her anger talking.

"Silas will come back," she repeated.

"And what's he going to do until then? Live on grass and leaves in the bush?" She shook her head. "He knows that the police will come after him wherever he is in this country. He has nowhere to go but home. How's he going to earn a living in a country that's collapsing? What if he's thrown in jail again?" She started to cry.

Zak came striding down the hallway.

"What's happened? I just saw Silas running off toward the koppie." He saw the tears on Daphne's cheeks.

"You tell him," said Daphne.

Monica told him everything except the part about Daphne and Silas getting married.

He shook his head. "It's always the outsiders that get the blame." He looked at Daphne. "I don't know if Silas told you, but I've made an appointment for him with an excellent lawyer who handles high-profile asylum cases."

Daphne wiped her cheeks. She looked as surprised as Monica.

"South Africa grants asylum to a fraction of its applicants. I thought that if we could get Silas to tell the lawyer about what happened to him in prison, then he'd have a chance."

How many more secrets does Zak have? Looking at the face that had become so familiar to her, Monica realized she had something in common with Daphne: they both loved men with a past.

"I'll handle the police," said Zak. "You two make yourselves scarce."

His warning came too late. Dewald and Mike were walking up the steps when Monica opened the front door.

"You've got a good apprentice," said Dewald. He saw that Monica did not understand. "Dudu. She pushed that tape recorder in my face and fired away questions. It was Dudu who opened up our first avenue of investigation."

"What do you mean?"

"The last thing she asked was, 'Are you going to question the illegal immigrant in town?'"

Oh, Dudu, what have you done? But if Dudu hadn't told them, someone else would have.

"I don't suppose you know anything about this illegal immigrant? Or are you not in a position to say anything, just like with the abalone poachers?" Dewald's voice dripped sarcasm.

She opened her mouth to answer Dewald, but Zak beat her to it. "Is there anything I can do to help you gentlemen?"

Dewald gave Monica a scorching look as Zak motioned for them to come inside. He was still looking at her when Zak closed the front door.

She hurried home, wondering if Silas might be there collecting a few of his things. He was not. She scanned the faces of the koppies, brown and dusty, thirsty for the winter rains. A man could make it up to the top of one and down the other side in under two hours. There was no sign of movement now. Had Silas already started the descent on the other side? And then what? He would have to keep away from the road and cut through the national park. If he headed toward Cape Town, he'd encounter more police, so more than likely he'd head inland, toward the Cedarberg mountain range, home of rooibos tea, or up the coast toward Namibia. A man could make a living there. She disagreed with Daphne; Silas would not head for Zimbabwe.

Word of Francina's skill in disguising nature's imperfections had spread; her new client was from Cape Town, her first from the mother city. In a spaghetti-strap top and short skirt, the lady displayed far too much flesh for Francina's liking. The skin on her face was strangely tight, but her neck was wrinkled and she had lines on her chest from too much time in the sun.

Francina sighed inwardly. Why did women resist nature? Resisting nature was resisting God Himself. Was it entirely due to vanity or was it perhaps that they were scared to age in a world that no longer valued old people? Nobody listened to what old people had to say anymore. The world could do with some lessons from the Zulu people. Zulus respected their elders—or at least the majority of them did. Some of the children nowadays had heads filled with foreign ideas picked up from nasty television shows, films and books.

Francina showed the lady a picture of a dress.

"I'd like the neckline a little lower."

Francina frowned. The lady didn't have much to show off, but it would still be indecent if Francina bowed to her wishes. Another seamstress who wanted to make a living might not have argued, but not Francina.

"I think that would be in poor taste."

The lady looked as though Francina had blown her nose on her sleeve. "I beg your pardon?"

Francina wanted to be perfectly clear. "If I lowered the neckline, it would be vulgar."

"You have no idea what you're talking about. All the ladies in Cape Town are wearing dresses like this."

"Well, then, I very much doubt that they are ladies."

"What? I can't believe this! I've obviously wasted my time coming to a village dressmaker." She slid her sunglasses off the top of her head and onto her face. "I'll tell my friends not to bother making the trip to this godforsaken place."

Francina shrugged. "I wouldn't be able to help them anyway. I've been known to work magic hiding a belly here, bony shoulders there, but I can do nothing with poor taste."

"How dare you speak to me like that!" The woman slammed the door so hard that for an instant Francina worried the glass might shatter.

Well, she thought, this was a time when honesty was not appreciated.

That evening, Francina had another opportunity to be honest, but this time she couldn't do it.

"What do you think?" repeated Hercules.

He had unveiled his finished painting for her. Time had not improved the effort, as Francina had hoped it would. The houses were crudely finished; the doors looked as though they would not open, they were so crooked; the sea was a bright food-coloring-blue, and the seagulls flying overhead resembled squirrels. She stepped back, hoping that she may have just been too close to get the full effect. There was no improvement.

Hercules looked at her eagerly. Francina gazed at the painting.

Perhaps if she stared at it long enough, she'd think of something safe to say. How could she tell him it was awful? But she, Francina Shabalala, had never told a lie her entire life—and she was not about to start now.

"It's colorful."

Hercules pulled his mouth.

"And cheerful, too. Let's not forget cheerful. When I look at it I feel immediately cheered up after my awful morning in the shop."

Francina hoped that this would do the trick. Hercules was too kind to let a comment like that go by without a discussion.

"What happened?" he asked on cue.

She told him about the lady—if she could call her that—from Cape Town, and he shook his head. Hercules did not approve of vulgarity, in women or men.

"You don't need a client like that. It is not necessary to compromise your standards."

She put an arm around his waist, thinking how fortunate she was to have found this man so long after her youth had faded. If only she had married him when she was sixteen and not Winston. But then, Hercules might not share her wish for a different past; he had loved his wife dearly. She tried to push this thought aside, as though it were a tricky piece of sewing that required more concentration than she could possibly give at this moment.

Hercules covered up his painting again.

"I'll take this to be framed tomorrow."

He had either decided to accept her reply as a compliment or to ignore her opinion entirely. The only way to discover the truth would be to ask him, and there was no way she was going to start that conversation.

He pointed at a blank spot on the wall above the couch. "If we place it right there, it will set the tone for the whole room."

Set the tone? thought Francina. The only thing it would do for this room was make people wonder why they'd hung a child's painting on the wall when they had no children of their own.

Later, at dinner, Mrs. Shabalala was pleased that neither her son nor daughter-in-law had heard about the robbery and she could be the bearer of this important news. She folded her arms across her chest as though she were a magistrate presiding over a case.

"People say it's the Zimbabwean."

Hercules frowned.

"Poor Daphne," said Francina. "It's dangerous to get mixed up with a foreigner. They're responsible for a lot of the drug dealing and crime in this country."

Hercules cleared his throat loudly. Francina had seen this look on his face before—when she told him she couldn't marry him the first time he'd asked. Her husband was disappointed with her.

"Okay, maybe not all the crime," she added sheepishly.

"The Zimbabweans are our neighbors," said Hercules quietly but with a sternness that Francina imagined he used with his most wayward pupils. "Remember Jesus's parable about the Good Samaritan. Does it not apply today? Who is my neighbor? My neighbor is the one who needs my help."

Mrs. Shabalala nodded. "They're starving up there."

Francina felt as small as the saltcellar on the table. She did not consider herself a modern woman with flexible ideas, but even if she was sometimes rigid, she was always fair. Now her husband had shown her attitude to be unjust.

"It could be him," she said in a petulant voice. "We never had any crime before he came to town."

"We're new to town, too," said Hercules. "Am I to expect a knock on my door from the police this evening?"

Hercules was right, but this evening Francina did not feel like acknowledging it. Today it seemed that everyone had ganged up on her. She longed for dinner to be over so she could make her getaway to a hot bath and a magazine. She'd stay submerged for so long that Hercules would be asleep when she finally got into bed beside him.

Mrs. Shabalala had cut fruit for dessert and brought a tub of ice cream from the freezer. Francina felt her spirits rise. There had not been any treats in the house for ages because of Mrs. Shabalala's diet.

"It's frozen yogurt," beamed Mrs. Shabalala. "With a fraction of the calories of ice cream." She looked as happy as if she'd discovered a vaccine against malaria.

Francina ate her dessert slowly, savoring every spoonful, half listening to Hercules's plans to help a particularly trying child at school. Her thoughts were of Silas, the Zimbabwean. One evening, returning home from babysitting Sipho and Mandla, she had met him and Daphne on the street. They had been taking an evening stroll. Daphne had introduced him, but he had not made eye contact with her. Francina prided herself on being able to see things that other people with two eyes couldn't, and what she had seen was that Silas was not a man to be trusted.

16

¤¤¤¤¤¤¤¤¤¤¤¤

DAPHNE WENT AROUND AS THOUGH IN SHOCK. SHE would not speak unless asked about a patient and she left work the minute her shift ended. Monica tried to visit her at home, but Miemps told her that Daphne did not want to see her. The heartbreak was worse than the first time, Miemps said, because now Daphne was worried for her boyfriend's safety.

Dewald and Mike had scoured the town and the surrounding areas for Silas without success. The bulletin they'd put out on the police radio would stop him from getting far, said Dewald.

Oscar had changed the locks on the rear door of the gallery, and Nalini had resigned herself to the loss of one morning's cash. As far as everyone in town was concerned, the case had been decided. Silas's flight was an admission of guilt. It was no wonder that Daphne had stopped coming to Main Street to do her shopping.

It had been a horrible week, and Monica was looking forward to Saturday, when she and Zak had planned a picnic on the beach with the children. Being with him would calm her.

On Saturday morning Monica took the boys shopping for new school shoes. Sipho's uniform required that he wear black lace-up oxfords, but Mandla pounced on a pair of sneakers with soles that lit up when he moved. He refused to take them off. While packing his old shoes into the box, a movement at the window caught Monica's eye. Yolanda was strolling by with a boy. Something made her go to the door and call Yolanda's name, an act of unthinkable humiliation to a young teenager.

Yolanda spun around, saw Monica and flushed bright red. Monica recognized the boy, the eldest son of the new family in Sandpiper Drift, who had moved into Zukisa's old house near Miemps and Reginald and whose mother had wanted her son away from the gangs in Cape Town.

"See you later?" said Monica.

For an instant Yolanda's expression was blank.

"The picnic," offered Monica.

"Oh, yes. The picnic."

On face value, the words meant nothing, but Monica was certain that they were a brush-off. She waved as the teenagers continued down the street. When had Yolanda gotten to know this boy? He had joined Green Block School after she had started school in Cape Town.

Monica closed the door and immediately bumped into Sipho, who had come closer to witness the encounter on the sidewalk. Mandla was too busy jumping up and down in front of the mirror to notice anything other than his new shoes.

"So Yolanda has a new friend?" she said.

She could tell by Sipho's expression that he had not warmed to this boy. Zak had to be working this morning, which was the only reason he would not be with Yolanda. There must have been an emergency at the hospital. And even then, Monica was sure Zak would have told Yolanda to wait at home for him.

"He smokes," said Sipho.

"Who?" Monica was still thinking of Zak, who definitely did not smoke.

"Jake's big brother, Montgomery."

Monica nodded, digesting this new information. "Let's take your brother away from the mirror and get that picnic packed."

"Picnic!" screeched Mandla, causing the shop assistant, who was perched on a ladder, to wobble precariously.

Monica paid for the shoes and then led the way across the road to pick up some rolls from the bakery.

At home, she instructed the boys to get their jackets. The sun was shining, but as soon as it went behind a cloud the air would be chilly.

Zak should have already arrived at their house. She toyed with the idea of calling him and decided against it. Only something serious would have prevented him from calling, and she did not want to interrupt whatever that might be.

"I'm hungry," moaned Mandla.

She gave him a slice of bread with peanut butter to keep him going.

Zak and Yolanda finally arrived at one o'clock. Monica had been right; there had been an emergency at the hospital. She got the feeling that there was something Zak was not telling her, but there was no time to ask if they were going to settle on the beach and get lunch into these children before dinnertime.

Yolanda avoided Monica's eyes. What had gotten into the girl? Yolanda was acting as though Monica were the enemy. If she feared Monica would tell Zak that his daughter had been alone in town with a boy, this was a strange way of trying to prevent that happening.

Since it was so late, they decided not to walk to the beach, and Zak offered to drive. Monica fetched the booster seat for Mandla and buckled him in. As she turned to get in the front seat, she saw that Yolanda had beaten her to it.

"Let Monica sit in the front," said Zak. He sounded shocked.

"Mandla irritates me."

"Yolanda!" said Zak, his voice rising.

"It's okay, I'll sit in the back," said Monica, wanting to defuse the situation but at the same time feeling bewildered by Yolanda's change in attitude. The day she had looked forward to was not turning out as planned.

At the beach they spread the picnic blanket on the sand and Yolanda went off alone to the water. Monica looked at Zak, expecting him to use the opportunity to explain his daughter's behavior, but he had busied himself unpacking the food. She watched Mandla run up to Yolanda and give her a playful shove. Yolanda did not chase him, as she usually did, but turned around and shouted something at him. Monica did not have to hear the words to know that they were unkind, because Mandla came running back in tears.

"What's the matter?" she asked.

"Yolanda said I'm a pest."

Zak looked at his daughter, who was throwing shells back into the ocean, and let out a long sigh. He said nothing.

The uneasy feeling that Monica had carried all the way to the beach turned to panic as she recognized the guarded expression on his face. It was the same look he'd worn the night he'd refused to come in for dinner. She had considered herself exempt from Miemps's theory about the blindness of people in love because she had sensed that something was wrong that night. But it had taken only one call from Zak for her to change her mind. To be fair to herself, though, she had not had much opportunity to discover the truth; she and Zak had seen each other just once since that night on the doorstep. Perhaps she should have taken that as a clue. He'd seemed distracted during their quick lunch in his office, but she'd assumed it was because he'd had a desperately ill patient in the ICU.

Did his ex-wife want him back? Had she made a play for him when she'd summoned him to Cape Town for a talk? Was he torn because to go back to Jacqueline would mean his family could be intact again?

"I'm hungry," said Mandla. He was never anything but hungry.

"Let's eat, then," she said with forced breeziness. She had lost her appetite.

Sipho, the most sensitive child Monica had ever known, looked up from his book to study her face. She waited for Zak to call Yolanda to eat, but he didn't, as though aware that his daughter's presence would cause even more friction.

A wash of thin gray clouds had formed above the horizon, making it hard to distinguish the ocean from the sky. Monica pulled on her jacket. Zak and the children were comfortable in the warm autumn sun, but she felt cold. They ate in silence, while gulls gathered nearby in anticipation of a feast.

"Can I give them my crusts when I'm finished?" asked Mandla.

"In a minute. If you toss the crusts up now, you know what will happen."

"Yep, bird droppings in the salad." Mandla laughed.

They had almost finished eating when the wind came riffling up the beach from the ocean and tugged at the paper plates. Monica and Zak packed away the leftovers as the children put on their jackets.

If Monica had not been there for the silent lunch, she might have thought that the glum faces were for the approaching winter. Soon they would spend many days indoors listening to the icy rain on the tin roof, playing board games while the wind raced around the house, drinking hot chocolate. Would Zak and Yolanda be with them? Would she and Zak dress up in coats and rain ponchos to spend time alone together walking on the beach?

Yolanda picked up a handful of sand and let it fall through her fingers. Of course, the wind blew it everywhere.

"Hey, you put sand on my sandwich," complained Mandla.

Yolanda shrugged. Monica watched to see if Zak would insist Yolanda apologize. But he seemed to be lost in thought and had not even heard Mandla's complaint.

Mandla looked at Monica, waiting for her to mediate.

"I think you should say sorry to Mandla."

Zak ended his reverie and frowned at Monica.

"Sorry," mumbled Yolanda.

Monica got a new sandwich for Mandla and patted his head. It didn't matter that he had already eaten quite a bit and probably wouldn't finish it. It didn't matter that Yolanda was Zak's daughter. Monica would not stand back and let anyone treat Mandla rudely.

Two hundred meters offshore, past the breakwater, a dive boat headed for deeper waters. The cold weather did not deter tourists, many of whom had expensive dry suits to keep them warm. Kitty had told Monica that the shark diving business owned by her husband James was making more money than the inn.

Sipho watched the boat disappear into the distance without saying anything, and Monica wondered if he had finally decided that he could not win a battle against the shark divers—not now, anyway, at the tender age of eleven.

"Can we go now?" whined Yolanda.

Zak looked at Monica and shrugged. Monica felt her anxiety turn to anger. Was a shrug all he was capable of when his daughter was impolite?

"Mandla hasn't finished eating," she said, her tone curt.

Rolling her eyes, Yolanda turned to face the waves. Monica wondered why Zak had agreed to come; he had barely said three words to her the whole time. As they watched Mandla throw his crusts to the gulls, Monica hoped that Zak would suggest they all go for a pizza or something tonight. But he didn't. If they had been alone, she would have asked him what was the matter.

Yolanda got into the backseat of the car for the return journey, and Monica wondered if Zak had had a word with her, because the girl did it with a sullen expression on her face.

"Don't touch me," she warned Mandla.

Monica reached back and squeezed his knee.

When they arrived at Monica's house, she invited Zak and Yolanda in for tea, but he motioned in the direction of the backseat and shook his head. Monica waited for him to say something about his plans for the evening.

"I'll call you," he said. "Thanks for packing the food."

As he left, he winked at her, and she felt her stomach drop. Surely this was just a bad patch they had to scrabble over.

The telephone did not ring that evening, and Zak was not in church the next morning.

"Are you and Zak fighting?" asked Francina after the service.

"No, why?"

Francina shrugged. "I can tell something's wrong."

Monica would have liked to tell Francina about her insecurities, but this was not the time or place.

"I may only have one eye, but you know I see all."

"I'll tell you later," said Monica.

Suddenly she was scared. The look on Francina's face made it a reality—her relationship with Zak was in trouble.

He knocked on her door later that afternoon after driving Yolanda back to Cape Town. "Can we talk?"

She glanced inside to where the boys were doing a jigsaw puzzle. "How about in the garden? I'll grab my jacket."

She cleared the leaves from the patio chairs and indicated for him to sit. In spite of the cold, her palms felt clammy.

"Monica, I've had a difficult week."

She felt a sudden calm. The anxiety of not knowing was over; the inevitable had been set in motion.

"Do you remember when I had to meet Yolanda's mother?"

So she'd been right all along; the source of their problems was his ex-wife.

"She told me that Yolanda has been wetting her bed, not obeying instructions and getting into trouble at school. We had a family conference, and it seems that Yolanda thinks there's a chance her mother and I might get back together."

"And her mother gave her this idea." It was not a question, but Zak thought it was.

"I don't think so. Jacqueline is still with her boyfriend."

Monica watched him grapple with the possibility and realized that it had never occurred to him. Was he pleased at the prospect? She couldn't tell.

"Monica, there's no other way to say this. Yolanda thinks you are the one preventing her parents from being together."

"Me? Why not her mother's boyfriend? Did you correct Yolanda's impression? She is wrong, isn't she?"

"I think we should stop seeing each other for a while."

The strange calm remained with her.

"Can you tell me your interpretation of *a while?*"

He shrugged.

"Is that all you ever do?"

He grabbed her hands, but she pulled them away.

"I don't want to hurt you, Monica."

"Then don't do this. We can work it out. Yolanda will get used to the idea." She heard the desperation in her voice but didn't care.

He bowed his head. "I can't take the high emotion anymore," he said quietly. "My daughter is unhappy and she's at a very vulnerable age."

"Are we talking weeks, months, years?"

He started to shrug and then thought better of it. "I'm sorry, I can't say."

Monica stood up. "I'm a mother. I understand that your child is your priority. But you should know that I won't wait forever."

Her words were brave, but deep down she was terrified that her patience would not be tested at all, that he would simply go back to his wife in the next few days.

He stood up and moved toward her, but she stepped back from him. How dare he try to torment her with a tender goodbye embrace?

He headed for the garden gate. Monica knew it was because he couldn't face the boys inside. She pushed the gate shut behind him, shoved her hands deep into her pockets and went back to sit in the garden by herself. Her mind was frozen, like the water in her neighbor's birdbath. Stunned, she sat there feeling only a gnawing emptiness in her chest. Her nose started to drip—from the cold, not from crying.

A crested barbet, confident now that the cat Ebony was no longer a threat, hopped on the ground, trilling loudly for the crazy woman to take shelter.

The boys would be wondering where she was. Dinner had to be made, school clothes ironed, shoes polished, homework supervised. There was no time for self-pity in a house with children.

She stood up, wiped her nose on a tissue and walked toward the house. In the distance, the wind howled up the sides of the koppies, sounding like a woman crying.

17

THE NEXT MORNING MONICA TURNED OFF HER ALARM clock when it buzzed and went back to sleep. Dudu would wonder about her absence, but somewhere out there in the bright light of morning was a hulking truth she wished to escape.

She awoke two hours later to Sipho shaking her.

"I'm late for school."

Her alarm clock showed ten to nine. She braced herself for the impact of her misery. But it did not come. Instead the numb sensation of the previous evening returned. She was a factory that had lost power; from the outside unchanged, but inside, lying in wait, mute and dangerous in the darkness, were the sharp blades and teeth of disabled machinery.

"We're all taking a day off." She heard her voice float in the air around her.

"But I'll get into trouble."

"I'll sort it out, don't worry."

But Sipho would not be appeased. "Why didn't you tell me the plan?"

She looked at his big eyes, always so serious, and had a feeling that he saw more than she wanted him to.

"Something happened, okay. I'm not ready to talk about it, but I need to be with you and Mandla."

He nodded. Monica knew he would not ask her about it but that if she didn't tell him soon he would fret, and his imagination would conjure up far worse scenarios than a severed relationship. The thought made her push her legs over the side of the bed. Her boyfriend had broken up with her, but today eight hundred people would die of AIDS in South Africa, many of them parents of small children.

Mandla was delighted at the change of plans.

"Should we go somewhere different?" he asked.

That set off an idea in Monica's head. They would visit Zukisa at her aunt's house.

"Yes, let's go to Cape Town." She forced brightness into her voice.

The boys ate their breakfast quickly and got into the car. Mandla brought along a tote bag full of toys.

"So I don't get bored," he explained.

He was so like his mother, Ella, who'd found enjoyment wherever she went, in bright rooms and dark corners.

There were no tortoises on the road this morning and the boys were disappointed.

"They didn't know you'd be coming on a school day," said Monica. Mandla laughed, but Sipho shook his head at her weak joke.

The directions to Zukisa's aunt's house lay beside her on the passenger seat. Zak's handwriting, once illegible to her, seemed perfectly clear now. His squiggles were consistent, so once she had identified them, they were nothing more than a code.

How long would it take, she wondered, to remove all traces of his presence in her life—the sweaters left draped over the back of the sofa, the shells he'd collected for her on their walks on the beach, the CDs of bossa nova music he'd lent her, as well as the book of short stories by South Africa's bright new literary stars?

Their first meeting since the breakup would come soon. You could not hide for long in a town as small as Lady Helen—not if you wanted to eat and work. If she didn't see him in town this week, she would see him at church on Sunday. Would they talk about the weather? About Daphne? Monica would not be able to bring herself to ask after Yolanda. Her throat felt tight and tears sprang to her eyes, but now was not the time for crying. She blinked furiously.

Zukisa's aunt lived near the docks, in a neighborhood of identical rows of two-story apartment buildings. Monica drove slowly, searching for the number Zak had written. When she'd located it, she parked as close as she could to the stairwell and unbuckled Mandla from his booster seat.

Nobody answered their knock at the door, but from inside came the sounds of a television and a baby crying. Mandla pounded on the door.

"Who's there?" said a child's voice.

"It's Monica, a friend of Zukisa's."

They heard whispering and a series of locks being opened, and there stood Zukisa, smiling broadly, a baby on her hip. The boy next to her scowled at the visitors.

"I'm happy to see you," she said.

She did not introduce the boy, who was a head taller than she was. Her sweatshirt kept falling off one shoulder, and Monica was shocked to see the sharp ridge of her shoulder blade. The boy wore a blue tracksuit with grass stains on the knees. From inside came the smell of cabbage cooking.

"Come in." Zukisa's hand went to her uncombed hair. "I wasn't expecting anyone." She swayed as she spoke to calm the baby, who had begun to fuss.

"Is your aunt at home?"

The boy left them and walked toward the television. Zukisa closed the door behind them. Away from the street noises, the extreme volume of the television was immediately apparent.

"She cleans the café down the road after the dockworkers have finished breakfast."

Monica wondered why Zukisa was whispering when the television was blaring, but then remembered that the aunt collected a pension. The aunt had probably warned her niece not to tell anyone about the job. Monica knew the government pension scale; the monthly check would not be enough to feed all these children.

"Are you back at school?"

Zukisa shook her head. "I have to look after the baby, cook, clean, see that the boys get to school on time. My aunt says I must help with her grandchildren and earn my keep."

Another boy appeared in the doorway and smiled shyly at the visitors. He was a head shorter than Zukisa.

Zukisa saw the question in Monica's eyes.

"They didn't want to go to school today." She sighed. "I'm going to get into trouble when my aunt comes home."

"When will that be?"

"At lunchtime. Would you like to come into the kitchen with me? The boys will never turn off that TV."

They followed Zukisa into the tiny kitchen and settled themselves around a table covered with a patterned vinyl tablecloth. Mandla fingered the little rows of blue anchors while Zukisa put the baby in a high chair and gave him a piece of toast. Two pots simmered on the electric stove. Monica knew it would be only a couple of minutes before Mandla, tormented by the aroma, declared that he was hungry. She was wrong; it took only one minute.

"Would you like a slice of bread and jam?" asked Zukisa.

Monica was seized by a wave of sadness. Zukisa's question and tone of voice were mature beyond her years. She watched the girl cut thick slices of white bread. The younger of the boys appeared in the doorway.

"I'm hungry, too."

"Okay. I'll bring it to you."

Monica found herself wondering how many meals Zukisa had served those boys in the living room.

"If the boys fill up on bread and jam, I might be able to keep some of this stew for tonight's meal." Zukisa put her hand to her mouth. "I'm sorry. I shouldn't have said that. You're very welcome to stay."

"Thank you, but we've already eaten."

Monica was glad that Mandla was too busy licking jam off his fingers to contradict her. She pulled the sweatshirt over Zukisa's exposed shoulder, but it slid back down again. They heard the front door slam.

"Smells good, Zukisa," shouted a voice.

Monica stood up as the aunt walked in and dumped two plastic bags of leftovers from the café on the counter. Money was scarce in this household, and yet this woman had given a share of her pension every week to support her late brother's dying wife and child. Her brusque personality may not make her easy to like, but sometimes the purest hearts belonged not to those who smiled broadly and talked in kind tones but to those who faced hardship every way they turned and understood suffering. Now she was providing a home for Zukisa.

"I'm Monica Brunetti. We spoke on the phone. We came to say hello."

"Well, hello, then."

She did not indicate for Monica to sit down again, and Monica wondered whether this was because the woman was unsure of herself or if she actually wanted to make her guest feel awkward. Either way, Monica was very uncomfortable.

Mandla took a step toward the aunt and stuck out his hand. "Good afternoon," he said.

She looked down at him in surprise, as though she hadn't noticed him before. Her eyes moved to Sipho, who was leaning against the counter. Mandla did not withdraw his hand. The expression on her face softened and she bent down to take his hand.

"And who's boy are you, cutie pie?"

Mandla pointed at Monica.

"No, I meant where is your mother?"

Monica could hear the ticking of a large plastic clock that hung over the sink. She wanted to scoop Mandla into her arms and tell him that he didn't have to answer. But people would be asking him this question his whole life and he had to get used to it. She held her breath, wishing she could say the words for him.

"My mother is in heaven," he said. "Monica is my new mommy."

Monica heard Sipho let out a small puff of air.

The aunt stared into Mandla's eyes. Then she put a hand in the small of her back as though to massage an ache. "You're brothers?" she asked, looking at Sipho.

"Yes," said Sipho quietly.

"Monica, could I talk to you in private?"

Zukisa took Mandla's hand and indicated for Sipho to follow her out of the kitchen.

Monica heard loud commentary from a soccer match on the television. Sipho would not be content out there for long. She looked at Zukisa's aunt expectantly, but the woman seemed lost in thought. A moment later, she sighed and sat down heavily at the table. Monica took a seat across from her.

"It's not easy raising children at my age."

Monica nodded in commiseration. "And their mother…?" She let her question hang in the air.

"In Cape Town." She was silent a long time, and Monica wondered if she was trying to decide how much information to share. Finally she said, "She drinks."

"She could get help."

The aunt shook her head. "That's for people who want it."

Monica was sorry that the woman had to use money that could be spent on the children to support her alcoholic daughter.

"She works," said the aunt as though reading Monica's thoughts. Her voice dropped to a whisper. "Drink makes a person do things they normally wouldn't."

As her meaning became clear, Monica felt a surge of compassion for this woman who harbored such sorrow in her heart. Suddenly she was aware of the aunt's eyes on her.

"Can you take Zukisa?"

Monica was sure she hadn't heard correctly. "Excuse me?"

"I can't feed them all and I can't afford a school uniform for Zukisa. She's a clever girl. She needs to go to school."

"Do you mean take her forever or just until your financial situation improves?"

The aunt gave a tight little laugh. "What do you think—one day my fairy godmother is going to wave her wand and fill my bank account? I mean until Zukisa finishes school."

"I see."

She saw Monica's hesitation and added, "It's not safe for a girl around here."

In telling her this, the aunt had made Monica complicit in the preservation of Zukisa's well-being. Emotional blackmail or desperation, it did not matter; the result was the same. Either Monica left with Zukisa or with a heavy burden of guilt that would become impossible to bear if anything happened to the girl.

Monica thought of the vision she'd had for her life up until late yesterday afternoon. She would marry Zak and they'd have a child of their own—a little girl, perhaps. But this day had brought a new reality. Zak had left her, and although he'd said it might only be a while, it might be forever. So why not take in this poor orphan? Monica could afford to bring her up. It was not a decision that should be made on the spur of the moment, but it seemed God was telling her that this was the right thing to do.

"Do you want to go away and think about it?" asked the aunt.

Monica shook her head. For a few seconds she remained still, absorbing the enormity of what she was about to do.

The aunt took her silence as a refusal. "Don't worry, we'll find a way to make it." She pushed her chair back and started to stand up.

Monica touched her arm. "I'd love to take her."

The aunt did not smile, and it was then that Monica realized just how hard it must have been for her to make this request.

"Should I come back in a few days to get her?"

The aunt shook her head. It was clear that she did not trust herself to speak—or to delay the parting.

"I'll wait outside in the car," said Monica. "If she doesn't come out in twenty minutes, I'll know you've changed your mind."

She wrote her address and home phone number on the back of her business card. The aunt put it in a biscuit tin in the cupboard.

In the other room, the boys were all at the window watching a fight on the small rectangle of grass between the buildings.

"Stop looking at the hooligans," said the aunt. She pulled her grandsons away from the window. "Why are you two not at school? We're going to have a serious talk this afternoon."

Monica noticed Zukisa wince. "It was good to see you," she said, touching the little girl's arm.

"Goodbye," said Zukisa. "I hope I'll see you again."

Monica found that she could not reply and was relieved when the aunt closed the front door before they had even taken a step down the corridor.

In the car, Monica did not strap Mandla into his booster seat.

"The police will catch me," he complained.

"We have to wait here for a while."

She turned around in her seat to face both her boys. "I have something important to tell you." She should have consulted them when making this decision, but there hadn't been time or opportunity, and now she braced herself for their reaction. "Zukisa may be coming to live with us."

She watched their faces. Mandla's registered surprise and joy. Sipho's was blank. "Her aunt may change her mind or Zukisa may refuse to come with us. We'll wait twenty minutes to see."

It was not fair to break the news to them this way, yet she couldn't tell them the minute they saw Zukisa coming down the stairs with a suitcase.

"She can sleep in my room with me," said Mandla.

Monica had not begun to consider the practical arrangements. If Zukisa came, the boys would no longer be able to have their own rooms. "I suppose you could sleep with me if you wanted," she said to Mandla.

Why not? It was not as though she was getting married anytime soon.

A smile spread across Mandla's face as he considered his choices.

"How many more children are you going to adopt?" asked Sipho.

Monica had not anticipated this response. Did he think she was making a collection? That would diminish the importance of his presence in her life.

"I hadn't planned on adopting any others, but Zukisa's aunt is struggling."

"Who will look after the baby?" asked Mandla.

"I presume the aunt will take him to work with her."

His question made Monica think. In letting Zukisa go, the aunt was making a sacrifice.

She turned around to see what Sipho was looking at and saw a group of boys passing the front of the car. Two of them had bloodied noses. They were all laughing. They took no notice of the small family in the car.

"This will not change the way I feel about the two of you."

"Mothers always do more stuff with their daughters," said Sipho.

"I promise you, Sipho, it will not change anything between us."

He sighed, and she knew then that she would not get his blessing, but he would not make a fuss.

Fifteen minutes went by and Monica started to think that she had caused Sipho to worry for no reason.

"There she is," shouted Mandla, pointing at a bright red dress on the second-floor corridor.

There were two arms around Zukisa's shoulders. Monica felt a sob catch in her throat. Zukisa and her aunt stayed pressed together for almost two minutes.

"She better hurry." Mandla breathed heavily.

"We're not going to lock the doors if she doesn't make the cutoff time," said Sipho.

Monica smiled at him gratefully.

Zukisa's aunt pulled away, kissed her fingers and placed them on Zukisa's face. Then she turned around and shut the door behind her, to spare her niece, Monica knew, from seeing her break down in tears.

Mandla waved frantically as Zukisa peered over the railings. She stood for a minute, as though trying to gather the strength to leave.

"Come on," said Mandla quietly.

She picked up her suitcase and started to walk.

Monica got out of the car to greet her. The suitcase was a small cardboard rectangle, the type children used for school. Inside was everything the girl owned. Tears ran down Zukisa's cheeks and dripped onto the lace collar of her red dress.

Monica took her hand. "I know this must be hard for you. But I want you to know that we're very happy to have you."

The corners of Zukisa's mouth twitched, but she could not muster a proper smile. She climbed into the backseat next to Mandla and buckled her seat belt. The boys were suddenly silenced by the situation.

Zukisa looked up at her aunt's door as they drove away, perhaps hoping to catch a glimpse of her relative one last time.

"You can visit here whenever you want," said Monica.

Zukisa let out a squeal and Monica glanced at her.

"He tickled me."

Even at a time like this, Mandla could not stop himself from tickling, poking and prodding.

"What did I tell you about that?" asked Monica, giving him a stern look in the rearview mirror.

"I don't mind," said Zukisa. "It surprised me—that's all."

Monica drove on.

This time it was Mandla's turn to squeal. Zukisa had tickled him back.

18

FRANCINA HEARD THE CAR IN THE DRIVE AND RUSHED outside. She felt weak with relief.

"Where have you been?" she cried as Monica rolled down the window. "I went to pick up the boys from school, and the teachers told me they hadn't showed up today. I phoned your office, and Dudu told me she had no idea where you were."

"I'm sorry, Francina. I forgot to tell anyone. This morning I was so—"

"As I walked through each room of your house, I held my heart, expecting to find the three of you lying murdered on the floor." Francina began to cry.

"I wasn't thinking straight." Monica got out of the car and dropped her voice to a whisper. "Yesterday Zak broke up with me."

"Why?"

"I'll tell you later."

"No, now. You owe me."

"Because of Yolanda."

Francina digested this new information for a few seconds. When she spoke, her voice was strangely flat. The prolonged tension of this morning had exhausted her. "I'm sorry. But you'll get back together."

Monica looked on the verge of tears.

The boys climbed out of the car. Francina saw that there was someone else still inside.

"Who's that?"

"It's Zukisa," announced Mandla. "She's going to live with us and be my big sister."

Francina felt her skin go cold. She looked at her arms and saw gooseflesh. "Is that true, Monica?" Her voice was tremulous.

"Her aunt asked me to take her."

"Another child." Francina's voice was soft, as though she were talking to herself.

Monica waved at Zukisa to get out. With her head down and her hands clasped in front of her, Zukisa obliged.

"*Molo*," said Francina, greeting the girl in her native Xhosa. Still using Xhosa, she asked after the girl's health.

"I'm fine, thank you," said Zukisa in English, looking shyly at Monica, as though she realized that Monica might not understand Xhosa.

Francina told her—in Xhosa—to come to her if she ever needed help. Zukisa smiled demurely.

Francina did not speak Xhosa fluently, but Monica did not speak it at all—and that was the point. Francina had never complained about her lot in life—even when she lost her eye—but today was different. Why was Monica entitled to another child and she couldn't have even one?

"I'm sorry I didn't tell you I was taking the boys," said Monica, interpreting Francina's silence as continued irritation at her disappearing act.

Francina wanted to shout, *How could you do this when you know how much I want a child?* But for the sake of the children she kept quiet.

She did not know if her legs would carry her home to her flat, where Hercules would have returned after searching—without success—for Monica and the boys on Main Street. She knew that she would be tempted to take out her hurt on him and her mother-in-law and, later, when she said her prayers before going to bed, on God. This expansion of Monica's family would eat away at Francina like a cutworm in a *mielie* field. Day after day, she'd feel the writhing weight of it, the silent painful gnawing, until, just like the young plants, she'd fall where she stood to be consumed by the pest.

"I've got to tell Hercules you're safe," she said through tight lips.

"Francina, I really am sorry."

And so you should be, thought Francina, *for a whole lot more than you realize.* She squeezed the boys' hands and felt a terrible temptation to call them "my boys" in front of Monica. It was childish, but she wanted to hurt Monica as she had been hurt.

"*Hamba kukule,*" she said to Zukisa, and the girl gave a little wave.

"Can I show Zukisa my toys?" asked Mandla, jumping up and down.

Francina could barely bring herself to say goodbye to Monica.

"I'll make it up to you," said Monica. "I'll personally bring you five new clients."

"I don't need any more white women from Cape Town," snapped Francina.

Monica's mouth fell open. Francina knew she had gone too far, but she did not care. Her heart was breaking.

As soon as she was far away enough that she knew Monica would not call her back, she allowed her tears to slide silently down her cheeks and drop onto the front of her dress. She was past caring that someone might see her. God had forsaken her. He knew her deepest desire and yet had chosen to reward Monica with the gift of this precious little girl.

When she arrived home, Hercules took one look at her face and froze.

"What happened to them?" he whispered.

"Nothing. They went to Cape Town."

"Oh, thanks be to God. So why have you been crying?"

Francina did not want to tell him—not because he wouldn't understand but because it hurt too much. All she wanted to do was climb into a hot bath and be alone.

"You got a fright," said Hercules, rubbing her shoulders.

She gave him a feeble smile.

"Since you have the rest of the afternoon off, do you want to see my new painting?"

This was the last thing in the world she wanted, but she allowed herself to be led to the living room window.

"It's also of Lady Helen," he said, setting the painting on its easel. "Ta-da!" He pulled off the sheet.

If anything, it was worse that the last painting, which now hung above the couch. The colors were so vivid the painting was like an illustration in a comic book. But how could she tell him?

"I've tried to capture the pioneering spirit of the town," he said shyly.

Francina burst into tears.

"Is it that bad?"

Francina shook her head, then changed her mind and nodded. "I'm sorry," she sobbed. "I just can't..."

She ran from the room and locked herself in the bathroom. Hercules knocked on the door, but she did not answer, and eventually he went away. She turned on the hot water, poured half a bottle of bubble bath into the tub and slipped in for a long soak.

Soon she heard whispers outside the door; Mrs. Shabalala had been summoned from the shop, and Francina would have to explain herself when she came out of the bathroom. Ducking under the hot water, she felt the tips of her ears burn, and when she could no longer hold her breath, she emerged, hair covered with bubbles, the skin on her face pinched and tight.

Monica had changed so much since she had been carjacked and shot. She had come to know and respect Francina as a human being, not merely the woman who washed her clothes. And now this. Francina knew that Monica had not set out to betray her, but that didn't soften the blow. Nothing had changed. Those who had something in life were rewarded with more, and those who had nothing suffered in silence. She topped up the tub with hot water.

When her skin felt as raw as her heart, she climbed out and prepared to face her husband and mother-in-law. Hercules stood up as she entered the room. Mrs. Shabalala hovered nearby, a glass of water in her hand.

"I'm fine now," said Francina.

"Sit down, dear," said her mother-in-law. She offered Francina the glass of water.

Why, wondered Francina, did people offer water in times of emotional distress? But although thirst was the furthest thing from her mind, she appreciated the concern behind the action.

"I'll let you two talk," said Mrs. Shabalala.

"You don't have to leave, Mama." Francina looked at her husband's face, creased with worry. "You both know that I would have loved a child." She sighed deeply. "Every day I thank God for bringing me you, Hercules, but I wish that it had been sooner, before I passed my time."

Hercules took her hand.

"Today Monica brought home another child—Zukisa—to be a sister to the boys."

She thought this announcement would elicit cries of disbelief from her family, but they waited in silence for the rest of the story.

"It's not fair," she added defensively. "Monica knows that I would have jumped at the chance to take that child in." Suddenly she realized what she had said. "Of course, I would have discussed it with you first, Hercules."

"Have you ever told Monica of your desire?" asked Mrs. Shabalala.

Francina shook her head.

"My dear, it's not fair then for you to blame her." A deep frown appeared on her forehead. This was the first time she had criticized her daughter-in-law, and she waited to be chastised.

But Francina merely nodded.

Hercules, who had been silent up till then, offered his opinion.

"Even if Monica had known of your desire for a child, what was she supposed to tell this woman? I have a friend who's desperate for a child? I'll pass Zukisa along to her like a sack of potatoes?"

Trust Hercules to be the infuriating voice of reason. No matter how high the waves rose around him, he never lost sight of a fixed spot on the horizon. His moral compass never wavered.

He was not finished. "Did you stop to think of Monica's wishes? She already has two children and will want some of her own when she marries. But she's a good woman and wouldn't have been able to say no even if she'd wanted to."

Francina hadn't thought of this. Hercules never took an issue at face value. He turned it upside down and examined it until all the angles were considered. It was quite possible that Monica felt she did not have a choice in this matter *and* that she had no idea of Francina's secret desire.

That evening Francina asked Hercules if they could skip her lesson. They went to bed early, but she could not get comfortable and, not wanting to disturb her husband, she got up and went into the living room. Light from the street spilled through a chink in the curtain onto the sweater her mother-in-law was knitting for Mandla.

Francina held it against her. She knew what was keeping her awake. It was her conscience, and she didn't have to think now to know what to do. In the cold silence of the sleeping flat, she got down on her knees next to the couch and asked God to forgive her for blaming Him for deserting her.

When she awoke the next morning, the pain was still with her, but it had dulled. On her way down to the shop she passed Hercules's covered painting, and suddenly it became clear to her that if she respected her husband, she had to tell him the truth. The important thing would be to do it gently.

She had just sat down to write invoices when the bells on the door tinkled and Monica walked into the shop.

"I don't want hard feelings between us," she said. "I should have told you I was taking off with the boys."

"Apology accepted." Francina knew that she owed Monica the truth, too, but she felt too fragile to do it now. "How is Zukisa?"

"A little shellshocked. Two moves since the death of her mother is a lot for a child. I've left her at the office with Dudu. There are a few things on my desk I need to handle before taking the rest of the day off."

Francina knew then that if she wanted to tell Monica the truth, this was the time. A few more days and Zukisa would be settled in and it would be too late.

She indicated for Monica to sit. The next client was not due for an hour—they would not be interrupted. She took a deep breath. As she told Monica of her desire for a child, she didn't dare look at her friend's face. And when she was finished, she felt Monica's silence as sharply as a slap.

Finally Monica spoke. "You want Zukisa." It was not a question.

"Yes," said Francina quietly. She had not discussed it with Hercules, though she'd said she would, but this opportunity had presented itself without warning.

Monica fingered the invoice book. She was deep in thought.

"It was not my plan to adopt another child. But it's not as though I'm going to have a baby of my own in the near future."

"He will change his mind." Francina knew that Monica would think that she'd said this because it would help her in her fight for Zukisa, but she believed it deep in her heart. Only a fool would give up Monica. Anton, her ex-boyfriend, had been a fool; Zak was not.

"We will have to talk to Zukisa's aunt first."

Francina felt her stomach turn over. She was afraid to say another word in case Monica changed her mind.

"She may say no," warned Monica.

In her mind, Francina was already rehearsing her plea to the aunt.

"The boys will be disappointed," said Monica.

"Sipho didn't look too excited to me. And Mandla could get very jealous after his excitement has worn off."

Monica did not respond, and Francina wondered if it was because she'd had the same concerns. They looked at each other, contemplating the magnitude of the decision they had made between themselves. Francina knew that Monica would want to end by saying something profound—Monica liked to leave things tidy—but just as she was about to speak, a customer came into the shop.

"Can we go today?" Francina asked quickly.

Monica nodded. They both knew it was not fair on Zukisa to delay this.

"Can Hercules or his mother watch the children this afternoon? I don't think they should come with us."

Promising that it would be done, Francina turned to assist the customer, who had come armed with a magazine picture of a party dress. As Francina took the lady's measurements, she pictured Zukisa sitting at the worktable stitching together tiny pieces of fabric Francina had cut out for her doll.

Thank you, God, she prayed silently.

It was not premature; she was as certain of this as she was that the sun would rise tomorrow. God had not intended for her to be childless her whole life.

Hercules had brought the children to the flat for dinner when Monica and Francina returned from Cape Town. In his eyes the two women saw the question that could not be answered with words. Francina gave a slight nod, and Hercules and his mother broke into smiles as wide as the dinner plates on which homemade pizza was being served. The menu had been Francina's choice, part of her plan for winning over Zukisa.

In the car on the way back, she and Monica had decided that Monica would take the girl home tonight. It would not be fair to spring this on her, even though the aunt had given her blessing. At one point in the aunt's flat, Francina had believed that she would not get her desire—the aunt did not know her; she had never even heard her sister-in-law speak of her. Francina had asked Monica to leave the room. She knew that Monica would think it was so she could make a case for the child being better off with someone of her own race, but it was because she was too timid to reveal her heart in Monica's presence.

She'd told the aunt how her first husband had ruined her chances of having a normal life. The aunt had declined her offer to take out her eye to prove that she'd been beaten, and Francina had gone on to explain how she had passed her childbearing time early and come to happiness later in life. The aunt had taken Francina's tears for sadness, but they'd been of desperation. Francina had pleaded her case as passionately as if she were standing before a judge who had the authority to put her in prison for thirty years.

"If Zukisa agrees, I will not fight it," the aunt had said, not smiling.

Now, as Mrs. Shabalala bustled off to get two extra plates, Monica inquired about the children's day. From her measured tone, Francina could tell Monica felt burdened by the task of having to break the news to Zukisa, and Francina felt a rush of love for the woman who had been only a little girl when they'd met, in Johannesburg, when Francina had first come to work for Monica's mother. Francina and Monica had gone through many difficult times together, and now Monica was prepared to grant Francina her heart's deepest wish: a child of her own.

Hercules and his mother were waiting for her at the top of the stairs when she returned from seeing Monica and the children off. Francina felt a tremor in Hercules's arms as he hugged her. Mrs. Shabalala looked away politely.

How on earth, Francina wondered, *did I manage to find this wondrous man?* Their discussion before she left for Cape Town this afternoon had been brief. Before last night neither of them had even mentioned fostering a child, and yet the very next morning he had agreed, and with wild enthusiasm.

"A child in the house," said Mrs. Shabalala, clapping her hands together and doing a little dance on the spot. "I never thought I'd live to see this day. Oh, my goodness, we have so much to do before she comes."

"Would you mind if she slept in your bed with you?" asked Francina.

"Mind? I would love that. I slept in my *gogo's* bed when I was a child." She did a little twirl. "And now that I've lost so much weight, there's extra space for a little scrap of a girl."

"We have to fatten her up," Francina and her mother-in-law said in unison.

Hercules shook his head, but there was laughter in his eyes.

"And buy her some clothes," added Mrs. Shabalala.

"Buy?" said Francina, hands on her hips. "I'm going to go downstairs right this minute and start making her a whole wardrobe of dresses in all the colors of the rainbow. Zukisa has style. She can't wear store-bought dresses. Sorry, Hercules—no studying again tonight."

"And I'm going to bake a cake for her arrival tomorrow," said Mrs. Shabalala, hurrying toward the kitchen.

Hercules yawned. "Do you two mind if I go to bed? I've been playing horse to Mandla's cowboy all afternoon."

"You get your rest, sweet husband—or should I say, sweet Daddy-to-be?"

Hercules kissed her on the cheek. He was still grinning when he came out of the bathroom after brushing his teeth.

A little before dawn Francina slipped out of bed and wandered into the kitchen to make herself a cup of tea. Again she had barely slept at all, but rather than feeling tired, she was quite capable of sewing four hems in quick succession. The only disadvantage of a shop on Main Street was that it was exposed to everyone who passed by—she couldn't go down there in pajamas.

With her cup of tea in hand, she opened the living room curtains and left the sheers drawn. There was no evidence that Mayor Oupa, whose office was directly across the street, would have the slightest interest in the goings-on in her flat, but one could never tell what people did in their spare moments. The baker lady across the street had left her curtains open, and Francina could see her in front of her television, doing some sort of exercises on a mat. As Francina sipped her tea, she watched the baker contort herself into positions that looked rather painful.

The mayor's office was still dark. He was up for reelection. Hercules would be an excellent replacement, and it would be an easy commute for him. But he would never agree to run; he loved teaching too much.

When she'd finished her tea, she turned away from the window, and her eyes rested on the covered easel. She took the sheet off.

"I hope you're not going to burst into tears again," said Hercules in his dressing gown.

She shook her head, smiling.

He came to stand next to her. "I could use some help, couldn't I?"

This was the moment she had dreaded.

"A little," she said. The understatement wasn't a lie.

"Do you think Gift will still be interested in giving me lessons?"

She took his hand and nodded.

"The teacher will have to be taught." He covered the painting. "This can be recycled."

"Keep it for a comparison. Before and after. I kept my first trial exam paper." She hoped he didn't remember that it was one Oscar had prepared.

"I'd better get dressed for school. Do you think Zukisa will be here by the time I get back for lunch?"

"I hope so. Monica hasn't enrolled her in school yet. That's up to us, Zukisa's new parents." Francina smiled shyly. She didn't mention the possibility that Zukisa might refuse to come.

"I don't know how I'll get through the morning." It was not like Hercules to be emotional.

"Zukisa's name means 'be patient' in the Xhosa language. Parents who have planned and waited for a child choose this name."

Neither of them mentioned the possibility that Zukisa might not agree to come. Francina believed with all her heart that it was God's will for her to have a child. He had made her wait, but it would happen.

After she'd kissed Hercules goodbye, Francina went down to the shop to wait. With her hands occupied by a particularly slippery fabric for an evening gown—one of her clients was going to a wedding in Johannesburg—she listened to the ticking of the grandfather clock and imagined old Richard Kumalo, the late owner of the shop, hearing the same sound as he peered through his watchmaker glasses at minuscule cogs and springs. Had he worried, as he'd worked, that his son was showing little interest in learning the trade and that, after his own death, the shop might be sold? Had he, like Francina, matched the tempo of his thoughts to the enduring rhythm of the clock?

On the stroke of eight—the start of the school day—she noticed dark patches on the fabric; her hands were sweating. Monica would have dropped the boys off by now and would be on her way to the shop. Was Zukisa with her? With her heart in her mouth, Francina watched the clock tick away the five minutes she had calculated it would take Monica to get from the school to the shop. A car pulled up outside, but she did not dare lift her head from her work. "Please, God, let her be with Monica," she whispered.

The bells on the door tinkled. Her stomach lurched and she felt nauseated. Monica was alone.

"She doesn't want to get out of the car." Monica saw the anguish on Francina's face. "No, no, she wants to come. She's just shy."

"Really? She agreed happily?"

Monica shrugged. "She agreed. I won't say happily. But it's too soon after her mother's death for her to be happy about anything. Why don't you go out and persuade her to come in?"

Francina approached the car and saw that Zukisa was staring at her hands in her lap. She waited until the girl became aware of her presence and rolled down the window.

"We have a cake for you," she said. "And when we've finished, we can go to the school and enroll you so you can start tomorrow."

Zukisa nodded but did not smile.

"It's a lot of change in a short time," said Francina.

"My daddy brought his watch to this shop when it was broken."

"The big grandfather clock is still here."

"Really? I remember watching the pendulum swing and wishing I could hear it chime."

"You'll hear it on the hour all day and night now."

Zukisa thought about this and smiled wanly. "My mother and father didn't know they were sick then. It was hiding in their bodies like a burglar."

"I know, baby. I want to hear all about them."

"Really?"

"You can write it all down in a journal so that one day, when you're a mother, your children will know their grandmother and grandfather."

"I think I'll come inside now."

Francina opened the car door. She wanted to take Zukisa's hand, but she thought it might scare the girl.

"I like the name of your store." Zukisa pointed to the sign on the window.

"Jabulani is the name of my village."

"Happiness dressmakers," said Zukisa, translating.

"The happiest," said Francina.

19

THE KNOCK ON THE DOOR CAME, AS EXPECTED, AT SIX in the morning. Monica was already dressed and sitting at the kitchen table. A cold draft ran through the house as she let Oscar in.

"I'm glad I'm not a fisherman," he said, rubbing his hands together.

"Or a poacher," she added, handing him a cup of coffee.

Dawn came later now, with the change in season, and she was bargaining that the poachers would, too.

"This is crazy, Monica. The police should be doing this."

"They'll force me to reveal the name of my source, and I can't get her into trouble."

"But these men arc armed."

"Yes, but this time I'm not going to be stupid. We'll wait in the car, at a distance, and then follow them. I only want to know where they come from. I have a hunch that these are the men who broke in and robbed the gallery."

"If I get nervous, I'm calling the police."

"Of course."

There was another knock at the door, and Monica hurried to let in Kitty, who had agreed to watch the boys. Monica had not wanted to ask Francina, since this was Zukisa's first day of school, and Monica imagined Francina already in the kitchen, cooking a breakfast fit for a princess.

"You got a pregnant woman up at this hour?" said Oscar.

Kitty groaned and clutched her growing belly. "I don't sleep very much nowadays. I can't get comfortable."

"Thanks, Kitty. I really appreciate this," said Monica.

"Tell me again what time school starts."

"Eight."

"If you're not back by seven-thirty, I'll take the boys."

Monica gave her friend a kiss on the cheek. "You're a star."

As Monica reversed out of the driveway, she saw a light on in S.W.'s studio and wondered if he'd stayed up all night. One of the joys of old age, he'd said, was having more time to work since he needed less sleep.

She drove down to the beach where she had seen the poachers before and parked up a darkened side street. She and Oscar had a clear view in front of them of the rocks she'd hidden behind last time and, beyond the rocks, the white sand.

"Lucky for us nobody's replaced the lightbulb in this streetlight," said Oscar.

They sat in silence, watching, checking the time, their warm breath forming circles of condensation on the windshield.

Oscar broke the silence. "I'm glad you took my advice. Zak is a good choice."

Monica sighed deeply. "It's over."

"I wondered if something had happened. He was miserable yesterday."

"You spoke to him?"

"I went in to have a bad toenail pulled. He looked terrible."

"I didn't end it, he did."

"Not willingly, by the looks of it. You should see him. He hasn't shaved, his hair looks like mine after a month at sea and he's got dark raccoon circles around his eyes."

Knowing that Zak was suffering should have given her some satisfaction, but it didn't. It only made her recognize the futility of their pain once again, and that, if they'd handled things differently from the beginning, they might still be together. Perhaps if she'd told Yolanda that day on the beach that she did not want to come between her and her father, the girl might not have felt so threatened. If Zak had explained that there was no chance of him reconciling with her mother, Yolanda might have slowly let go of that hope. But Zak had obviously not done that, and perhaps it was because he didn't believe it himself. History had a strange pull on people. Was an emotional investment early on in one's life always more valuable through time than a new attachment?

"Is that them?" asked Oscar.

A blue truck was approaching the beach. This time there was only one man in the back.

"Yes, hide," said Monica, sliding down in her seat.

Three men got out of the front cab, leaving the truck running with its lights on, and unloaded the scuba gear.

"I wonder if those are dry suits. It's got to be freezing in the water," said Oscar.

He cleared a patch on the foggy windshield with his hand. The men walked in the strong beam from the truck's headlights to the water, burlap sacks flapping at their legs. Once they'd entered the water, the driver of the truck killed the lights.

"And now we wait," said Monica. She opened a flask of coffee and poured it into plastic mugs.

Sunlight had started to spill over the koppies, making the faint white crests of the waves visible on the ocean. A lone pelican drifted past, so slowly that Monica marveled it could stay aloft. She hoped that the residents of this street were used to fishermen parking outside their houses, so no one might grow suspicious and call the police.

As she and Oscar waited, counting the slow minutes, the sunlight reached the beach, but the street remained in the shadow of the koppies.

"Here they come," said Oscar.

They saw a diver emerge from the water, dragging a full sack. The others were not far behind.

"They were down longer last time," said Monica.

Someone in a nearby house let a dog into the garden and it ran over to the fence, barking.

"Oh, no, we're going to have to move," said Monica.

"Get back in here and be quiet," a man's voice called, and the dog scampered back into the warmth of the house.

Monica and Oscar watched the truck's driver tip the contents of the sacks into a chest in the tailbed and stow the diving equipment.

Within a few minutes he had started the truck and was turning it around. Monica and Oscar ducked as the headlights swept over the hood of their car.

Monica gave the truck a short head start. When she and Oscar reached the foot of the koppie, they spotted the truck rounding a bend on the winding road up ahead. From the top of the koppie, they saw it reach the Cape Town road and take a left, away from the city.

"What if they're heading as far as Port Nolloth? Or the Namibian border?" asked Oscar.

"Please call Kitty with my cell phone and ask her to take the boys to school."

Oscar smiled at Monica. She refused to reveal her source to the police and yet she wouldn't think of breaking the law by talking on the phone while driving.

The truck, as it turned out, was not heading for Port Nolloth. Just after crossing the Berg River, it took the exit for Velddrif.

"You'll have to catch up or we'll lose it in town," said Oscar.

Velddrif was small, but the truck could disappear into a garage at any of the houses. Morning traffic clogged the road, and the best Monica could do was stay four cars behind. She kept up with the truck through the central business district and into a residential neighborhood north of town. The fronts of the small brick houses had verandas, many of them enclosed to make sunrooms, and tiny patches of grass encircled by chain-link fences. A group of women had congregated on one driveway, some with babies strapped to their backs with blankets, others in aprons as though they'd just stepped out of their kitchens.

The truck turned a corner and when Monica reached the intersection, she and Oscar saw the taillights vanishing down a driveway.

"Should I drive past?" asked Monica.

"Go around the block to give the men time to go inside. Then we'll drive past to take down the address. That is our plan, isn't it? Just to take down the address? You don't have any crazy ideas of bursting in there?"

"You've been watching too many bad movies," laughed Monica. "I'm going to make an anonymous tip to the police."

When they arrived back in Lady Helen, Monica drove straight home.

"What about the police?" asked Oscar.

"Please could you drop off the tip? I'll write it all down."

Oscar thought about this for a while. "I presume you know what you're doing."

Throughout the rest of the long morning Monica fought the urge to call the police and find out what had happened. That was the problem with an anonymous tip—you didn't get any feedback.

At lunchtime, while Dudu was out buying sandwiches, Oscar walked into her office, surprising her.

"They got them," he said.

"How do you know?"

He threw up his hands. "What did you expect? They saw me leaving after I slipped the note under the door and called me. I had to promise to go back to the police station after they'd investigated the house in Velddrif."

"I'm sorry, Oscar. Did you tell them anything about me?"

He shrugged. "I had no choice."

Monica knew she had to warn Anna not to go out tomorrow for abalone.

Dewald had contacted the police in Velddrif, and a squad car had met him and Mike at the entrance to the neighborhood. The Velddrif police had taken two Taiwanese nationals into custody after discovering them in a back room off the garage, packing abalone into foam chests filled with dry ice. The men had confessed to poaching abalone all along the West Coast and shipping one ton of the delicacy to the Far East each month.

"And the gallery robbery?"

Oscar shook his head. "The men they apprehended have alibis to prove that they were in Velddrif at the time. Monica, Dewald and Mike want to talk to you—now."

She had known all along that it would come to this. Lady Helen was far too small to keep secrets.

After leaving a note for Dudu, she accompanied Oscar to the police station. Every step of the way she thought of Anna's baby and what this would mean to him. Dewald's face lit up when she walked through the door.

"Hey, Mike," he called. "She's here."

Mike entered the office, grinning broadly.

How would Monica tell Anna that she had betrayed her confidence?

"Your check will take about six weeks," said Dewald.

"Check?"

Dewald, Mike *and* Oscar grinned at her.

"The police in Saldanha have been after this gang for two years. One of the fisheries there put up reward money." Mike looked bemused. "You really didn't know?"

She shook her head.

"We have what we want, so you can keep your source secret—this time," said Dewald.

"Thank you," she said quietly.

As she left with Oscar, Mike called her back. "We want to know if you hear from your friend Silas." His look told her that she would not get off so easily if she hid anything about that situation from them.

Oscar waited for her to catch up with him. "Please go and see Zak."

She was too shocked to reply.

"He looks terrible."

"He doesn't want me, Oscar."

Oscar shook his head. "I don't believe that."

"It's complicated."

"Love always is. But sometimes one person in the relationship has to make a surprise move. If you always do what's expected of you, then..." He trailed off, and Monica sensed that he was speaking of his own past.

"Oscar—"

"I've got to hurry to my next job." He put up a hand to wave goodbye—maybe to stop her from asking the question she had been about to ask, she wasn't sure.

When she returned to her office, Dudu told her that Nick had called.

"Nick?"

Dudu looked at her message pad. "Nick Stavos. He said he knew you from Johannesburg."

"Of course. He helped with the adoption papers for the boys." Monica hadn't spoken to him in two years.

"He's staying at the golf resort." Dudu handed her the message. Her curiosity was poorly disguised.

Nick Stavos in Lady Helen? And staying at the golf resort? Monica hadn't pegged him for a golfer. She went into her office and waited until she heard Dudu answer another call before dialing. She wondered if she was banned not only from visiting the resort but also from calling there. But the switchboard operator cheerily offered to put her through. There was a click, and then a recorded voice with an affected British accent began to extol the virtues of the championship golf course and the world-class spa.

"Hello?" Nick's voice sounded thick with sleep.

"It's Monica. You were having a nap. I'm sorry."

"It was either that or join my friend on the golf course," explained Nick. "I'm no golfer."

Her assumption had been correct. Nick explained that an old friend from university had persuaded him to come away for a long weekend. "I heard that you'd moved to Lady Helen…" He drifted off.

Monica was immediately on edge. If Nick had accompanied his friend for the sole reason of looking her up, then that meant only one thing. She had once said that if she ever married, she hoped it would be to a man like Nick—but she had never said that she was attracted to him.

Nick sensed her hesitation and quickly added, "I've heard how beautiful this part of the country is. Now if I could just get my friend to leave the golf course, we might do some sightseeing."

He was putting the ball in her court. Whatever she said next would determine the nature of their meeting or whether they met at all.

Monica wondered why Nick hadn't asked her out in Johannesburg.

Whatever his reason, her reluctance now was due to one thing only: Nick was not Zak. But he was a good man, too, and what harm could an hour or so bring?

"I could show you around if you'd like." Somewhere in the back of her mind a voice told her this was a mistake, but she silenced it by recalling the grim expression on Zak's face the last time they'd spoken in her garden. She could almost feel the cold again of that day.

"Thank you."

Monica heard the smile in Nick's voice.

They arranged to walk around town on Saturday morning. Monica told him that her two sons would be with her, and she was pleased when he sounded genuinely happy about seeing them again.

20

FRANCINA PAUSED AT THE DOOR. FROM INSIDE CAME the soft snuffling noise—not quite a snore—her mother-in-law made when sleeping. Zukisa had gone to bed at eight, but an hour later, when Francina had checked, the girl had been staring at the ceiling, thinking perhaps about her old life and nervous about the future. Now Francina hated to wake her, but it was time to start the morning, a new routine, a whole new life. Breakfast was on the table. All Zukisa had to do was put on the uniform Francina had bought yesterday, eat and brush her teeth.

Monica had waited patiently while the boys decided what to call her, but Francina and Zukisa had sorted it out on the first day. Francina had offered her Auntie or Francina; Zukisa had chosen Mother. Mother and daughter. Francina was no longer a battery hen keeping another's egg warm until the baby's beak pecked out of the flimsy shell. This time the little chick would stay close to the nest.

She heard the bedsprings squeak, and there was a lull in her mother-in-law's snuffling. A minute later the doorknob turned, and there was Zukisa, dressed in her navy pinafore and freshly ironed white shirt.

"Good morning, Mother." Zukisa's eyes shone as brightly as her new black shoes.

"Good morning, my dear." While she worked today, Francina would think carefully of a pet name for her new daughter. Monica used "sweetie." Francina would choose something just as charming. "Breakfast is ready. In a minute Hercules will join us for story time."

"What do you mean, Mother?"

"Oh, just you wait and see." Francina smiled as she led Zukisa by the hand to the dining room, where the table was set with bowls for porridge, freshly baked muffins, cantaloupe slices and orange juice.

Zukisa looked at her plate when Hercules sat down at the table and did not speak. Francina understood the girl's awkwardness; Hercules was not a man one warmed to immediately, but in time Zukisa would fall in love with him just as Francina had.

Francina could tell by Hercules's choice of stories this morning that he was also nervous. Steering clear of politics and crime, he read about the birth of an orangutan at the Johannesburg zoo, an upcoming fashion show in Cape Town with designers from all over Africa and the lineup of children's television for that week. Francina wanted to put her hand over his and tell him to be himself.

When they had finished breakfast and Zukisa had gone off to brush her teeth, Mrs. Shabalala appeared in her dressing gown.

"Did I miss breakfast?" she asked, yawning.

"Since when do you get up this early?" asked Hercules.

"I wanted to see Zukisa in her school uniform. That child was as still as a log in my bed. A couple of times in the night, I put my hand on her back to feel if she was still breathing. I can't tell you how long I've dreamed of..." She let her sentence hang in the air.

"It's okay, Mama. Me, too," said Francina.

Zukisa returned. "Good morning, *Gogo*."

And now Mrs. Shabalala had two children who called her *Gogo*—Mandla and Zukisa.

As this was Zukisa's first morning at Green Block School, Francina wanted to accompany her on the walk there with Hercules. Her husband's smile told her that he was grateful he'd be spared any awkward silences.

Francina insisted Zukisa put on her school sweater, as well as the navy blazer with the brass buttons. The wind hit them as soon as they stepped out of the shop.

"Pull your collar up, dear," said Francina. "I'll start knitting you a scarf as soon as I get back."

At the entrance to the school, Francina gave Hercules a peck on the cheek, and then she and Zukisa went off to find Mr. D, who would show Zukisa to her new classroom.

A few girls said hello to Zukisa along the way, and Francina hoped that Zukisa would find at least one familiar face in her new class. Francina wondered if Zukisa's mother had walked her to school every day—and then she tried to block the thought from her mind. If she compared herself to Zukisa's mother in everything she did for the child, she would make herself sick.

* * *

All morning long, while the dress orders hung untouched on the rack, Francina sat knitting a scarf in navy wool and hid it under the counter whenever the bells on the door chimed. With watery sunlight falling across her lap like a soft blanket, she thought of mothers all over the country—on factory assembly lines, behind desks and shop counters, pushing brooms—performing their duties with a smile but all the while wondering if their child had found his or her backpack or made it to school on time or was listening in class or getting into trouble again today. As with most of her theories, Francina had no proof, but she was almost sure that men could stash thoughts like these away in a cubbyhole for the day and retrieve them when it was time to go home, while women could never turn off their concern.

She arrived at Green Block School fifteen minutes before the end-of-the-day bell.

"I'm the first *mother* here," she said aloud.

Yesterday she was a babysitter, picking up another woman's children; today she was a mother picking up her own daughter. She felt like giving a whoop of joy but restrained herself in case someone overheard and went running to tell Hercules that he was married to a crazy woman.

She remembered then that she had not discussed the afternoon arrangements with Monica. No, *discussed* was not the right word— she had not *informed* Monica that Zukisa would be coming along every afternoon when she looked after the boys.

At the sound of the bell, she went to Mandla's classroom and hurried back with him to wait at the gate for Zukisa and Sipho.

Zukisa came out of school swinging her backpack and talking to another girl.

"Hello, my angel." Francina watched Zukisa's face to see if the new term of endearment was acceptable or not.

Zukisa smiled at her and took Mandla's hand.

Sipho came out of the school last, in the company of none other than Yolanda, Zak's daughter. Francina wondered if Monica knew of this change in arrangements.

"Hello, Yolanda. What are you doing back here?" she asked.

The girl shrugged.

Realizing that her question might have sounded a little abrupt, Francina added, "I'm happy you're back."

"Bye, Sipho. Bye, Zukisa," said Yolanda, and she walked off in the direction of the hospital.

"She didn't say bye to me," complained Mandla.

"I wonder why she's here?" said Francina.

"She doesn't like her mother's boyfriend," explained Sipho.

"Poor girl." Francina watched her disappear around a corner. She thanked God that she was able to offer Zukisa a stable home.

When Monica arrived home from work later that afternoon, she was surprised to hear that Yolanda was again living with Zak.

"He didn't tell you?" said Francina.

"We don't speak anymore."

"That's plain ridiculous," said Francina. "Two people in love with each other and not talking. Would you like me to have a word with him?"

Monica smiled.

"I'm serious."

Monica's smile disappeared. "Please don't."

"If we happen to meet—"

"Francina, I'm begging you not to."

"I'll judge the situation when it arises," said Francina.

When Francina picked up the children the next day, she saw Yolanda in the company of the boy whose family had moved into Zukisa's old house in Sandpiper Drift. What was his name again? It was something funny. Montgomery! That was it. Who on earth called their son Montgomery? Someone with a sense of humor, that's who—or someone who wanted their son to be teased mercilessly. She watched as the boy took a shiny new camera from his bag. Yolanda struck a pose and he took her picture. The two of them laughed. There was something about this boy that Francina didn't like; something told her that he was not to be trusted.

That afternoon she casually mentioned to Monica that Yolanda had walked home with Montgomery. There was a brief look of surprise in Monica's eyes, and then her face became expressionless, as though she'd purposefully shut out all thoughts that had anything to do with Zak.

"I don't trust that boy," continued Francina. "Maybe you should talk to Zak. He's at work all day and can't know what his daughter's getting up to."

"You don't think that…? Oh, no, please don't say that."

The appeal to Monica's nurturing instincts had opened up a chink in her armor.

Francina shrugged. "He's an adolescent boy. They have ideas." She twisted her mouth. "Actually, they never grow out of these ideas. Except for Hercules, of course."

Francina had said what she needed to say. What Monica did now was her business. But Francina would warn Zukisa about that boy Montgomery—and all other boys for that matter.

21

SIPHO OBSTINATELY TOOK HIS TIME DRESSING AND spooned his oatmeal into his mouth at a rate of one bite every three minutes.

"I wanted to go to the lagoon today," he whined.

Monica knew the real reason for his sullen protest was because he hated the idea of Monica meeting anyone but Zak.

"Nick was very good to us in the past. We'll give him a little tour of our town and we'll be cheerful about it."

Sipho grunted.

If Monica had allowed her childish instincts to show, she would have behaved the same way. She would rather be going for a walk around town with Zak. Nothing was going as planned. She'd lost the love of her life; Silas was still missing; Daphne had told Miemps that she never wanted to see Monica again; and now that the gang of poachers had been apprehended, Monica was sure that the abalone ladies were continuing to break the law. So much for being a problem solver. So much for nudging people to do the right thing. She couldn't even solve a single one of her own problems.

Nick was waiting outside the newspaper office at ten sharp, as planned. He had lost weight—or was it only that he was not wearing the dark rumpled suit that she was accustomed to seeing him in?—and his face had a little more color, perhaps due to the past couple of days in Lady Helen.

"Hi, Monica. Hi, Sipho. Hi, Mandla."

She was touched that he remembered the boys' names.

With a forced smile, Sipho shook the hand Nick offered. Mandla tried out an intricate handshake he had learned from Oscar, and after a fumbled start both he and Nick were laughing.

"I was wondering if you wanted to walk up the koppie to get a view of the town and the ocean or whether you wanted to have a look around Main Street and go to the park and the beach."

Nick shot a look at Sipho. "What does everyone else think?"

Sipho did not respond.

"No climbing," moaned Mandla. "My legs get too tired."

Monica tickled him in the soft hollow of his neck. "How do your legs get tired when you're riding piggyback?"

Mandla laughed.

There was no wind for a change, and with few clouds to hide the sun, the day was quite warm. They strolled slowly down Main Street, Mandla greeting everyone with a smile and an imperious wave, as though he were mayor, Sipho feigning interest without success. Nick spotted a painting of the town he thought he might like to purchase in the window of Nalini's gallery. Monica was about to join the boys, who'd continued on and were half a block ahead, when she saw the abalone ladies walking toward her. It was strange for them to be in town together. They stopped in front of her. Not one of the women returned her greeting.

Anna spoke first. "We were on our way to your house. The police were on the beach this morning. We couldn't collect anything."

Monica had called Anna to tell her that this might happen now that Mike and Dewald were aware of the serious poaching problem on the West Coast, but Anna had obviously chosen to ignore her warning.

"How are we going to earn money now?" the oldest woman wanted to know. "You haven't solved the problem, you've made it worse."

Monica was aware of Nick shifting his weight from one foot to the other beside her.

"Innocentia has no other way to feed her two children," snapped Anna.

Innocentia sniffed into a handkerchief.

"I'll come up with something," said Monica.

"That's what you said last time," said the oldest woman.

"I tried to do—"

"Well, it didn't work. Let's go, ladies."

As they walked away, Anna looked back over her shoulder. Her eyes were cold.

"You don't have to explain if you don't want to," said Nick.

Monica sighed. "I thought I was helping them, but I wasn't." She told Nick the story.

"The situation is not as irredeemable as you think. All you have to do is find alternative employment for the women."

This was one instance where Nick beat Zak; Zak had not given her any advice.

"But where?"

Nick shrugged. "Surely one or two of these business owners—" he waved at the stores on Main Street "—could do with extra help. And if you can convince a couple of the others to create jobs, you'll be set."

"I don't know if I'm capable."

"I've seen you at work. If I remember correctly, you were quite assertive getting interviews from that crabby public prosecutor."

"Being assertive may work in Johannesburg, but it doesn't here. People in Lady Helen don't like to be told what to do."

Monica was glad when the boys turned back and joined them again. Nick was well-meaning, but he had no idea how things worked in a small town.

"I don't think you should buy that painting," said Mandla. "A photo would be better. My mom can take one for you."

Nick smiled. "Thanks, Mandla. I'll think about that. We haven't been in the general store yet. What about a treat for you boys?"

Mandla clapped his hands in glee.

"No, thanks," said Sipho. "Aren't we going to have lunch soon?"

She had planned to take Nick to the park before lunch, but they might beat the rush of diners if they ate now. Although there were fewer tourists around in winter, there were still many regulars who came up from Cape Town on weekends. Mama Dlamini said it was for her daily cake or pie specials, but Monica knew, having lived in a big city herself for many years, that the real reason was to have a little breathing space for a while. The drive north up the coast, with glimpses of the ocean on the left, could ease even the most jangled nerves. There was less chance of running into Zak at Mama Dlamini's if they went early.

Mandla slid into one of the two booths available. He looked around the café, but there weren't many familiar faces. Most of the diners were day-trippers. Mama Dlamini appeared from the kitchen and gave each of her favorite two boys a chocolate milk shake on the house.

"This is Nick from Johannesburg," said Mandla. "He helped Mom adopt us."

"Is that so? Well, a chocolate milk shake on the house for him, too. You, too, Monica." She bustled off to get them.

Monica could tell from Sipho's sudden look of panic that Dr. Zak had entered the café. There was no need for her to turn around. Mandla, happy at last to see a familiar face, called out, "Zak, Yolanda, over here. There's a booth open next to us."

Monica could feel the color draining from her face.

"Are you all right?" asked Nick.

She nodded and quickly grabbed a menu and, although she knew it by heart, pored over it. "I can recommend the snoek," she said. She sensed Zak approaching. It was infantile to hide behind a menu, so she looked up. Oscar was right; he did look terrible. He was clean shaven, but his hair was in desperate need of a cut and his skin looked sallow. His eyes were not on her but on Nick. She had no choice but to pretend that everything was normal and introduce them.

"Hi, Zak, Yolanda. I'd like you to meet a friend from Johannesburg.

This is Nick Stavos." She could have explained that he was the attorney who had assisted in the boys' adoption, but she felt suddenly impatient with herself for feeling uncomfortable. She didn't owe Zak any explanations. He was the one who had rejected her.

Zak shook Nick's hand, more vigorously than was necessary. She didn't know if Sipho was about to slide under the table in embarrassment or burst into tears. Smiling broadly, Yolanda took the hand Nick offered.

"A beautiful town you have here," said Nick, trying to make small talk. Monica guessed he had pieced together the evidence and come to the correct conclusion.

"It's a slice of paradise," Zak replied.

Monica had never heard sarcasm in his voice before. He was clearly upset, and although her immediate elation horrified her, knowing Zak still cared gave her a measure of comfort.

"We'd better sit down before we lose the booth," said Zak.

Yolanda gave them a cheery wave and took a seat in the empty booth.

"Good to meet you." Zak did not even make an attempt to sound sincere. "Goodbye, Monica."

Monica felt the weight of the world descend on her, and her brief, childish surge of happiness disappeared, leaving her more miserable than before. She watched Zak and Yolanda pick up their menus. There was an air of possessiveness about Yolanda. This was the future and Monica hated it. If Zak had found another woman, it might have been easier; at least she could have vented her fury and disappointment. But since he had chosen his daughter, Monica was expected to maintain her dignity and even feel compassion for him.

She became aware of Nick watching her—and Sipho, too. Why couldn't she be one of those enigmatic women who hid their true feelings behind a veneer of sophistication? Concern was plain in both Sipho's and Nick's eyes, but for different reasons.

The snoek Nick had ordered took longer to prepare than Zak and Yolanda's sandwiches. Monica would have liked to have left the café first, to give a cool wave on the way out. But instead she had to smile when Zak and Yolanda departed as though her heart didn't ache. Sipho pushed his plate aside and refused to eat the rest of his meal.

"Is Zak angry with us?" asked Mandla.

"No, sweetie," whispered Monica, hoping that Nick was too engrossed in the exquisite flavors of his first-ever West Coast snoek to hear. "He just has things on his mind."

"Yes, he does," said Nick. From his wry tone, it was clear that he had reached the correct conclusion about the nature of Monica and Zak's friendship.

After the meal and a short argument over who would pay the bill, which Monica won, they walked down Main Street toward the park. Nick wanted to know the details of how Monica had helped save Sandpiper Drift, but she didn't want to talk about it and told him instead how Daphne and the women had climbed onto the roofs of their houses. When they reached the park, the boys ran ahead toward the beach.

"I'm sorry if my presence made you uncomfortable at lunch," said Nick. "Tell me if I'm being too intrusive, but I sensed that you and Zak were once an item."

Monica wanted to tell him that this didn't begin to describe what she and Zak had shared, but she felt herself tearing up and so merely nodded.

Nick stopped walking. "I'm probably going to make a giant fool of myself, but I have to tell you something. One day I just woke up and realized that I'd been an idiot not to have had the courage to ask you out. A reporter from your old radio station told me you'd gone to Lady Helen. I jumped at the chance to come down here with my friend." He paused, and Monica knew that this was where she was supposed to say, *I'm glad you did.* She could taste the words in her mouth, but she couldn't say them.

She wondered if she could grow to love Nick. He might even be able to accept a pale substitute to what she felt for Zak. But it would not be enough for her. Hadn't she, in the past few years, realized that nothing was more important than living an authentic life?

"If anything changes, I'll contact you," she said.

A stranger eavesdropping at that moment might have jumped to the conclusion that here was a woman giving a man the brush-off with an insincere promise. But it was not true, and Nick, thankfully, seemed to realize it. He seemed to understand that he'd simply chosen the wrong time to reappear in her life.

As she watched him show his guest pass at the gate of the golf resort, she felt a strange sense of loss. This chance for romance had failed before it had even gotten off the ground. Anton, Zak, Nick— all of these relationships fraught with problems. Would she ever have an intimate partnership that was smooth sailing? She glanced in the rearview mirror and saw a satisfied smile on Sipho's face.

22
///////////////

THE FOLLOWING MONDAY AFTERNOON, WHEN MONICA came home from work, she took Francina into the kitchen so they could be alone.

"You didn't tell me about Montgomery's new camera."

"I didn't think it was important."

Monica put her head out the door to make sure that Sipho and Zukisa were still busy with their homework at the dining room table. Mandla was coloring in a picture of a famous children's singing quartet. When selecting it, he'd told Monica, "One day I'm going to sing on stage, too."

Monica dropped her voice to a whisper. "I think we have our thief."

Francina put her hand over her mouth.

"I cornered Yolanda after church yesterday when Zak was speaking to Reverend van Tonder. Yolanda says Montgomery bought her a silver locket."

"Why would she tell you anything? Aren't you her enemy?"

"Ah, Francina, this is something I learned as a journalist. When you want information from a person, you offer them something first to gain their confidence."

"So what did you offer?"

"I told her that I understood why she felt I was a threat to her."

"You sold yourself out!"

"I *do* understand how she feels."

"Monica, you're brilliant. Telling her this might be the first step toward getting Zak back."

"I never said—"

"And here I thought you weren't going to put up a fight." Francina clicked her tongue. "Silly me."

"Francina, that wasn't—"

"So the money Montgomery used to buy the camera and locket came from the gallery. He'll just deny it."

Monica's eyes narrowed. "I'm not going to put pressure on Montgomery. I'm going to put pressure on Yolanda. Call it a hunch, but I think she knows something."

"Your brother used to get that look before rugby games."

Monica froze at the mention of her brother. "Do you think he would have liked it here?" she asked softly.

Francina nodded. "But he wouldn't have stayed long. This place would have been too small for him."

They smiled, remembering the spirited boy they had both loved. Francina knew that Monica was pleased to have someone here who knew her history and her people.

* * *

The next day Monica scanned the crowd of children coming out of the school. Francina and Mandla were at the gate, waiting for Sipho and Zukisa. She hoped they wouldn't notice her. Yolanda came out a few minutes after Sipho and Zukisa. She was alone.

Monica gave her a head start. She didn't want to approach the girl where anyone could see, but she had to do it before Yolanda reached the hospital—if that was where she was headed. Monica didn't feel like crying when she thought of Zak now; she just felt empty.

Yolanda stopped at the end of the next block, turned around, and, with her arms folded, waited for Monica to draw alongside.

"Why are you following me?"

"I wanted to talk to you in private."

"You mean without my dad around?"

Yolanda was once again the sullen girl Monica had picked up from her mother's house.

"Can we talk?"

Yolanda shrugged.

"Let's go for a milk shake at Mama Dlamini's."

"I'm supposed to go straight to the hospital and do my homework in my dad's office." Monica wondered if she was imagining the emphasis Yolanda placed on the word *my*.

"Get in. The wind is cold."

Yolanda got into the passenger seat, settled her backpack at her feet and stared straight at Monica. The engine clicked as it cooled. Monica found herself longing for the distractions of Mama Dlamini's Eating Establishment. She tried not to let Yolanda's scowl disconcert her, but all she could think was, *Here is the girl who won the battle for Zak, the person who ended our happiness.*

She had planned to start by reassuring Yolanda with words of support and understanding, but now she discovered that she couldn't get her tongue around them.

"I know that you know something about the robbery at the gallery," she blurted out.

Yolanda's hand went for the door.

"Wait! Where will you run to? You can't disappear like Silas." Yolanda's eyes widened at the mention of the Zimbabwean's name. "Did you know that he and Daphne were planning to get married?"

Yolanda nodded. Misery had replaced the sullen look. "I saw her outside the hospital, crying."

Monica said in a gentle voice, "You and I both know Silas is not the one who robbed the gallery."

Yolanda looked away, out the passenger window.

"It's hard to keep a secret," said Monica.

Yolanda's head whipped around. "How would you know?"

"I've kept my fair share." She thought of the abalone ladies. It was time to make Yolanda nervous. "The police could have taken me in for questioning if they'd wanted to."

Mention of the word *police* did the trick.

"My dad will kill me if the police arrive to question me. You won't tell them, will you?"

Monica shook her head. "I know you'll do the right thing."

"Montgomery said he needed the money so he could run away. He misses his friends in Cape Town."

"Is he in a gang?"

Yolanda nodded.

Monica fought the urge to ask why Yolanda would be friends with a boy like Montgomery. One day the story would come out, and Monica suspected it would have something to do with how the girl had felt toward her parents at the time. Zak would do well to send his daughter for counseling.

"I have to go to the police, don't I?" Yolanda began to cry.

Monica put her hand on the girl's shoulder. "It's the right thing to do. Silas is an innocent man."

"How am I going to tell my father?"

Monica reached across and hugged her. "I'll come with you. And if you want, I'll help you tell him."

Yolanda stopped crying. "Can you? I can't do it myself. He's going to be so angry."

Monica handed her a tissue. On the way to the hospital, Yolanda began to cry again.

Zak's face twisted with controlled rage; his fists clenched and unclenched at his sides. Monica thought of her father, who did the same thing with his hands when his temper threatened to get the better of him.

"Yolanda, I can't believe you kept this a secret."

Yolanda had not said a word while Monica had told Zak the story. The girl had just stood looking at her shoes and biting her lower lip.

"Poor Silas, running away like an animal when my own daughter knew he was not the culprit." Zak shook his head in disbelief.

"I'm sorry, Daddy."

He looked at her as though he'd never seen her before.

"It's not too late to put things right," said Monica.

Yolanda's face silently begged her father to believe Monica. "I'll tell the police," she said. "And then we can find Silas."

"Where? He could be in Botswana by now."

Monica took Yolanda's hand. "It was very brave of you to tell us the truth now."

Zak let out a long sigh. "It was," he agreed. His shoulders sagged as his anger subsided. In its place was resignation. His baby girl was growing up and he had lost control of her.

"I'll let the staff know I'm going out for a while." He left the office.

Yolanda burst into fresh tears. "He's so disappointed in me."

Monica put her arms around Yolanda. "He'll forgive you," she murmured.

At the sound of her father's returning footsteps, Yolanda pulled away and dried her tears.

"Let's go," said Zak.

"Do you want me to come along?" asked Monica.

Zak looked at Yolanda but she didn't respond.

"Thanks, but I don't think it's necessary," he said. He gave Monica a smile she could not decipher. Was it wistful or just sad?

On her way to the hospital entrance, she caught a glimpse of Daphne through one of the open doors. Daphne noticed her, she was sure of it, but the nurse kept her head down and continued checking the patient's IV fluid. Monica wondered if she should tell Daphne that the real burglar would soon be apprehended. Perhaps it was best for Zak to deliver the good news after he'd been to the police.

Monica could not get the image of his smile out of her head. The more she thought about it, the more she believed he missed her.

What if Francina were right and this whole horrible episode led to Yolanda's changing her mind about their dating? Was it possible? Or would Yolanda think back over the day's events and decide that without Monica's interference she would have been free to keep her secret?

23

ONE NIGHT, TOWARD THE END OF WINTER, HEAVY RAIN struck the tin roof with such ferocity that Mandla left his bed for Monica's, and they both lay awake, pretending together to be on a pirate ship in the middle of a stormy ocean.

In the couple of months that had passed since Monica had gone with Yolanda to tell Zak about Montgomery, she had not come face-to-face with Zak again. He had not contacted her, as she'd thought he would. The only times she saw him now were at church, and he always arrived late and was the first to leave. Monica could not forgive herself for having believed Francina that the episode with Yolanda would lead to the girl changing her mind about Zak and Monica's dating and the two of them getting back together. In spite of this, Zak was in her thoughts every day, no matter how hard she tried to block him from her mind.

The rain continued in the morning, and the boys pulled on their raincoats, hats and boots and waded through the puddles from the car to their classrooms. As Monica was getting back into her car, a milk truck raced by, and she couldn't close her door in time to avoid being drenched by its spraying tires.

Dudu handed her a towel when she arrived at the office. "It feels as though the whole town is going to be washed into the ocean."

"But the spring wildflowers will be spectacular after this," said Monica, drying her hair.

Through her office window she saw that the park and the ocean had merged in the gray light. Only the frayed tips of the palm trees, flapping wildly like rags in a car wash, were visible in the gloom. On Main Street, the irrigation ditches had overflowed, and cars were making their way slowly through two inches of water. Shivering, Monica turned up the heat to dry her clothes. She was just sitting down at her desk to begin a story on S.W.'s new art exhibit when her direct line rang.

"They're back," said Kitty.

"More poachers?"

"No, that university professor who came to look at the rock art. This time he's brought three colleagues."

Monica had spoken to this professor the last time he'd visited, and he'd assured her that he wanted only to photograph the work in order to place it in a catalog he was compiling of all the rock art in the Western Cape. It was for academic purposes only, he'd said, and would not be published.

"Where are they now?"

"Pacing the living room. As soon as the weather clears, they're going up the koppie."

"I think you'd better get out the board games. They're in for a long wait. How's baby coming along?" she asked, knowing that Kitty could go into labor at any time.

She heard her friend laugh. "I think he's almost finished cooking."

At eleven there was a break in the rain, and a wan sun sliced through the low clouds. Storekeepers and gallery owners ventured outside and stared up at the sky as though they'd been deprived of sunlight for months. The water on Main Street would take a couple of days to subside, but because the street was lower than the buildings, there would not be any damage.

Monica telephoned Kitty and was told that the university researchers had raced out the door the minute the rain stopped.

"They haven't had lunch, so I don't think they'll be away long," said Kitty.

Shortly after three, Monica drove to Abalone House. Kitty had the door open before she'd even walked up the steps.

"Come in quickly and warm yourself next to the fire. They're in there, half-frozen, muddy and as hungry as wolves. Do you want something to eat, too?"

"No, thanks. You look ready to pop."

Kitty stroked her round belly. "I certainly hope so."

Monica joined the researchers at the fire.

"Nice to see you again," said the professor she'd met before. "Let me introduce you to my colleagues."

Monica shook hands with all three men.

"So what brings you back here?" she asked.

The professor looked at the eldest of his colleagues, who shrugged.

"There has been a contention that the paintings might not be authentic."

"You mean someone other than the San people painted them?"

The professor nodded.

"But why?"

He pursed his lips. "Rock art attracts tourists. We've seen it done before."

"Nobody here would do such a thing."

He held up his hands. "Wait a minute. We have not determined that the paintings are fake. We're still comparing the photographs to others in our catalog, but my colleagues wanted to see the paintings with their own eyes. By the way, I thought you should know that a vagrant is using the cave. I suggest that you assume the paintings are genuine and get your police officers to remove him immediately."

A flash went off in Monica's head. Who else could the vagrant be but Silas?

She thanked the professor and asked that he let her know the results of his study. Kitty met her at the door to the kitchen.

"You're not leaving without having a cup of tea, are you?"

"I'd love to stay, Kitty, but I have to find Oscar to come up the koppie with me. I'll explain later. Call me if you need help getting to the hospital."

Kitty nodded. "I might need to if James is out on his boat."

"Still shark diving, even in this weather?"

Kitty nodded. "There are more crazy tourists out there than I thought."

Monica called Oscar as soon as she got into her car. He was waiting on her driveway when she arrived home.

"Dress warmly," he said, looking at her light jacket.

She rushed inside, changed into jeans and a heavy jacket, kissed the boys and told Francina that she would be back by five.

"Are you sure?" asked Francina, eyebrows raised.

"Okay, five-thirty at the latest."

Oscar was fit from hiking up and down the coast, and he and Monica reached the cave in half the time it took with Mandla and Sipho. Dark clouds had drifted in again from the ocean, enveloping the tops of the koppies and obscuring the view of the town below. Another onslaught of rain was not far off.

Oscar got down on his hands and knees and crawled into the entrance of the cave.

"There's a pile of newspapers," he called back to her. "And a bottle of water." He crawled back out again. "I wonder where he's gone."

"The mist's getting thicker." Monica could no longer see the path on which they had come up.

"He'll return soon to be somewhere dry when the rain starts again," Oscar assured her. "Don't worry, I know this koppie as well as I know my own face—and I have to tell you that I can shave in complete darkness."

"I'm not even going to ask how you discovered that talent."

They settled themselves in a crevice between boulders to escape the wind. Monica hoped that Oscar was correct when he said that it was too cold for snakes to be out.

"I saw Zak today." Oscar blew in his hands to warm them. "I don't know why you broke up, since it has made you both so miserable."

Monica was taken aback; she thought she'd done a good job of hiding her feelings.

"It wasn't our choice." She didn't offer to explain. That was up to Zak.

"Well, I still think you were made for each other."

"And what about you?"

Oscar looked away, into the mist. "There was someone once, in Trinidad."

The girl who had done what was expected of her? Monica wondered, remembering Oscar's advice about how to save a relationship. "What happened?" she asked now.

"Her father would not let her marry me because I was a white South African. He said that if I wasn't allowed to marry his daughter in my own country, then he wouldn't allow me to marry her in his country."

"And yet you still came back here?"

Oscar shrugged. "Where else would I go? I can move to another country, get a foreign passport, even learn a new language, but my heart will always be South African."

They sat in companionable silence, listening to the wind whistling through gaps in the rocks. She thought about both their hearts—his that had brought him back to South Africa, hers that had never allowed her to leave. Her introspection was interrupted by a rustling sound too marked and irregular to be the wind. They peered around the boulders to see the soles of two shoes and a man's rear end disappearing into the cave.

"Silas!" shouted Oscar, standing up.

The man stopped.

"Come out!"

The man crawled backward and ducked his head as he emerged. It *was* Silas. Monica ran toward him. His eyes scanned the boulders behind her, narrow with fear.

"It's okay, Silas. We're alone. You can come back now. The police know who really robbed the gallery."

Silas wrapped his blanket tightly around him. He did not speak.

"Daphne's going to swoon when she sees you," said Monica.

"The police will still arrest me now that they know I'm here illegally."

"You can't stay here anymore, man," said Oscar. "It's too cold. We'll wait until it gets dark and then sneak you into my house."

"And what happens tomorrow morning?" Silas did not look convinced.

An idea occurred to Monica. "Silas, if you and Daphne are planning to get married—"

"*Were* planning to get married."

"What if I can get Reverend van Tonder to come to Oscar's house first thing tomorrow to marry you? Then you can go straight to Cape Town to apply for legal residence."

Silas's eyes lit up. "Do you think he'll agree?"

"Of course," said Monica, sounding more confident than she felt. Reverend van Tonder was not known for his willingness to find a way to maneuver around the law. It would take a persuasive argument to get him there in the morning.

"I'll just clear out my bedding." Silas went back into the cave and retrieved the stack of newspapers. "I promise you that I didn't touch the paintings."

Monica could see that Oscar was itching to double-check, but out of consideration for Silas's feelings, he would restrain himself.

"Silas is not your real name, is it?" she said.

He shook his head. "I can never use my real name again, not with my family still in Zimbabwe."

"What did you survive on up here?" asked Oscar.

"Roots, berries. You know—what these guys survived on." He thumbed in the direction of the San paintings.

"Really?" Oscar's eyes were wide.

Silas shook his head. "No, those guys are amazing. I couldn't find anything. And when I did, I wasn't sure if it was safe to eat. No, I snuck down at night and got food from the Dumpster behind the dairy farm and drank from Peg's garden hose."

"You were in Lady Helen at night?" said Monica.

Silas nodded. "Once, I crept up behind Daphne's house and watched through her window as she slept. I wanted to leave her a note, but I didn't have a pen or anything to write on."

Monica prayed that Reverend van Tonder would be touched by the plight of the sweethearts who had been separated against their will.

Oscar guided them down the koppie, stopping periodically to check that Monica was keeping up in the strong wind. At Peg's farm, Oscar and Silas hid behind the barn to wait for full darkness, while Monica made her way home to alleviate Francina of her duties.

As she approached her front door, she wondered if it was futile to hope that her own bittersweet love affair would also have a happy ending.

Reverend van Tonder, as feared, was not keen on Monica's idea when she telephoned him that night.

"The man is wanted by the police."

"But you know they found the person who really robbed the gallery."

"Silas is still wanted by the police."

Monica sighed. It would not be respectful—or productive—to argue with him. Perhaps it would be better to place her appeal in the context of history. "Think about the past in this country. There were times when churches went along with the law even though that law was immoral."

"This is hardly the same, Monica."

She didn't like to beg, but if there ever was a situation that called for it… "Please, Reverend van Tonder, Silas is not a criminal. If he and Daphne don't marry, Silas will have to go away again. They're in love. Do you really think God cares about stamps in passports?"

Reverend van Tonder's sigh was deep. "Tell me where I have to go."

"They'll be at Oscar's house at seven tomorrow morning. Thank you, Reverend."

The first cool rays of the sun outlined the koppies when Monica and the boys climbed into the car. Mandla counted fading stars. He had reached forty-five by the time they arrived at Oscar's house.

Miemps and Reginald were standing close together in the living room, Reginald in a suit and tie, Miemps in a navy dress that Monica knew Francina had made a few weeks ago.

"Oh, my dear, I can't believe this is finally happening to our Daphne." Miemps squeezed Monica's hand. "Silas is the sort of man I would have chosen for her—a man of principle. And he adores her.

Last night, after you phoned, she got down on her knees and begged God to forgive her for being angry with Him. Thank you, thank you, thank you once again, Monica, for helping my family."

"Don't thank me, thank Reverend van Tonder." Monica was worried that if he wasn't swept up in the excitement of the morning, he might change his mind and return to his warm bed.

Daphne and Silas sat on the sofa, holding hands and beaming at each other. Daphne wore a flowing dress in cream floral organza and a beaded headband in her hair. Monica had never seen her looking so beautiful. Silas had bathed and shaved and no longer looked like the wild mountain man of yesterday. The suit Oscar had lent him was a little long in the pants, but nobody cared about such a small detail.

Reverend van Tonder positioned himself in front of the fireplace and welcomed everyone. As he ran through the familiar words of the wedding ceremony, Silas and Daphne clutched hands as though afraid someone would burst through the door and try to separate them. Monica wished the reverend would cut corners and get to the part where he pronounced them man and wife, but looking at Miemps and Reginald as they gazed at their daughter with pride, she knew that this was the right way.

"Do you, Daphne Cloete, take this man to be your lawfully wedded husband, to have and to—"

The doorbell rang.

"Go on, please," Monica told the reverend.

Oscar made a move toward the door.

Monica mouthed the words, *I'll deal with them.*

Icy morning air slapped her in the face as she opened the front door. "Good morning, Dewald. Good morning, Mike. Cold, isn't it?"

Dewald took a step forward, but Monica did not move out of his way. "Is Oscar home?" he asked.

Monica could hear Silas saying his vows.

Dewald heard it, too. "Let us in, Monica."

"In less than two minutes Reverend van Tonder will pronounce Silas and Daphne man and wife, and it will be too late for you to do anything. Can we not talk about the weather until it's over?"

Dewald and Mike looked at each other.

"I'm warning you, Monica. Step aside." Dewald's voice was threatening.

"One and a half minutes," said Monica. "Come on, guys. This man is in the country illegally because he was imprisoned and tortured in his own country for speaking out against a dictatorship."

Mike looked uncomfortable.

Monica seized her chance. "Compared to what you've seen as policemen over the years, is his offense that important?"

"She's right," mumbled Mike.

Dewald made a halfhearted protest about getting into trouble with their superiors in Cape Town.

"Why will there be trouble?" asked Monica. "You came as soon as you heard Silas was here, but you were too late. That's all."

Inside they heard clapping.

"See?" said Monica. "It's all over. Now come in and have some cake. I made it myself last night."

24

THE DAY AFTER THE HASTY WEDDING, THE RESIDENTS of Lady Helen awoke to find their dusty brown sentinels, the koppies, wearing ruffled skirts of lilac, orange, crimson and golden yellow. The wet end to the winter rainfall season had created perfect conditions for the germination of millions of seeds that had lain dormant under the sandy shale, and now vygies, lilies, violets, gladioli and daisies covered every inch of the slopes and, below in town, laid claim to grassy medians, sidewalks and an untended strip at the edge of the park.

In any other town, this colorful display would have heralded the start of spring. But the residents of Lady Helen were waiting for the return of the birds.

Zukisa's first days in the flat above Jabulani Dressmakers had passed too quickly for Francina, who had wanted to commit every first to memory: first dinner, first homework session, first fitting in the shop. And so now poor Zukisa had become like a celebrity, with a camera shoved in her face every time she moved. Francina did not, as she thought she would, worry about the years she had missed of Zukisa's life. Those were not hers to claim. She would never have an album of her daughter's first year of life, but she could have one for her own first year of motherhood.

At dinner that night, talk was of the wildflowers and the busloads of tourists to follow. When the meal was over, Zukisa stood up and, as she had done every evening for months since her arrival, began clearing away the plates. Francina said the same thing she'd said every evening.

"You don't have to do that."

Both Hercules and his mother gave her imploring looks.

"I don't make Sipho and Mandla help," said Francina, lifting her shoulders as though to suggest she had no idea why they didn't agree with her.

"I want to be useful," said Zukisa quietly. "I want to pay my way here."

Francina shot Hercules and his mother a look and quickly went to put her arm around Zukisa.

"You are our daughter now," she said. "You are not a lodger who has to pay her way."

Zukisa considered this for a while. "I want to be a good daughter—and a good daughter helps."

Out of the corner of her eye Francina could see her mother-in-law nodding.

"Well, okay," said Francina. "But remember that your homework comes first. You're not going to be like me, cleaning houses and trying to get an education at forty-one. You're going to finish school and then you're going to university."

Zukisa hovered, as though waiting to be dismissed.

"To study anything you want to. Right?" said Hercules, looking pointedly at his wife.

She narrowed her eyes as she held his gaze.

"Right?" repeated Hercules.

Francina gave a stiff nod and rose from the table to help Zukisa before Hercules could roll up his shirtsleeves and put his hands in the sink.

With Francina washing and Zukisa drying, the work progressed quickly. Francina held her tongue as Zukisa opened and shut all the kitchen cupboards to find the correct homes for pots, plates and cutlery. This was one way she could prove to Hercules that she could be hands-off. When Zukisa opened a third cupboard to find the place for the grater, Francina hummed a tune to distract herself.

"I'm glad to be back at school," said Zukisa when she found what she thought was the right place and put the grater away.

Francina winced. It did not belong with the mixing bowls, but she would force herself to let it be for now.

"You quickly caught up what you'd missed."

Zukisa smiled. "My new father helped me a lot. He's a patient teacher."

Francina had suspended her own lessons with Hercules while the child had caught up the work she'd missed.

When the sink had been emptied, Francina sat down at the tiny kitchen table to wait for Zukisa to finish the last of the kitchen cleanup, and as she did, she heard the crinkle of paper in her pocket. She hadn't meant to keep the letter a secret from her family, but her concerns were not meant for the ears of a ten-year-old child, who might conclude that her new mother did not approve of interracial marriage when that was far from the truth.

Against Francina's advice, her brother Sigidi had married his white girlfriend before the year of mourning for their father was over. How would Francina explain to Zukisa that it was a combination of events that made Sigidi's written words taste sour on her lips as she read them out loud? In some parts of the country, especially rural ones, acceptance of change came slowly. Nobody in Francina's village had ever married a white person, and that alone would set tongues wagging—even more so on top of the marriage happening before the one-year anniversary of their father's death.

Sigidi had been raised in the same house as Francina, but by moving away he had become part of the new generation that had no patience, wanting everything yesterday. Francina wondered if her brother's bride was pregnant; this would be a reasonable explanation for rushing into marriage. One day Francina might have a niece or nephew with skin as light as Monica's.

A letter like this begged a response, but what would that be? It was too late to change the action. Sigidi had proved that he didn't listen to his sister's advice. Would he heed it this time if she told him not to take his bride home until the year was up?

She watched Zukisa shining the sink with an old rag, and tears filled her eyes. Her brother might have a baby on the way, but she had hers already. Praise be to God. He had certainly rewarded her patience.

* * *

Monica sat at her desk in her office, admiring the bowl of yellow-and-white daisies Mandla had picked for her on the outskirts of Peg's Dairy Farm. It was against the rules to pick flowers, but he'd presented them to her with a look of such pure adoration on his face that she couldn't bring herself to reprimand him.

Next to the flowers, her in-box of story ideas beckoned, but Monica was too irritated to concentrate. Earlier that morning she'd run into Anna, who was on her way to the golf resort with a bag of abalone. Anna had simply lifted her hands, as if to say, what did you expect? And what had Monica expected? She hadn't offered the abalone ladies an alternative, and it was obvious that the police would not keep up their daily watch of the beach. The boxes of groceries she left outside their houses every week were only a temporary patch on a more serious problem.

Dudu poked her head through the doorway. "Tea?"

"Yes, please."

At least there was one person in the office this morning whose spirits were high. Dudu had not finished her graphics course yet, but she loved it so much that Monica had already given her the responsibility for laying out the newspaper.

Monica stared at her computer screen where she had typed the words *Researchers test rock art for authenticity*. She thought of Silas and Daphne, the newlyweds, happily settled in the Old Garage. Had Silas carried his bride over the threshold after the wedding? Monica had scattered bougainvillea petals all over the studio apartment in anticipation of their arrival. She pictured the smile on Daphne's face, all the more dazzling for its rarity, and wondered if she, herself, would ever fall in love again.

The computer's screen saver appeared. Fifteen minutes and she'd only written a title. When Dudu returned with two cups of tea, Monica invited her to sit down.

"Phutole's doing much better at school," said Dudu, setting her cup on its saucer. "Your advice about taking him outdoors to play before school really worked."

"I'm glad."

"You're definitely a natural at solving problems."

Monica could not stop a sneer from forming on her lips. "Not everybody's."

Dudu put her hand to her forehead. "That reminds me. He sounded as though he had a big problem."

"Who?"

"He called while you were in the bathroom, and I got so involved in doing the layout that I forgot to give you the message. Dr. Niemand. I'm sorry."

Monica tried to speak evenly. "That's okay."

She drank the rest of her tea as fast as she could without burning her mouth. Dudu, she noticed, tried to do the same but could not. When Monica's cup was empty, Dudu rose.

"Stay and finish," said Monica.

"The layout is calling me."

They both knew it was a pretense, and Monica was not surprised when Dudu closed the door—that usually remained open—behind her.

She wondered if she would catch Zak on his private line in his office or if she would have to page him and interrupt his work.

She dialed his office. He usually picked up on the second ring. She was about to put the receiver down when she heard his voice.

"Zak Niemand. Hello."

Her courage failed her.

"Hello? Hello?"

"Hi, Zak."

"Monica!" It was an exclamation, the kind usually followed by an explanation for the speaker's excitement, but Zak gave none.

"Dudu said you phoned." She was not going to make this easier for him by initiating small talk.

"I hate telephones. Can we meet? Please."

"I have some time free this afternoon at around four."

"I meant now."

"Oh."

"It's important. Can you meet me in the park in five minutes?"

The wind was gusting down Main Street. Near the beach it would be even more powerful.

"It's the only place we can be sure there won't be anyone else."

She replaced the receiver, grabbed her coat and told Dudu that she had a meeting to go to. The success of her subterfuge, she had learned, could be gauged from the angle of Dudu's eyebrows. This time they swooped right up like swallows taking flight. Monica hurried out, afraid that every emotion she felt was shining on her face.

Zak was waiting on the bench for her, hunched against the cold. She paused to pull her collar up and tighten the scarf around her neck before walking toward him. He stood up when he saw her.

"Thanks for coming." She read his lips, but the words were whipped away by the wind.

They would have to be close to hear each other. He pointed at the bench, and she sat down, leaving a space between them. There were dark shadows under his eyes and his face seemed thinner.

"I wanted to say thanks—a very belated thanks."

"What for?" She knew it was a stupid reply.

"You saw that something was up with Yolanda when I didn't. You helped her get out of a situation she would have regretted for the rest of her life."

"Sometimes a little push in the right direction is all it takes. And it wasn't just me who noticed something was amiss. Francina did, too."

Although she didn't hear it, the way he raised and dropped his shoulders told her that he'd let out a loud sigh. "I'm making a mess of being a single parent. Girls do better confiding in their mothers."

"Some of this may be my fault. Yolanda felt that I was elbowing her out."

He took off his glasses and rubbed his eyes.

"You didn't deserve this, Monica. You always wanted what was best for her."

"You did what you had to. Yolanda has to be happy with things—" she wanted to say *us* "—or it will affect her for the rest of her life." She thought of her own parents' dysfunctional marriage.

He sighed again, and she sensed that there was something he wanted to say but lacked the nerve. Did he want to ask for her forgiveness so they could greet each other like old friends whenever they ran into each other in town? Or was he working up the courage to ask her for another chance?

"Over the past couple of months, Yolanda has changed her mind about you." He had to shout to be heard over the wind.

She moved closer to him so that he could speak normally, and he smiled at her.

"I know that this might not make any difference to you now and I know that you might despise me for choosing my daughter over you, but—"

"I don't despise you, Zak. You're a wonderful father who doesn't want his daughter to be hurt any more than she has been. Perhaps it was only our timing that was wrong."

A slow smile spread over his face as he realized the full import of her words. "Does that mean we can try again?" He wanted to hear her say it.

She smiled at him and touched his cheek. If she could do anything for him now, she would tuck him into bed for a long nap.

Lightly he took her cold hand and brought it to his lips. Then he moved in close till their faces were an inch apart.

"I love you, Monica. I don't want to be without you." He leaned in and kissed her.

When they finally pulled apart, the wind had died down. Five or six palm tree fronds lay on the grass. Monica touched her face and realized that she was covered in a fine layer of beach sand. Zak was, too. In their absorption with each other, they hadn't noticed the consequence of their open-air privacy. Laughing softly, Zak shook out his scarf and then used it to gently wipe her face.

25

〈〈〈〈〈〈〈〈〈〈〈〈〈〈〈

THE FOLLOWING WEEK, THE DAYS GREW WARMER, AND
Monica and the boys exchanged their jackets for light sweaters,
which were not needed by noon. Wispy clouds skittered across the
sky, pure white against the arching blue. The koppies' colorful skirts
had faded slightly, but still drew busloads of tourists daily.

On Saturday afternoon, at Sipho's urging, Monica, Zak, Yolanda and
the boys set off from the church parking lot across the mud, heading
toward the sharp glint of the lagoon. As they listened to the sucking
sounds of their boots in the mud, they became aware of another
sound, high-pitched and frantic, coming from behind the church.

"They're here," shouted Sipho, taking off at a sprint.

Monica had wondered if the migratory birds would again make
an appearance, to great fanfare, during the Sunday church service,
but it seemed that this year they had chosen to avoid the Sabbath.

At first, Monica thought Sipho's shouts were of excitement, then she realized that he was in distress. She and Zak took off running at the same time and found Sipho at the edge of the lagoon, throwing stones into the water. When Mandla had caught up, he gazed at his brother with joyful disbelief—this was something *he* liked to do and Sipho usually restrained him. The object of Sipho's fury was standing knee-deep in the water, the pale, limp leg of a bird hanging from its mouth.

"Go away!" Sipho threw another stone that missed its mark by a wide stretch.

A writhing, shifting shadow covered the lagoon as the birds hovered and drifted and made wide circles in the air, waiting for the predator to leave. Unwilling to give up its catch and waiting for more to fall from the sky, the bat-eared fox remained immobile in the water, while the shrieks of the birds rent the air, growing louder, shriller, more desperate. In the distance, a dog began to howl.

Zak bent to pick up a stone. His shot hit the fox squarely on the back. The indignant animal turned his sharp head to look at the waving figures on the bank of the lagoon and then looked up at the flurry of agitated birds, as though weighing the reward against the risk. His jaws opened and the limp leg slid down his throat. If he couldn't have more of them, he was not going to lose this one while making his getaway. As he churned through the water, his legs lost touch with the bottom of the lagoon and he was forced to swim to the far bank. When he reached the other side, he shook his wet fur, gave one last desultory glance in his spoilers' direction and crashed through the papery reeds.

"Thank you, Zak." Sipho's face glowed.

"I spent my holidays on my grandparents' farm trying to hit anthills and tin cans. I'm glad it wasn't a pure waste of time."

"I didn't know you were a farm boy," said Monica.

Zak put his arm around her. "There's a lot you still have to find out about me."

It was the first time since they'd made up that Zak had touched her in front of the children. She saw Yolanda looking at them, her face impassive. Monica wanted to smile at her, but she didn't want it interpreted as a smile of victory. As Yolanda continued to stare, Monica considered politely stepping away from Zak's embrace. But then Yolanda's face broke into a wide grin, she tossed her hair over her shoulder and ran off to join Mandla at the water's edge.

Monica and Zak watched the birds landing: dropping out of the sky like dive-bombers, coming in slowly with air under their wings, making a loud splash, or landing almost soundlessly. There was no sign of the seagulls that had lorded over the lagoon in the winter. Like the fox, the gulls had heard the approaching birds, but had responded by skulking off back to the beach, squawking in impotent fury. The season had changed. Spring was officially here. Sipho punched the air in excitement.

That night, Zak and Yolanda joined Monica and the boys for their special Saturday dinner.

"Don't touch the candles," warned Mandla.

Zak rubbed Mandla's head. "Good advice, my little man."

After they'd finished eating, Zak helped Monica clear the table while the children went into the living room to set up a board game. Monica was standing at the sink when Zak came up behind her and nuzzled her ear.

"We make a happy little family, don't we?"

It sounded like a rhetorical question. Was Zak working himself up to ask *the* question?

"Mmm," she said, scrubbing a pot.

"I was thinking that——"

The telephone rang in the entrance hall.

"Leave it," he said as she hurriedly dried her hands.

She flicked him on the chest with the dish towel and went to answer it. He had started on the pots when she returned.

"It was James. Kitty's gone into labor."

He quickly rinsed the pot. "Adelaide's on call tonight. She'll be paging me any minute. Can I leave Yolanda with you?"

"Of course."

He stooped to kiss her. "We'll finish our conversation another time."

So he had been working himself up to something.

"If I'm late…" he began.

"Yolanda can stay overnight. Sipho will be disappointed. He was hoping to beat you at checkers tonight." Listening to herself, she was struck by how domestic—and right—her words sounded.

He kissed her again and then went into the living room to tell Yolanda he had to leave. Strange as it was, not one word of complaint had come from the children about how long it was taking for the grown-ups to start the game. It was as though they'd decided to give their parents time alone together.

As Monica waved goodbye to Zak, she saw a light go on in the Old Garage. Silas and Daphne had arrived home after having dinner with Miemps and Reginald. They would be moving in a week, not to Cape

Town, as Miemps had feared, but to a one-bedroom flat on Main Street. Mama Dlamini would be their new landlady. When Silas's permanent-residence permit arrived, he would resume doing odd jobs at the hospital, since his real job would not pay a living wage, if anything at all. Silas had contacted an ex-colleague who he'd heard was in Cape Town, and together they were starting a weekly newspaper, which they planned to truck into Zimbabwe as traded goods. They had already enlisted a group of secret correspondents in the country to supply them with news, and Gift's son Justice had designed a Web site to solicit donations from people all over the world who were concerned about the demise of democracy and freedom in Zimbabwe.

Monica would miss Silas and Daphne, but her mother would be arriving soon, and Monica wanted to show off how comfortable life could be in the Old Garage.

The next morning after church Monica took the boys and Yolanda to the hospital to see Kitty and her baby girl.

The new mother had just finished nursing when they entered the ward. The new father, James, was slumped in a chair in the corner, asleep.

"She looks like you," whispered Monica to Kitty.

The baby girl's dark hair stood up just as Kitty's did in the morning.

Kitty put the baby back in the bassinet so the children could admire her from all angles. She lowered her voice to address Monica. "I have a feeling that Zak came straight from dinner to deliver her. I wonder who he was with?"

Monica turned away, but not before Kitty saw the blush on her cheeks.

"I knew it," whispered Kitty. "Abalone House will be the perfect place for your wedding."

"Stop it." Monica was nervous the children would hear.

"He seems very relaxed and happy."

Monica changed the subject. "You look tired. How are you going to manage running Abalone House?"

Kitty looked at her sleeping husband, who had stirred briefly when his hand slipped off the armrest of the chair. "He's so busy with shark diving, I suppose I'll have to hire someone."

"I have the perfect person for you. She's the mother of a baby herself, so she'll be able to give you advice and help you in that department, too."

"If she has a baby, she won't have much time, will she?"

"Longer than you think, if you allow her to bring her baby to work with you. And if you need more help, I have someone else in mind, too."

Kitty agreed to interview the two women as soon as she was home from the hospital. "You know, Monica, you should register as a candidate for the mayoral race."

Monica shook her head. "Oh, no. I'll put profiles of the candidates in the paper, but that will be the extent of my involvement in the election."

"You'd make a great mayor."

"Not while the boys are still so young."

Kitty was too exhausted to argue.

James woke up as Monica and the children were leaving.

"Congratulations," she said, shaking his hand. Despite knowing him a long time, she still didn't feel comfortable enough to give him a kiss on the cheek. Mandla shook his hand, but Sipho only mumbled hello.

That evening, she racked her brain to think of possible positions for the remaining two abalone ladies.

The next morning, a plate of Mama Dlamini's scones was waiting for her in her office. Dudu's gesture was not only thoughtful, it gave Monica a brilliant idea. Mama Dlamini needed help in the busy summer season; all Monica had to do was persuade her to take someone on full-time. Before the lunch rush, Monica would take a walk to the café and speak to Mama Dlamini. Three down, one more to go.

Dudu put her head in her office.

"Be careful going into the storeroom. A delivery of supplies arrived early this morning, and I haven't had time to unpack the boxes. I'm trying to finish the layout."

Of course! The answer was under her nose. If anyone needed help, it was Dudu. Now that she was doing the layout for the *Lady Helen Herald,* Monica could not expect her to still do all the filing, cleaning, organizing, tea brewing and countless other things that made the office run smoothly.

"I'm going to get somebody to help you," said Monica.

"Does this mean I'm being promoted?"

Monica thought for a couple of seconds. "I suppose it does. Congratulations. You're the *Lady Helen Herald*'s new design director."

Dudu clapped her hands together. "This calls for a cup of tea."

"I'm sorry, but I won't be able to pay you more."

"That doesn't matter."

"And I won't be able to give you a new office since you'll still need to greet visitors in reception."

Dudu shook her head. "I've found something that I'm good at. You don't know how happy that makes me."

Monica smiled mischievously. "Maybe *I* should make the tea to celebrate?"

Unaware that she was being teased, Dudu shook her head dramatically. "Oh, no. Promotion or not, that will always be my job."

That afternoon, after having secured a promise from Mama Dlamini to hire one of the abalone ladies, Monica set off for Anna's house. She owed Nick an apology; he knew more about small-town life than she'd presumed. People in Lady Helen could be persuaded after all. She should have plucked up the courage to test his suggestion long ago.

Standing at Anna's door, Monica heard low voices inside. She had called to tell Anna that she was coming, and Anna had reluctantly agreed to invite the other ladies. The voices stopped when Monica knocked.

Anna opened the door. "They're all here."

The ladies stared in silence as Monica sat in the chair offered to her. How did she begin? As with everything she did in Lady Helen, this required a delicate touch—and a bit of what Ella used to call the "Ella Nkhoma shake and bake" and Monica called spin.

Here we go, she thought. "Ladies, I have wonderful news." She looked from one face to the next. "We all know jobs are hard to find in this country, but I have managed to find something for each of you."

The ladies looked at each other in surprise.

"We had perfectly good jobs selling abalone," said Anna, handing her baby a teething ring.

Monica searched the ladies' faces for the light of recognition of the irony in this statement, but there was none. Selling abalone was something these women had done for so many years that the matter of its legality had long been forgotten. They were unable to comprehend how the law could control what nature provided, what was right outside their doors, ready for picking.

"What kind of jobs?" asked the oldest lady.

Monica explained the options and told them the salaries. Before she had finished speaking, the ladies were shaking their heads.

"We were earning more in a couple of hours than what you're offering for a whole day," said the oldest lady.

It was time for Monica to play tough. "Yes, but it's an illegal activity."

"What about my baby?" said Anna.

Monica smiled. She had made a breakthrough. "Kitty says you can take him to work."

"We need time to think about this," said the oldest lady.

Monica stood up to leave. "I'll come back in fifteen minutes."

As she walked toward the beach, she saw a group of pelicans flying low along the water's lacy edge. There was nobody in sight, only a few sullen seagulls pecking at strands of washed-up seaweed. With the beach so close, it was easy to see why Anna was frustrated that a piece of paper drawn by parliament could prevent her from doing what was natural.

If the women formed a small company, they might be able to apply for a commercial abalone license. These were scarce and, as word had it, not allotted fairly, but Monica might be able to find a way to help them in the future; stranger things had happened in Lady Helen.

She turned to look at the whitewashed fishermen's cottage and wondered if the thick walls were masking the sounds of a heated argument between Anna, who was obviously ready to accept Monica's proposal, and the oldest lady, who was cantankerously resistant to change. Or perhaps the ladies were having tea and playing with the baby, their last stand nothing but a show to make the capitulation, when it came, less mortifying.

When the fifteen minutes were up, Monica knocked on the door and was admitted to the living room by an obviously less stern Anna.

"We're all in agreement," said the oldest lady. "And we've decided who wants to do which job."

Monica had thought that the employers would be the ones to decide this, but she decided to allow the power to shift to the abalone ladies in this area; they were giving up so much already.

"Good," said Monica. "I'll tell Kitty and Mama Dlamini. They'll be pleased."

"So you came through after all," said the oldest lady. "It wasn't the solution we hoped for, but it's a solution."

And Monica knew that this was all the thanks she would get right now. In the months to come, when the ladies considered what might have happened to them if the police had caught them poaching, they might look back on Monica's efforts with more generosity. But she did not need thanks; solving a problem was a reward in itself.

26

FOUR AIRLINERS FROM EUROPE HAD TOUCHED DOWN within minutes of each other, and people were crammed around the baggage-claim exit, craning their necks, waving signs, clutching bouquets of proteas and digital cameras.

"Excuse me, I've got to see my nonna," said Mandla, diving into the crowd.

Monica had no choice but to follow, apologizing profusely.

The spring flowers were gone, but every summer the warm sun and sandy beaches of Cape Town lured hundreds of thousands of Europeans from their artificially heated homes under low, sodden skies.

Mandla had made it to the guardrail.

"I'm sorry," said Monica as she and Sipho squeezed between two scowling heavyset men to join him. She ought to have stopped him, but his excitement gave her pleasure; her mother was clearly not just a lady far away who sent him birthday and Christmas cards.

Mirinda Brunetti would arrive looking as though she'd stepped out of a fashion magazine, but she didn't seem to be as concerned about sticky hands and muddy shoes as she had been when Monica was a child. Monica wondered if she had noticed the change in herself.

"There she is!" shouted Mandla with such unadulterated joy that the people around him smiled.

Mirinda, wearing a cream linen suit and high heels, hurried forward to greet them and pick up Mandla. Monica noticed a few hands cupped over mouths for privacy—some people needed more time to get used to certain sights, such as a little black boy greeting his white grandmother. Mirinda hugged Sipho and kissed him on the neck. She turned to Monica.

"You look wonderful. Who is he?"

"Mom," said Monica, feeling herself blush for the umpteenth infuriating time since she'd first developed an interest in Zak.

"He's Dr. Nobody," said Mandla, slapping his thigh. "Get it, Sipho?" Sipho rolled his eyes.

Mandla looked to Monica to explain his joke to Nonna.

"His name is Zak Niemand."

Her mother's face, makeup perfectly reapplied before landing, registered surprise.

"Afrikaans *and* a doctor?"

"His father's Afrikaans."

"Why didn't you mention him in your letters?"

Monica waited till the boys were engaged in conversation with each other before answering. "We had a few problems."

"And now they're sorted out and you're getting married?"

"There's been no talk of marriage."

Monica tried not to be irritated that her mother was enthusiastic about a man she had never met, simply because he was a doctor.

"He's very nice," she said, hoping to make her mother feel guilty.

"I'm sure he is. He's a doctor."

Monica knew that she had to change the subject; she couldn't allow her mother to get under her skin before they'd even left the airport.

"Sipho, Mandla, let's go show Lady Helen to Nonna."

Mandla skipped to his grandmother's side and took her hand. "Did you bring me a present?"

"Mandla!" said Sipho.

"Of course I did. We'll pop open my suitcase as soon as your mother leads us to her car."

Monica was secretly pleased at the easy way her mother referred to her as the boys' mother.

On the way home Monica stopped at the top of the koppie and watched her mother's expression as she looked down on beautiful, seductive Lady Helen. In a way, Monica was glad that her father was not here to rush the moment. Mirinda was more appreciative than her husband of aesthetic beauty—sometimes a little too much—but Monica planned to make use of every tactic she could to get her parents to move to Lady Helen, at least for part of every year.

After Mandla had taken Mirinda on a tour of the house and garden, he led her to the Old Garage.

"Don't worry, there's no tools and lawn mower in here anymore," he told her.

"It's lovely."

Monica stopped to listen at the door.

"I hope you don't get scared out here, because Sipho and me want you to come and live here."

Monica strained to catch her mother's reply.

"We'll have to get Nonno here on holiday first. And then we'll all work on persuading him."

Monica smiled. Gift was right when she said that once you saw Lady Helen you always returned.

"Monica, stop eavesdropping and come in."

Rolling her eyes, Monica joined her mother and son on the bed.

"So when are we going to meet your boyfriend?"

"Mom, please." Next, Mirinda would be asking Mandla what he thought about having Zak for a father.

"Mandla, tell me about this—"

"It's time to wash your hands for lunch," interrupted Monica.

Mandla rose and moved slowly toward the door. "He's funny. You'll see, Nonna—tonight when he comes for dinner. And Yolanda used to be mean, but now she's nice."

"Yolanda?"

"His daughter."

"So he's been married before?"

Monica saw a shadow pass over her mother's face. "Yes."

"Never mind. You can't have everything."

Monica had to force herself to accompany Mandla out of the room. Before falling asleep last night, she had promised herself that she would not bicker with her mother in front of the children, as her parents had done incessantly for years. But her memory of her mother must have deceived her, because last night this goal had seemed attainable.

Francina's flat was lemony-clean, as always, the table set with teacups and a freshly baked cake, and downstairs, waiting for Mirinda's critical eye, were two completed and three nearly completed orders. But Francina had more on her mind than the impending visit of her former employer. If not for the crinkle of paper in her pocket every time she moved, she would feel excited about showing off her new life to Mirinda.

It was a shame that the second half of her mother's letter had upset her so much when the first half had made her whoop with joy. Two weeks ago a crew of government workers had arrived in her family's village and begun digging trenches. This past week they had laid pipes. By the end of the month every home would be connected to municipal water.

Can you just imagine? Francina's mother had written. *No more going to the communal tap in the village, and a flushing toilet just like the ones in the lodge? God has truly blessed us.*

But then the news of her brother. Sigidi had ignored Francina's advice again and taken his new white bride home. Her mother was sad that he had shown disrespect for his father's memory by marrying during the period of mourning, but not wanting to ruin Sigidi's obvious happiness, she'd said nothing. In her mother's words, the girl was *friendly and sweet.* But the villagers had not been kind. They'd stared and whispered, and the elderly women had refused to greet her. Sigidi had taken her back to Durban in tears.

As the minutes before Mirinda's visit ticked by, Francina's outrage grew. For years the villagers had treated her much the same way. Tomorrow after church, when she was calmer, she would write to her mother and tell her to warn the villagers that if they didn't change their attitude toward her new sister-in-law, they would get a tirade such as they'd never heard before when she came home for the one-year anniversary of her father's death. If she could make their chief, Winston, see the error of his ways by threatening to expose his past life of drinking and gambling, then the villagers wouldn't amount to much of a challenge. This wife of a history teacher would not allow history to be repeated.

With a plan formulated at last, she began to relax, and when the knock came on the shop door, she hurried downstairs, eager to welcome for the first time into her home the woman for whom she had cooked and cleaned for more than twenty years.

The whole time they were at Francina's flat, Monica prayed her mother wouldn't say anything insensitive. Francina had long out-grown her role of humble maid and would be a fiery match for Mirinda. But it didn't happen. The two women, who had once seemed as likely to become friends as a cat and a mouse, found some-thing that put them on an even footing: fashion.

"If only I'd known you could make dresses like this," Mirinda kept saying.

She marveled at the half-made creations hanging on the rack, at the two completed dresses and photographs of orders that had long since been picked up and worn to special events. She felt the fabrics between her thumb and forefinger and paged through design magazines. At one point Monica realized that if she slipped away, neither her mother nor Francina would notice. If Mandla hadn't complained that he was thirsty, they all might have been there the whole afternoon.

As Francina led the way upstairs, Monica sensed apprehension in her mother; never before had she been invited into Francina's home.

The fact that Mirinda was unable to hide her surprise when she entered the flat should have angered Francina, but she seemed genuinely pleased with the compliments on her decor, drapes and furniture and not at all offended when Mirinda mentioned—without even the slightest embarrassment at her patronizing tone—that Francina's was the cleanest flat she had ever been in.

The absurdity of the situation did not escape Monica; Francina knew things about her mother that her father might not even know, and yet when it came to knowing Francina, Mirinda was as ignorant as if this had been their first meeting.

Downstairs, the bells on the shop door tinkled.

"My family," announced Francina with obvious pride.

Mrs. Shabalala came up the stairs first, puffing only slightly after her considerable weight loss. She was followed by Hercules and Zukisa. The three of them had been to church to meet a visiting choir director.

"This is my husband, daughter and mother-in-law," said Francina, spreading her arms as though she might gather them to her bosom.

Hercules shook hands with Mirinda, but Mrs. Shabalala, who was part of the old school in which ladies did not shake hands, nodded and smiled.

At the end of the visit Francina asked Monica if she would be taking the boys to hear the visiting choir that evening in the amphitheater at the park.

"They're from near my village," she added.

"Zak's coming to dinner," said Mirinda.

"Ah, I see." Francina gave Mirinda a knowing look and nodded to show her appreciation for the man.

"Don't worry, you'll hear the choir in church tomorrow," said Hercules. He gave Francina a sideways look. "Our choir will also be singing something in Zulu."

"We will? None of the other ladies speaks Zulu."

"I know," said Hercules. "But you do."

Francina shook her head. "Oh, no, I'm not singing a solo."

"You have a great voice."

"Maybe, but it's one that harmonizes well with others, not one that wants to be heard alone."

"Reverend van Tonder requested it."

"You just take note of this, Monica, for when you and Zak get married. What's the English word I'm looking for? Something to do with trains. *Railroaded*—that's it."

Francina and Mirinda nodded at each other like members of a secret club.

Monica's face burned with the talk of marriage in front of Hercules and his mother. Mrs. Shabalala's best friend was Mama Dlamini, the most socially connected person in Lady Helen. If she got wind of this, by lunchtime tomorrow Zak would learn from someone else that he was about to be married. As they filed downstairs, she heard Francina inviting her mother to come back for a fitting.

Gift arrived to pick up Mrs. Shabalala for the concert while the family was still eating their dinner of *bokkoms* soup. Zukisa, who had grown up on the West Coast, adored the salted, dried mullet that was caught locally, but Francina thought it tasted like seaweed.

Hercules went to answer the door while his mother fetched her sweater for the cool summer evening. Francina would never have guessed that these two women would become friends. Gift had traveled all over the country exhibiting her art and had even gone to Europe once. Before she had moved to Lady Helen, Mrs. Shabalala had only left the small town of Dundee twice—to attend funerals for her aunts in Durban—and since her marriage had never worked outside the home.

Francina and Zukisa heard Gift laugh; Hercules could be amusing sometimes without intending to be. It was the serious voice he used, even for ordinary, everyday observances. Another person might tell you that rain was expected and you'd remind yourself to take your umbrella; with Hercules you'd be forgiven for wanting to go out and make sandbags to protect your house. Some giggled politely, but Gift always laughed out loud.

Francina and Zukisa were doing the dishes when Hercules returned.

"I don't know if I'll ever understand artists," he said. "Some don't want to talk at all when you meet them on the street. And then there's Gift, who laughs at everything I say as though I'm the most amusing man in the world. I know I'm not."

Francina found it funny that he thought it necessary to point this out to her. "*I* think you're amusing."

Twenty minutes later, the three of them were walking down Main Street, Zukisa skipping a few paces ahead. Hercules followed the girl with his eyes.

"I want to make this a permanent arrangement," Francina said.

Hercules understood immediately. "Then we'll visit Zukisa's aunt and ask if we can legally adopt her."

"Monica knows a lawyer in Johannesburg who can help us."

Zukisa waited for them at the entrance to the park. A fresh breeze blew off the ocean, and Francina made Zukisa put on her jacket. More than half the town had turned out for the concert, and since Francina's family was not on time, they would not be able to get closer than the back row. The wonderful thing about an amphitheater was that latecomers always got a good view from high up. Tonight, however, the waves were especially loud, and though Francina could hear the singers' voices, she would have preferred to feel the vibrations of sound, as she and Hercules had when their choirs sang indoors at competitions.

Hercules squeezed her hand as the visiting group began a hymn of praise that had once been the signature song of Francina's choir back in Johannesburg. Hercules had a deep respect for music and would not talk while the concert was under way. Listening to the language of her people, her daughter's small fingers entwined with her own, Francina stopped worrying that her voice would falter in church tomorrow. This beautiful language deserved to be shared, and she would do it with such enthusiasm that the members of her congregation would *feel* the music deep in the marrow of their bones.

After the concert, Hercules introduced Francina to the portly choir director who would be attending their church service the next day.

"Thank you for coming." The pastor gave her a warm hug and then took a step forward to hug Hercules, but Hercules quickly bent down to answer a question that Francina knew Zukisa had not asked. She wanted to laugh at the look of horror on his face. Hercules would never be comfortable with casual physical contact.

"We hope that you can join us for lunch tomorrow." Without looking in her husband's direction, she knew that he was staring at her in disbelief. "And bring your group, too." She didn't dare meet Hercules's eyes. There were ten people in the group.

"Thank you," said the choir director.

A waitress from Mama Dlamini's Eating Establishment approached the choir director with an invitation for the entire group to enjoy a late dinner. Judging by the size of the man's waistline, invitations to celebratory meals were a common occurrence.

The waitress addressed Francina and Hercules. "Mama Dlamini told me to invite you, too."

"Please thank Mama Dlamini for her invitation," said Francina, "but we are very tired and have to get up early to rehearse for my solo."

Renewed panic at the thought of performing in front of these gifted singers welled up inside her like nausea.

"Thank you for not accepting Mama Dlamini's invitation tonight," said Hercules as they walked toward Main Street.

"Husband, I know your wishes before you even utter them. And I promise you, tomorrow's lunch will be our last social event for a while. Zukisa and I need to start preparing for the end-of-year exams."

27

THE BLEARY-EYED VISITING CHOIR UNEXPECTEDLY CUT
their program short by two songs, and Francina was caught unawares
when Reverend van Tonder announced her Zulu solo.

Monica could tell she was nervous by the way she held herself completely still, like a soldier waiting for orders. Hercules raised the famous
retractable baton that had been in his possession ever since he was a
teenager, and as he lowered it, Francina began to sing unaccompanied
in her mezzo-soprano voice. Since the congregation had not been given
a handout with the English translation, Monica listened as one might
to the beautiful playing of a harp. Hercules's baton moved more rapidly
and Francina's voice increased tempo. She swayed from side to side,
and the other ladies of the choir followed, clicking their fingers to
keep time.

Out of the corner of her eye Monica saw her mother watching Zak. Today, at his suggestion, they all sat together in church.

"I don't care if the whole town knows about us," he'd said.

At dinner the previous evening Monica had come close to kicking her mother under the table for hanging on to his every word like a love-struck teenager. Just after nine her mother had gone to bed, claiming to be exhausted. This was a lie, since she'd slept for eight hours on the flight, and Monica was reminded of the time her mother and father had made an excuse to leave her alone with Anton so that Anton could propose. How different—and empty—her life would have been if she'd given in to habit and history and accepted his proposal.

The visiting choir director stood up to dance and urged his singers to join him. Only five did; unbelievably, the others had fallen asleep. In one of the back pews, Mama Dlamini and the small group of Zulus that belonged to the Little Church of the Lagoon clapped in accompaniment. Francina carried the final note for a full thirty seconds—Sipho timed her—and then she bowed as the congregation erupted into applause.

After the service, Monica and Sipho joined the throng gathered around Francina.

"How's my big boy?" Normally Francina would have put her hand on Sipho's head, but she knew better in a public place. She had often remarked that Sipho could be Hercules's son, they were so alike.

Monica and Sipho went to get Mandla and found him sitting on his Sunday school teacher's lap, listening to a Bible story.

"You can leave him with me for as long as you want," said the teacher, a high school senior. "He's a sweetheart."

Mandla looked up at her with the face of someone who had never done anything naughty in his life. Sipho rolled his eyes.

"Let's go, sweetie," said Monica.

Mandla reached up and hugged his teacher's neck. If the girl had been a cat, she would have purred.

"The whimbrels had the most babies this year," commented Sipho as they stepped into the bright sunshine and heard the cries of thousands of birds.

Monica held Mandla's collar to stop him from running up to the water's edge and clapping his hands. He loved to see the birds take off together.

Francina and her family left with the visiting choir, and before long the only people at the edge of the lagoon were Monica, her mother, Zak and the children. Mandla's shirt was spattered with mud, and there were two dark patches on his knees from where he'd fallen. Sipho and Yolanda wandered off to get a closer look at black-and-white baby shelducks learning to swim. Mandla grabbed Mirinda's hand and dragged her toward a pile of stones he had collected the previous Sunday.

"Watch this, Nonna." He skipped a smooth flat stone across the water. Monica watched him instruct her mother how to do the same.

Zak put his arm around Monica's waist. It was the first time that day they could be alone together. "Have you heard the news around town?"

"No."

"We're getting married."

"Really?" She didn't know where to look. Mrs. Shabalala must have said something to Mama Dlamini last night at the concert.

Zak turned to face her and put his other arm around her waist. "So what do you think?"

She was forced to look at his face. "About what?" This pretense was infantile, but she was so flustered it came without thinking.

"About getting married."

"In general?"

Zak gave an affected sigh. "It looks as though I'm going to have to do this the traditional way." He got down in the mud on one knee. "Monica, will you marry me?"

Mandla squealed nearby and they heard Sipho shout, "Stop it immediately!" Monica knew without even checking that her mother and Yolanda were watching.

"Yes, my answer is yes. Please get up out of the mud."

He stood up and pulled her toward him. "I'm sorry, but I didn't ask your parents' permission."

"You saw my mother last night. Do you honestly think she'd mind?"

Zak laughed. As they kissed, Monica saw her mother smiling at them.

"Who's going to break the news?" she asked. "You or me?"

"You. I already discussed this with Yolanda last night."

Her mother, the boys and Yolanda rushed over when she called. Since her mother already had an inkling of what she was about to say, she addressed the children.

"Sipho, Mandla, Yolanda, Zak and I are going to get married."

"Can I carry the rings?" Mandla jumped up and down. "I did a good job at Francina's wedding."

"Of course you can, sweetie." She bent down, and he stopped jumping to wrap his arms around her neck.

"Where will we live?" Sipho's face was serious.

Monica and Zak looked at each other. They had not had time to discuss this.

Zak put his hand on Sipho's shoulder. "Yolanda and I were saying the other day how much we love your house. What would you say if after the wedding we moved in with you?"

Sipho's smile returned and Monica shot Zak a look of gratitude. The house would be full until they added a bedroom or two, but the boys didn't mind sharing their home.

THREE WOMEN
ONE MAN
A GATHERING STORM

In the path of a devastating hurricane, three very different women find themselves trapped in the elevator of a high-rise office building. All three conceal shattering secrets—and all three are unaware that their secrets center on the same man....

"Guaranteed to wring tears from
even the hardest-hearted reader."
—*Publishers Weekly*

From *USA TODAY* bestselling author

TERESA HILL

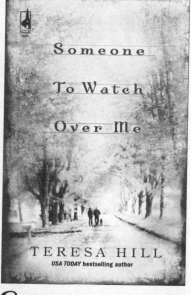

Someone To Watch Over Me

A family death leaves Jack "Cal" Callahan with Romeo…
a spoiled, aptly named dog who seems to have taken
charge of Cal's life. Deciding the dog has to go, Cal finds
the perfect owner in Gwen Moss…who also turns out
to be his perfect match in love, life and faith.

"Teresa Hill…is pure magic."
—*New York Times* bestselling author
Catherine Anderson

Available wherever paperbacks are sold.

Steeple
Hill®

A town scorned them both.
Could faith and love bring them together?

RUTH AXTELL MORREN

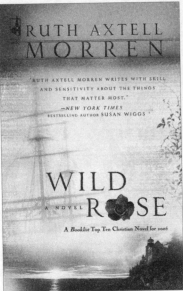

An outcast all her life, Geneva Patterson endured the cruel
taunts of the New Haven townspeople in solitude—until
Caleb Phelps came to the small Maine town. Once a respected
sea captain, he'd been wrongly accused of a shameful crime
and now held only pain in his eyes. Through God's grace,
Geneva and Caleb try to find redemption and love.

WILD ROSE

"Ruth Axtell Morren writes with skill, sensitivity
and great heart about the things that matter most....
Make room on your keeper shelf for a new favorite."
—*New York Times* bestselling author Susan Wiggs

Available wherever paperbacks are sold.

Steeple
Hill®